JOURNEY TO PARADISE

'It is with great pleasure,' Marcus Pleyton went on, 'that I can inform you, Kamala, that General Warrington has asked for your hand in marriage.'

'General Warrington?' The words seemed to be forced between Kamala's lips. 'But he is an old man, very old!'

'He is a man of sensible age,' Marcus Pleyton replied, 'not yet sixty, and as a widower he is an experienced husband. He will know how to deal with your somewhat exceptional qualities, Kamala.'

Arrow Books by Barbara Cartland

Autobiography

I Search for Rainbows
We Danced All Night

Polly: the Story of My Wonderful Mother
Josephine Empress of France

Romantic Novels

1	*Sweet Punishment*	36	*A Light to the Heart*
2	*The Black Panther*	37	*Love is Dangerous*
3	*Stolen Halo*	38	*Love on the Run*
4	*Open Wings*	39	*Theft of a Heart*
5	*The Leaping Flame*	40	*The Enchanted Waltz*
6	*To Mend a Heart*	41	*The Kiss of the Devil*
7	*Towards the Stars*	42	*The Captive Heart*
8	*Armour Against Love*	43	*The Coin of Love*
9	*Out of Reach*	44	*Stars in my Heart*
10	*The Hidden Heart*	45	*Sweet Adventure*
11	*Against the Stream*	46	*The Golden Gondola*
12	*Again This Rapture*	47	*Love in Hiding*
13	*The Dream Within*	48	*The Smuggled Heart*
14	*Where Is Love?*	49	*Love Under Fire*
15	*No Heart is Free*	50	*Messenger of Love*
16	*A Hazard of Hearts*	51	*The Wings of Love*
17	*The Enchanted Moment*	52	*The Hidden Evil*
18	*A Duel of Hearts*	53	*The Fire of Love*
19	*The Knave of Hearts*	54	*The Unpredictable Bride*
20	*The Little Pretender*	55	*Love Holds the Cards*
21	*A Ghost in Monte Carlo*	56	*A Virgin in Paris*
22	*Love is an Eagle*	57	*Love to the Rescue*
23	*Love is the Enemy*	58	*Love is Contraband*
24	*Cupid Rides Pillion*	59	*The Enchanting Evil*
25	*Love Me For Ever*	60	*The Unknown Heart*
26	*Elizabethan Lover*	61	*The Reluctant Bride*
27	*Desire of the Heart*	62	*A Halo for the Devil*
28	*Love is Mine*	64	*The Secret Fear*
29	*The Passionate Pilgrim*	65	*The Irresistible Buck*
30	*Blue Heather*	67	*The Odious Duke*
31	*Wings on my Heart*	68	*The Pretty Horsebreakers*
32	*The Kiss of Paris*	69	*The Daring Deception*
33	*Love Forbidden*	70	*The Audacious Adventuress*
34	*Danger by the Nile*	71	*Lessons in Love*
35	*Lights of Love*	72	*The Complacent Wife*

Barbara Cartland

JOURNEY TO
PARADISE

ARROW BOOKS

ARROW BOOKS LTD
3 Fitzroy Square, London W1

An imprint of the Hutchinson Publishing Group

London Melbourne Sydney Auckland
Wellington Johannesburg Cape Town
and agencies throughout the world

First published by Arrow Books 1974

Set in Intertype Pilgrim
Made and printed in Great Britain
by The Anchor Press Ltd
Tiptree, Essex
ISBN 0 09 908960 2

Author's Note

The cruelty and discipline of parents and guardians in the 19th century is an historic fact. My Grandfather always made his four daughters read aloud at breakfast the letters they received from their friends.

Vaccination for Smallpox was introduced to the world by Dr. Jenner in his book published in 1789. Bavaria made it compulsory in 1807, Denmark in 1810, Sweden in 1814. It was not compulsory in Great Britain until 1853.

When I was in Mexico I was given a fascinating and most detailed diary written about a visit to the country in 1839 by Fanny de Caldeion de la Barca. All descriptions in this story which is set in the same year therefore come from an authentic eyewitness.

With the ending of the East India Company's monopoly of trade with the East in 1833, owners of ships began trading on their own with fast vessels capable of carrying large cargos.

The first Clipper Ships were built in the U.S.A. in the same year and by 1840 were being produced in large numbers both sides of the Atlantic.

I

1839

'I see you have a letter, Kamala.'

The heavy voice seemed to boom down the breakfast table, making Kamala jump before she replied.

'Yes . . . Uncle Marcus.'

She had seen the letter as soon as she entered the room. The Butler's instructions were to place the post on the table at breakfast, an order which Kamala knew was one of the many ways in which her Uncle kept track of what was happening in his household.

There was in fact little that escaped his sharp eyes and he saw with a faint smile of satisfaction that the colour had left Kamala's face.

'Who is your correspondent?'

She might have guessed, she thought, he would not leave the matter alone.

'I do not . . . know, Uncle Marcus.'

'You were not expecting a letter?'

'No . . . Uncle Marcus.'

'Then naturally you must be curious to know who the writer may be . . I suggest you open the letter and read its contents aloud to us.'

Kamala looked towards the end of the table nervously.

Her Uncle was a large, red-faced, over-powering man. He ruled his wife and his servants with a rod of iron. He was in fact a domestic tyrant whom few were brave enough to defy.

'I do not know why Kamala should have a letter,' Sophie complained petulantly.

She was a large and plain girl not unlike her Father, and Kamala knew only too well that Sophie was jealous of her. The mere fact that her cousin should receive a letter addressed to her individually, even if it were only from a shop, would arouse Sophie's envy.

Kamala was quite certain that if her Uncle did not make a scene about the letter, Sophie would do so later.

'I do not know ... who it could be ... from,' Kamala said miserably, staring at the envelope in front of her as if it contained a booby-trap.

'Then let us not prolong our speculation on the identity of your correspondent,' Marcus Pleyton said sarcastically.

His hard eyes seemed to linger on Kamala's pale cheeks, and there was a cruel smile about his lips as he saw that the hand she put out towards the letter was trembling.

It would have been difficult to find two girls in such complete contrast to each other as Sophie and Kamala. It was in fact hard to believe that they could be related.

Kamala was small, fine-boned and very lovely.

She had eyes that seemed almost too big for her small pointed face, and her hair was the colour of the first golden fingers of dawn creeping up the sky.

Her eyes were deep blue, the colour of a stormy sea, and some Irish ancestor had given her dark lashes to accentuate the pale fragility of her skin.

She had a grace of movement which made her slim figure seem to sway like a flower in the breeze, and everything about her had an exquisite perfection.

Sophie on the other hand was fat, clumsy and commonplace.

Her hair was a straight and uncompromising brown, her skin inclined to be sallow and was not improved by the quantities of sweet-meats and chocolates with which she stuffed her already over-fat body.

She had little intelligence, unlike her Father who was extremely clever, and had little desire to improve herself.

8

She just wanted what other people had, and apart from being petulant and self-assertive, would not even struggle to fulfil her own ambitions.

Kamala picked up the letter and opened the envelope. The writing was unknown to her, but as she saw the signature she drew in her breath. She had met the writer only once.

'Well,' her Uncle asked, 'can you tell us now who has written to you?'

'It is ... Mr. Philip ... Radfield ... Uncle Marcus,' Kamala faltered.

'Why has he written to you?' Sophie screamed from the other side of the table. 'He came to see me! He is my friend. The letter must be for me.'

'Yes, I am sure it is for you,' Kamala said quickly, holding out the letter to her cousin.

'Let me see the envelope,' Marcus Pleyton demanded.

Kamala picked up the envelope she had laid down on the table and passed it to her Uncle. He scrutinised it, his heavy eyebrows meeting across his forehead as he did so.

'The address appears to be quite plain,' he said. 'Miss Kamala Lindsey—that is I think your name?'

'Yes ... Uncle Marcus.'

'Then let us hear what this young man has to say.'

Kamala opened the folded writing-paper with trembling fingers then began in a voice so low it was hardly audible.

'My dear Miss Lindsey ...'

'I cannot hear!'

With an effort Kamala began again:

'My dear Miss Lindsey,

It was a very great pleasure meeting you last Sunday and I have found myself thinking of you ever since. Would it be possible for us to meet somewhere where we can talk? Perhaps in the park or anywhere you suggest. Please do not refuse to see me as I have matters of the utmost importance to discuss with you. May I say once again what a very deep and lasting pleasure it was for me to make your acquaintance and I shall wait impatiently for your reply.

Yours most sincerely and admiringly,

Philip Radfield.'

Kamala had read the letter hesitantly with little pauses between the sentences. When she had finished her voice seemed to die away into silence.

She did not raise her eyes from the letter and sat staring at it as if she hoped it might vanish into thin air.

'Why has he written to you?' Sophie stormed. 'Why does he not want to meet me? He was my friend, mine, until you took him from me. I do not believe that letter is for you.'

She sprang up from the table as she spoke, ran round behind her Mother's chair and snatched the letter out of Kamala's hands.

She stared at the writing for a moment before she screamed:

'You did it deliberately, you enticed him into talking to you and now you have concocted some secret that he wishes to discuss with you. I hate you, Kamala! Do you hear? I hate you!'

As she spoke Sophie flung the letter down on the table and then with her right hand she slapped Kamala hard across the cheek.

Kamala sank back in her chair while her pale skin flared crimson from the impact of Sophie's hand.

'That is enough!' Marcus Pleyton commanded from the end of the table. 'Come and sit down, Sophie, I have something to say to you.'

'It is not fair, Papa, it is not fair!' Sophie cried. 'Kamala gets all the men who come to the house. She sets herself out to bewitch them. She uses black magic to lure them to her side.'

'Sit down at once, Sophie! I wish to speak to you,' her Father said sharply.

Tossing her head, pouting her thick lips, Sophie obeyed him, casting a glance of enmity and hatred at her cousin as she did so.

'You will give me that letter, Kamala,' Marcus Pleyton said, 'and I will send that impudent young puppy a reply he will not forget in a hurry.'

As if she knew what was expected of her, Kamala picked up the letter from the table where Sophie had thrown it, placed it in the envelope and rising set it down at her Uncle's side.

'I am so sorry, Uncle Marcus,' she murmured as she did so.

'Sit down and hear what I have to say,' Marcus Pleyton commanded.

Kamala returned to her seat glancing as she did so at her Aunt at the other end of the table.

During the screaming from Sophie and the orders from Marcus Pleyton she had sat still as a silent spectator.

Her expression was quite inscrutable and for a moment Kamala could not help wondering what she felt about the scene which had just taken place.

'I have been thinking about you, Sophie,' Marcus Pleyton said to his daughter. 'And I have certain plans for your future which I think will meet with your approval.'

'My future, Papa?' Sophie asked in surprise.

'That is what I said,' her Father replied. 'You are now twenty and it is time you were married.'

'Married!' Sophie cried, 'but to whom? No-one has asked for my hand? And what man is likely to do so with Kamala enticing them away from me!'

She seemed almost to spit out the words, but Kamala with her head bowed made no response.

'It is not my fault,' she thought desperately.

How was it possible to make her Uncle understand that if possible she avoided even speaking to the men who came to the house and certainly never tried to attract them.

She knew only too well what Sophie's feelings were on the matter, how she craved attention, how she longed to be courted, wooed by a man—any man—in order to boost her self-esteem.

But who was likely to look at the plain daughter of Marcus Pleyton, rich though she might be, when Kamala was about?

Kamala was not conceited. She had little opportunity to think of herself.

But she would have been extremely stupid and unintelligent if she had not realised that her looks attracted attention wherever she went.

Ever since she had been small there had been people to acclaim how lovely she was and to tell her that she was exactly like her Mother.

It was difficult to realise that Aunt Alice, Marcus Pleyton's wife, was her Mother's elder sister. There had in fact been ten years between them and it was almost impossible to believe that in her youth Alice Pleyton had been attractive.

Now with prematurely grey hair and a thin wrinkled face she seemed a nondescript, ghost-like figure, whose personality made no impact whatsoever upon her husband's household.

'Mama was so different,' Kamala thought to herself.

She remembered how lovely her Mother had been, how their house even though it was small and poor had always seemed filled with laughter and sunshine.

They had been so happy all together! So happy that even now the three years she had lived in her Uncle Marcus's house seemed but a nightmare, while reality was still a home with a Father and Mother who had adored her.

'As I have said,' Marcus Pleyton was saying in his harsh ugly voice, 'I have been making plans for your marriage, Sophie, and I have this morning heard that they are about to materialise.'

'What plans? Tell me, Papa! It sounds very exciting.'

'It is exciting,' Marcus Pleyton said. 'I have arranged, Sophie, that you shall marry the Marquis of Truro.'

'A Marquis!'

For a moment Sophie could hardly breathe the words, and then she said :

'Papa, how could you find anyone so important? Are you sure he will offer for me?'

'He has already done so,' her Father replied. 'It has all been arranged by his Trustee, with whom I have a personal friendship.'

'But he has not seen me,' Sophie said. 'And I have not seen him!'

'You will meet very shortly,' Marcus Pleyton replied. 'He is coming here to stay. He will make a formal offer for your hand in marriage which I shall accept on your behalf. After that your betrothal will be announced.'

Sophie drew in a deep breath.

'And what does he look like? Is he handsome? How old is he?'

'All these questions will be answered in due course,' Marcus Pleyton replied, 'and I think very much to your satisfaction. In the meantime, Sophie, you and your Mother will prepare to receive the Marquis in a proper fashion. We must entertain him. I wish him to realise how advantageous it will be to him to form an alliance with my only daughter.'

Sophie was silent for a moment and then she said:

'I think, Papa, you meant to imply that the Marquis is not well off.'

Her Father smiled.

'At times, Sophie, I find flashes of intelligence in you

13

which I know can only have been derived from me. Yes, of course, you are right! The Marquis is impoverished and you are an heiress. What could be more sensible that I should bring you both together?'

'I shall be a Marchioness!' Sophie said almost as if she spoke to herself.

And then the satisfaction faded from her face and she looked across the table at Kamala.

'I am not having Kamala here when he comes to stay,' she said spitefully. 'She will try to take him away from me as she has done with all the other men who have come to the house. Send her away, Papa, you have to send her away!'

'I have thought about Kamala as well,' Marcus Pleyton answered.

Now there was a note in his voice which made Kamala feel suddenly afraid.

'You will send her away?' Sophie asked impatiently.

'Kamala will be leaving here very shortly,' Marcus Pleyton replied. 'She too is to be married!'

Kamala's head came up with a jerk. She turned her face towards her Uncle, her eyes very wide and frightened.

'This may come as a surprise to you, Kamala,' Marcus Pleyton said, 'but I think that your disruptive influence and rebellious character would be best restrained by a husband. I have therefore chosen one for you.'

'You have chosen a husband for me,' Kamala said with a tremor in her voice.

'Yes, Kamala. I assure you, although you may not think so, I have your best interests at heart. And I consider you in fact an extremely fortunate young woman.'

There was silence as Marcus Pleyton expected Kamala to speak, but she was unable to do so. She could only sit looking at her Uncle, her face very pale save for the crimson mark left by Sophie's hand.

'It is with great pleasure,' Marcus Pleyton went on, 'that

I can inform you, Kamala, that General Warrington has asked for your hand in marriage.'

'General Warrington?' The words seemed to be forced between Kamala's lips. 'But he is an old man, very old!'

'He is a man of sensible age,' Marcus Pleyton replied, 'not yet sixty, and as a widower he is an experienced husband. He will know how to deal with your somewhat exceptional qualities, Kamala.'

Her Uncle was mocking her, and with a little glint of anger in her eyes Kamala said:

'I feel sure you will understand, Uncle Marcus, that I could not contemplate marriage with General Warrington.'

Her Uncle stared at her.

'Are you presuming to tell me that you wish to refuse such an offer?'

'I could not marry anyone so old,' Kamala replied, 'and I do not . . . like General Warrington.'

'Do my ears deceive me?' Marcus Pleyton thundered. 'Can it be possible for an insignificant chit, a pauper, living on my bounty, should take upon herself to refuse a man of such distinction as the General? A man of wealth and position, who would be accepted with alacrity by half the women in the county.'

'Then let him ask one of them!' Kamala retorted. 'I regret that I have no wish to marry the General.'

'Your wishes are of no consequence,' Marcus Pleyton snapped. 'I consider him a very suitable husband for you, and as your Guardian, I have, as you know, complete and absolute authority over you. You will marry the General whether you like it or not, because I say so.'

'Uncle Marcus, you cannot make me do this,' Kamala pleaded. 'He is a horrible man! It is rumoured that he beat his wife to death.'

'Stuff and nonsense!' Marcus Pleyton shouted. 'You have been listening to servants' gossip. The woman was a weakly creature who could not even give him a child. He wants

15

an heir, Kamala, and that you should be able to provide for him.'

Kamala clenched her fingers together in an effort to keep control of herself. She had met General Warrington on several occasions when he had come to luncheon, or to dinner.

She could remember the last time all too vividly. She had been next to him at dinner and she had thought he seemed over attentive, talking to her when she wished to remain silent and unobserved in case Sophie or her Uncle should think she was pushing herself forward.

'You have a very unusual name, Miss Lindsey,' the General had said.

'My Father chose it,' Kamala explained. 'He was very interested in Indian literature and Kamala means Lotus.'

'And a Lotus is soft and sweet to the—touch,' the General had said slowly.

Kamala had looked at him in surprise and then felt a sudden tremor of fear at the expression in his eyes.

There was a smile on his thin lips and she had thought as she had thought before he was a horrible old man. There was something almost bestial about him which made her believe that the tales of his brutality were not exaggerated.

Now she felt herself shiver, and difficult though it was for her to oppose her Uncle she managed to say firmly:

'I am sorry if I make you angry, Uncle Marcus, but I will not ... marry the General, not if he were the last ... man in the world!'

Marcus Pleyton brought his fist down on the table with so much force that all the plates and cups rattled.

'You dare to defy me!' he raged. 'Let me inform you once and for all, Kamala, that I will not tolerate your impertinence. You will do as you are told! I shall inform the General today that your marriage will take place almost immediately.'

'I will not do it, Uncle Marcus!'

16

Kamala rose to her feet as she spoke.

'I will not marry him . . . not if you drag me to the altar! Do you understand? Papa and Mama would never have made me marry anyone I do not . . . love.'

'Your impecunious Father is dead,' Marcus Pleyton sneered. 'He left you in my charge and I shall perform my duty as I believe it to be in your best interests. You need a strong hand, Kamala. You are wilful, rebellious and have an independence of mind which is most unbecoming in a female. I consider General Warrington an excellent choice on my part. He will school you as you need to be schooled.'

'I will not marry him!'

'Very well then, I will have to employ slightly more forceful arguments,' her Uncle said.

He rose as he spoke and drew his gold watch from the pocket of his waistcoat.

'I am going now to London to deal with Sophie's affairs, but I shall be back here soon after six. At six-thirty exactly, Kamala, you will come to my study and tell me you are prepared to marry the General. If you do not do so, I shall obtain your consent in a manner which you will find extremely painful.'

Marcus Pleyton turned as he spoke and walked from the Breakfast Room. He did not say goodbye either to his wife or to his daughter but Sophie ran after him calling, 'Papa! Papa!' as she followed him down the passage.

Kamala, her face very pale, turned to look at her Aunt. 'Aunt Alice, help me! I cannot marry the General!'

'There is nothing I can do, Kamala,' Mrs. Pleyton said in an expressionless voice.

'Please, Aunt Alice, surely you can say something. You can make Uncle Marcus see it is impossible for me to marry such a man.'

'Your Uncle always gets his own way,' Mrs. Pleyton replied.

'You were Mama's sister. You know how happy Mama

and Papa were together. They loved each other. Mama often spoke to me of ... marriage and said that when the time came, she hoped I would find someone like Papa whom I would ... love and who would, ... love me. She would never permit me to be forced to marry an old man with a ... reputation for cruelty.'

'I am sorry, Kamala,' Mrs. Pleyton said and for the first time there was something like sympathy in her voice. 'But you have no money and if your Uncle refuses to keep you any longer, what can you do?'

'Perhaps I could get a job,' Kamala replied, 'as a governess or a teacher.'

'You are so young, only just eighteen,' her Aunt said. 'Do you suppose anyone would employ you without a reference?'

'You mean Uncle Marcus would not give me one?' Kamala said incredulously.

'He does not like people to cross him, Kamala, you know that as well as I do. When you see him tonight, agree to marry the General! Otherwise he will beat you, as he has done before.'

'As he ... has done ... before,' Kamala said beneath her breath.

She knew only too well how savagely her Uncle could punish her and she always had the feeling he enjoyed being in the position to do so.

He disliked her, she knew that, and had known it ever since she came to his house. And she was sure that it was because of his dislike that he had deliberately chosen for her an unpleasant and cruel husband.

'Aunt Alice, what can I do?' Kamala begged.

'There is nothing you can do, Kamala, except obey your Uncle,' Mrs. Pleyton replied. 'I learnt many years ago that it is quite hopeless to oppose him. He always wins, Kamala —he always wins.'

For the first time since she had known her, Kamala thought her Aunt spoke as a human being.

There was something in her voice which proclaimed that she was suffering, and with a kind of sick horror Kamala realised now that her Aunt Alice's colourlessness was the direct result of being subjected to the will of Marcus Pleyton.

Perhaps she too had been happy and gay, like her sister, but he had either beaten it out of her or forced her by the sheer power of his personality to become the ghost-like creature whom nobody noticed.

'Aunt Alice . . . .,' Kamala said impulsively, putting out her hands towards her Aunt.

But already Mrs. Pleyton was leaving the Breakfast Room.

'There is nothing you can do but obey, Kamala,' she said in a flat voice.

Slowly Kamala folded her napkin, then went upstairs to her bedroom. She found it impossible to think.

She could only feel that the horror of this proposed marriage was like a great vampire hovering over her, menacing her so that she could only cower beneath it.

She looked at the clock on the mantelpiece.

She had nine hours in which to make up her mind whether she would defy her Uncle or acquiesce in his wishes and marry General Warrington.

She knew only too well what would happen if she continued to refuse.

Ever since she had come to the Castle, her Uncle had chosen to discipline her in a manner that was harsh to the point of cruelty. She had never experienced physical violence before.

'Corporal punishment' were but words in a book. But her Uncle soon made it clear that he considered her upbringing had made her pert and forward.

Her Father had always encouraged her to express her opinions, to discuss matters of national importance with him, to read the newspapers and to be well informed on current affairs as well as in the classics of English and French literature.

Her Uncle had, to her astonishment, acclaimed such accomplishments as being provocative and unfeminine. He restricted her reading, he denied her the newspapers.

For every remark that he considered impertinent and every opinion he considered unfeminine, he punished her. Whenever he could find a good excuse he beat her.

Kamala soon discovered that he enjoyed humiliating her, not only in public when he could pillory her in front of people but also in private.

When he beat her she was made to fetch the whip, kneel in front of him and ask him to correct her. When the punishment was over, she was made to kiss the whip and thank him for teaching her how to behave.

At first she had fought him wildly almost like an animal caught in a trap. Then when she realised there was no chance of her ever winning against his superior strength, she became more subtle.

She was quiet and subdued in his presence, and she felt almost a satisfaction in knowing by doing so she denied him the excuse to beat her.

At times it was almost easier to cope with her Uncle than with Sophie. Her cousin grew more and more dissatisfied with the difference in their appearance. Daily, Sophie became more jealous, more resentful as she focussed on Kamala all her own frustrations and limitations.

'What am I to do?' Kamala now asked herself.

It seemed incredible that in 1839 a parent or a guardian should still have the power to force a woman into marriage against her will.

But Kamala knew the law would uphold her Uncle's authority, and that legally he had a right to dispose of her in any way he thought fit.

Quite suddenly she put her hands up to her face.

'Oh Papa, ... Mama ...' she sobbed, 'how could you have died and let this ... happen to me?'

She knew now that her happiness had come to an end the day she learnt that the ship bringing her Mother and Father back from a holiday in Italy had foundered in the Bay of Biscay.

They had gone off so gaily.

'Our first honeymoon for sixteen years!' Kamala's Father had said. 'You must forgive me, dearest child, for not taking you with us, but I do so want to be alone with Mama, for us both to recapture our youth.'

Because one of her Father's books had been accepted and the advance from the publishers was nearly one hundred pounds, the journey had been possible.

'It is extravagant,' Mrs. Lindsey had said hesitatingly when her husband suggested it.

'Of course it is extravagant!' Kamala had heard her Father agree. 'But what is life unless we are extravagant? Not only with money, my darling, but with our happiness, our laughter and most of all our love.'

He had caught her Mother in his arms as he spoke and kissed her. She had looked up at him adoringly.

'Are you quite sure we should do anything so irresponsible?' she asked.

'I want, as I have wanted for years, to show you Italy,' he replied. 'Nothing and nobody is going to stop me now from taking you there!'

'Oh darling, it sounds so wonderful,' Kamala's Mother had cried. Then seeing her daughter's face she had put her arms round Kamala and held her close.

'Do not grudge me just a month alone with Papa,' she pleaded. 'We will leave you with your governess, and you will be quite safe until we return.'

'Yes of course, Mama,' Kamala had said, 'and I know you deserve a holiday.'

'No-one deserves one more!' her Father said positively.

Kamala had known he spoke the truth.

There had been years of struggle. Years when money had been very short, and they had not even been able to to afford a governess for Kamala and her Father had taught her himself.

She had much preferred to be taught by him, but it meant that he could not get on with his own work, the literary research on which he was always engaged and his self-enforced charity in looking after sick children.

It was strange, Kamala thought, how her Father had found children irresistible, specially when they were injured or ill.

The local Doctor was an elderly man who found his scattered practice almost beyond his powers.

He had been only too happy to let Andrew Lindsey set a broken leg, bandage a fractured arm, and even prescribe the herbs that he believed to be so efficacious instead of the more orthodox medicines.

It seemed to Kamala, looking back, that their life had been very full and varied.

They would drive miles in the ancient gig which was all her Father could afford in the way of a vehicle, to visit a farmhouse where a boy had fallen off a rick, or a child was coughing its heart out with some obscure complaint the Doctor could not diagnose.

Kamala often thought it was her Father's presence as much as his actual skill which put his patients on the road to recovery.

There was no doubt about it, the children he treated did recover and appeared to feel better almost as soon as he arrived.

He would explain it all to Kamala, and because he believed certain herbs and plants were more effective than the manufactured medicines, he would show her old recipes in manuscripts from the East, in books that he had collected to prove his point.

But Kamala thought personally that he had a kind of intuition and understanding that was more important than any traditional book-knowledge.

'Your Papa has green fingers, that's what he has,' one old woman said. 'When he touches me leg I feels the pain go. A man can't learn that! 'Tis somewat that be given him by God.'

How happy they had been, Kamala thought. Her Mother had seemed to radiate happiness however difficult the times through which they were passing, however hard the future might appear to be.

They died together as they would have wished to do, but Kamala had been left behind.

She could remember feeling numb with misery as she had begun to realise she would never see her Father and Mother again, and that her home henceforth must be at the Castle with her Uncle and Aunt.

There had been no other relations to whom she could turn, and when Uncle Marcus had arrived to look contemptuously at her home, sneering at the threadbare carpets, the wildness of the garden and the lack of servants, she had known that her own happiness was over.

Marcus Pleyton made no bones about despising her Father and having contempt for her Mother for marrying him. He looked down on anyone who was poor. He thought a man who was intellectual and uninterested in making money must be a fool.

Kamala soon realised that her Father had been everything Marcus Pleyton was not: a gentleman, a natural sportsman, a brilliant conversationalist, a man of taste, humanity and compassion.

It was perhaps the fact that Andrew Lindsey was well born which irritated her Uncle the most.

Kamala sometimes thought as she grew older that her

Uncle, in asserting his power over her, was attempting to convince himself that he was physically and mentally her Father's superior.

'Your clever Father who died without a penny to his name!'

'How intelligent is a man who cannot make enough to keep his wife and child?'

'Blue-blood does not fill an empty stomach!'

Jibes of this sort were flung at Kamala day after day.

She learnt by bitter experience not to answer them. Not to spring to her Father's defence. That he should provoke her into answering him back was just what her Uncle wanted.

Marcus Pleyton had made a great fortune in commerce, and Kamala soon realised that he was now anxious to buy himself a social position and the respect that went with it.

He had lived for not many years at the Castle, having purchased it from a family who had lived there for generations and who could no longer afford its upkeep.

Marcus Pleyton had embellished the interior with every expensive luxury that money could buy.

Yet Kamala could not help thinking that the Castle with its ancient walls and historical legends must have been far more beautiful before it was over-decorated with thick carpets, silk hangings and bright new furniture.

Sometimes she would creep up to the attic where pictures and furniture which the previous owners had left behind had been stored. There were portraits of their ancestors, so old that they had not thought them worth taking away.

The men had thin aristocratic faces with clearcut features and were very different from Marcus Pleyton's coarse, florid looks. And the women appeared gentle and well-bred and reminded Kamala of her Mother.

Also in the attic were curtains of faded velvet and torn

embroidered hangings which had once been tended by loving hands.

There were chairs with broken seats which had an elegance and delicacy very different to the heavy and over-ornamented chairs and sofas bought by Marcus Pleyton because they were expensive.

'What on earth do you find in that dirty old attic to interest you?' Sophie had asked once.

'History and people who lived it,' Kamala had answered, but her cousin had not understood.

Now looking at her bedroom with its shining brass bedstead and flowery patterned carpet, Kamala knew that wealth could buy none of the things which had been hers when she lived at home with her Father and Mother.

'I cannot marry without love,' she told herself.

But even as she spoke she felt the sting of her Uncle's whip and knew that if she defied him he would beat her until she was senseless.

Sooner or later she would have to give in. He would never allow her to defy him to the point when he must acknowledge her the victor and himself the vanquished.

Quite suddenly she made up her mind.

'I must go away,' she thought. 'I cannot stay here to be beaten into submission. And I will not . . . I will not marry the General whatever Uncle Marcus may do!'

She put her fingers to her forehead, trying to think. Where could she go?

She was well aware that if she left she must disappear. When her Uncle found she was gone, he would do everything in his power to bring her back. Then he would treat her as he had once treated a stable-boy who had run away after laming one of his horses by mistake.

Her Uncle had had the boy caught and brought back. He had then thrashed him, so that he had not been able to move from his bed for over two weeks.

'That is what will happen to me!' Kamala thought in a kind of sick horror. 'I cannot endure it!'

There was a knock on her door and she started.

'Who is it?' she asked apprehensively.

She felt as if her thoughts must be already known to other people in the household.

The door opened. It was only one of the maids.

'Madam's compliments, Miss Kamala,' she said, 'and she told me to tell you that she and Miss Sophie are going into the town to do some shopping and they will not be back for luncheon.'

'Thank you, Lucy, for letting me know.'

The door shut behind the maid and Kamala walked to the window. This was her opportunity. If she was going to leave she must leave now!

But how and where should she go? There must be somewhere where her Uncle could not find her! But where?

'I could go to France,' she said aloud. 'Perhaps it would be best if I went into a convent. At least then I should be free from anxiety and from the unwelcome attentions of men.'

Something young and resolute within her rebelled at the thought.

'Surely in France,' she thought, 'there must be people who wish to learn English.'

But she had to get there, and it would cost money.

Almost like pieces of a puzzle falling into place, she remembered the only valuables she possessed were her Mother's engagement-ring, which she had left behind when she went abroad in case it should be stolen, and a brooch that had belonged to her Grandmother. It was a star set with diamonds.

Unfortunately Kamala did not have them in her own possession. Her Uncle had taken them from her and kept them in his safe.

'It is not correct for a young girl to wear jewellery,' he had said.

Sophie wore pearls and owned several brooches. Kamala knew his decision was only an excuse to deny her something which might have given her pleasure.

Now she reckoned the diamonds must be worth at least a hundred pounds. She sat down at her desk and started to write a letter. When she had finished, she read it through.

Dear Uncle Marcus,

I cannot marry General Warrington and I know that Papa would not have wished me to do so. I am therefore going away where you will not be able to find me.

I must thank you for having housed me since my Parents' death, but I realise I have for a long time been an unwelcome member of your household.

You have in your keeping a diamond ring and a diamond brooch which are mine. These must be worth at least one hundred pounds. I have therefore taken with me twenty-five pounds in cash and Rollo the horse for which you paid seventy pounds a few weeks ago. The extra five pounds will pay for the saddle and bridle as I would not like to think I was in your debt.

Please forgive me for any worry and upset I may cause you by this decision, but I assure you that I will not marry any man I do not love.

I remain,

Your humble, if disobedient niece.

Kamala.

Kamala read the letter through again, placed it in an envelope, wrote her Uncle's name on it, and left it in her desk.

If it was not found for some time after his return, that would give her a better chance to get away.

Quickly Kamala changed. She thought for a moment and then put on under her riding-habit a thin silk dress as well as several petticoats.

She packed as many things as possible in a basket, including a nightgown, her brush and comb and the blouse she usually wore with her habit.

She covered the basket with a light wool shawl and putting it over her arm left the room.

She went to her Aunt's Sitting-room. As it was the end of the month, she knew there would be cash in the locked drawer of her Aunt's desk. This was for the wages of the women servants.

Her Uncle paid the men, but her Aunt was responsible for paying the housemaids, together with the Still-room and scullery-maids.

Kamala knew where the key was kept; for her Aunt had often taken it out in her presence. But when she drew it out from its hiding-place, she felt a sudden pang of guilt because in a way she was behaving like a thief.

Then she said to herself:

'I am taking only what I am owed. The ring and the brooch will undoubtedly fetch more than a hundred pounds, and when Uncle Marcus has got over his rage, he will in fact be glad to be rid of me.'

She took out twenty-five pounds and put it in the purse in her pocket. Then she locked the drawer and put the key back into its hiding-place. Taking up the basket she went downstairs and out to the stables.

'Will you please saddle Rollo?' she asked the Head-groom.

'Of course, Miss,' he answered. 'Are you going for a ride? I'll tell one of the grooms to accompany you.'

'No thank you,' Kamala said, 'I would rather go alone and I am not going far.'

The Head-groom glanced at the basket and thought, as

28

Kamala meant him to think, that she was visiting some sick woman in the village.

It was quite usual for her to be sent on an errand of mercy to a sick tenant or an aged pensioner. Sophie would never bother herself with such things.

'Very well, Miss,' he said, 'but be careful. Rollo be a bit frisky, he's not been out these last few days.'

As the horse was led into the yard, Kamala knew she had chosen well.

Rollo was a large roan, well-bred and also well-built. He had stamina, and she was pleased to see that he was full of high spirits, bucking a little to show his independence, fidgeting while she was helped into the saddle, and obviously impatient to be off.

She gave him his head as they crossed the Park; then just before they reached the main gates she pulled him to a standstill and dismounted.

Underneath one of the great oak trees she spread her shawl on the ground, rolled into it all the articles which the basket contained and tied the ends with pieces of ribbon.

Then she attached the roll to her saddle, threw the basket into a briar bush and mounted Rollo again.

Clear of the Park and the village, Kamala started off in a southerly direction. The land was open and she avoided the highways with their fast traffic and clouds of dust.

She must have ridden for nearly three hours before she stopped at a small wayside Inn to give Rollo a rest and a drink.

She also needed something herself. The agitation of seeing the letter in front of her place when she had come down to breakfast had made it impossible for her to eat and she was now extremely hungry.

There was only bread and cheese, but it seemed very palatable and the Landlord persuaded her to have a small glass of home-made cider which brought a faint flush to her cheeks.

The whole meal cost her only a few pence, and then she was on her way again still keeping to the fields.

It must have been two hours later when she realised that it was growing chilly. It had been such a fine warm Autumn that she had forgotten that, now they were in November, it could be cold when the sun began to set.

She wished now she had brought a cloak with her. Then she thought that would have been very difficult to explain to the Head-groom and quite impossible to conceal it in the basket.

Kamala was moving slowly over a ploughed field. There was a wood ahead. Suddenly she heard the sound of a huntsman's horn and out from the wood came a fox.

It ran across the field in front of her, its little body and red brush vivid against the dark soil, the swiftness of its movement having a grace which held Kamala spellbound.

She was watching the fox pass through a hedge and lope across the next field when from the wood there emerged a number of hounds, their noses to the ground, their tongues hanging out, their tails held high.

They tore after the fox who by now was a field and a half away from them.

Following came a lone huntsman. He was blowing his horn, but there appeared to be no-one to hear him. The field must have long been left behind.

'It seems an opportunity to be in at the kill,' a deep voice said beside Kamala.

She turned her head in surprise. While she had been watching the fox, a gentleman riding a black stallion had come up beside her.

Their two horses were standing together and she found herself looking into a handsome quizzical face and dark eyes which seemed to be appraising her almost critically.

'I am not hunting, Sir,' Kamala said quickly, with a dignity that she hoped rebuked him for speaking to her without an introduction.

'Nor am I,' he replied apparently unabashed, 'although, as I have just said, it seems a pity to miss such a glorious opportunity.'

Kamala looked to where the fox was just disappearing out of sight, the hounds still some way behind him.

Quite suddenly she felt the excitement of the chase well up inside her. It was, as the stranger had said, an opportunity that seldom came one's way, especially Kamala's.

Her Uncle seldom allowed her to hunt except when a meet was in the immediate neighbourhood. Otherwise she had to be content with riding round the Park.

But Uncle Marcus was no longer of importance and she could do as she wished. Kamala felt carefree and excited.

If she desired to follow the hounds, she could do so!

It was as if her unspoken decision communicated itself to Rollo .. Without her urging him, he broke into a trot, then into a gallop and in a minute they were tearing across the field, the stranger keeping pace beside them.

'We shall have to hurry to keep up,' Kamala thought.

The sound of the horses' hoofs, the wind in her face, the baying of the hounds, gave her a sense of exhilaration. She was conscious that the man riding beside her was big and broad shouldered, and she knew, without hardly looking at him, that he was smiling.

They reached the end of the field. There was a low fence. Rollo cleared it easily. The field ahead was a small one. Kamala saw the huntsman on whom they were gaining leap a gate at the far end of it.

The hounds were already out of sight, but she could hear them baying. Rollo was following the huntsman's lead.

As he reached the gate he braced himself and jumped magnificently.

They landed safely, then something made Kamala look back. The stranger on his big black horse had followed her lead, but either he had misjudged the height or his horse was tired.

The stallion's hoofs touched the top rail of the gate and he fell forward rolling sideways as he touched the ground.

Kamala saw the rider thrown from the saddle.

With difficulty she pulled up Rollo and turned him round. As she did so she saw the fallen horse scramble to his feet.

But his rider was still—lying hatless without moving, on the muddy ground.

2

'Where—am I?'

He opened his eyes and saw a kind of golden haze which made him think of sunshine. Then a soft voice said:

'You are all right, go to sleep.'

A cup was held to his lips, he drank a little and sank back into a deep, dark unconsciousness. . . .

He woke again and this time he realised it was night. The room was in shadows save for a flickering fire and two candles.

He must have moved, because someone rose from beside the fire and came to the bedside.

'Who are you?' he asked.

A vague memory came back to him of two very blue eyes.

'The—fox,' he murmured, 'were we—in at the—kill?'

'No, he escaped,' the same soft voice replied.

Again he was given something to drink. It was too much trouble to ask questions, he was too tired even to keep his eyes open. . . .

He came back to full consciousness to hear voices.

'Yes, he is much better this morning thank you, Mrs. Hayward.'

'I'll be a bringing ye somew'at to eat on a tray, Miss. Be there anything ye fancy?'

'The ham you gave me yesterday was delicious. I am sure you have a secret for curing hams which is better than anyone else's.'

'Get along, Miss, ye be a flattering Oi, that's what ye be a doing.'

'If I were, it would not be surprising, seeing how kind you are to us, Mrs. Hayward.'

'It be a real pleasure, Miss, an' that's th' truth. 'Tis not often we have th' Quality around here being so isolated, so ter speak.'

'We were very lucky to find your farm considering, as you say, you are so far away from any other houses or a village.'

' 'T'as its advantages and its disadvantages, Miss,' Mrs. Hayward said. 'Oi dunno' have no trouble with gossipin' neighbours.'

'I am sure that is a blessing!'

The two women laughed together. Then Mrs. Hayward said:

'Oi'll be a getting yer lunch, and mind ye have a bit o' a sleep this evening. Fred 'll watch th' Gentleman when he comes in from th' fields.'

'That is very kind of you, but I can manage. I slept in front of the fire yesterday afternoon and our patient was not half so troublesome last night as he had been the night before.'

'No, Oi be sure he be getting better,' Mrs. Hayward agreed and the door closed behind her.

The man in the bed opened his eyes. The girl with the soft voice was standing beside him, her eyes very blue, her hair as golden as he had remembered it in the pale sunshine coming through the small-paned casement window.

'What—happened to—me?' he asked.

'You broke your collar-bone,' Kamala replied, 'and you have had severe concussion.'

'I am sorry to have been such a—bother! It was stupid of me to try to jump the gate when I had been riding for so many hours. My horse was tired.'

'He is all right,' Kamala said. 'He was a trifle lame after

34

the fall, but I walked him round the yard this morning and I do not think there is anything wrong with him.'

The Stranger glanced round the room, tried to raise himself on his pillows and winced with the pain.

'Be careful!' Kamala exclaimed quickly. 'It will hurt you unless I help.'

She put one arm behind his back, lifted him expertly, and as she did so arranged the pillows under his elbow until he was comfortable. Now he could see her more closely.

'Where am I?' he asked, 'and why are you here? I do not understand.'

'You had a very nasty toss,' she replied. 'You were completely unconscious for over twenty-four hours. The men carried you here on the gate. It took all their strength, you are very tall and heavy.'

She smiled as she spoke.

'This is a farm,' he said slowly.

'The nearest house for miles,' Kamala answered. 'I cannot think what would have happened if you had fallen farther away.'

'You could have left me in the ditch,' the Stranger suggested. 'You have not yet explained why you are looking after me.'

Kamala smiled at him.

'I could not very well leave you in the charge of Mrs. Hayward. She is old and she already has five menfolk to look after. Besides, someone had to set your collar-bone.'

'You—set it?' the words were incredulous.

'There was no-one else,' Kamala explained. 'The Doctor lives over five miles away and they told me quite frankly that he would not come out at night. Apparently he ... indulges himself as soon as it is dark and he would not have been much use if he had come.'

'So you set it,' the Stranger said in wondering tones. 'But how do you know about such things?'

'My Father taught me.'

'He is a doctor?'

'Not exactly, but he liked looking after sick children. I must admit to being a little nervous, I had never set a man's bones before.'

It was true, she thought; she had been very anxious lest she should do the wrong thing.

But she had watched her Father so often and on one occasion she had herself actually set the collar-bone of a boy under her Father's instructions. He had a poisoned finger and had not been able to use his hands.

At the same time it had been frightening to handle a man as big as the Stranger.

The farmer and his two elder sons had carried him upstairs to the low-ceilinged, oak-beamed bedroom which they told her was their best.

' 'T'was always used by me mother-in-law,' Mrs. Hayward explained. 'Oi didno' fancy it meself when she died, so we keeps it for visitors, not that us have many.'

It was a comfortable room even though the furniture was poor. But the bed had a feather mattress and, Kamala noted with pleasure, everything was exceptionally clean.

As the men had put the unconscious rider down, she had hurried back to the kitchen to find Mrs. Hayward and ask for linen to make bandages.

They had found an old sheet and when they had torn it into strips, Kamala had come up to the bedroom to find the Farmer and his sons had divested the injured man of his shirt.

For a moment Kamala had felt confused and embarrassed.

She had never before seen a man naked to the waist, and the Stranger had such a strongly muscled body that he bore no resemblance to the children she had tended with her Father.

His skin felt cool and firm beneath her fingers and in a

panic she wondered if she would ever have the strength to reset the bones in the right position.

Then it seemed to her she heard her Father's voice instructing her, telling her what to do.

The unconscious Gentleman was not a man, but a patient, someone who was suffering, someone who needed her skill and her compassion.

She had set the collar-bone and bandaged his shoulder and arm into place.

Then Mrs. Hayward had brought one of her husband's night-shirts, well worn but also well washed, and the men had slipped the Gentleman into it, removing his breeches and riding-boots while Kamala busied herself in the other corner of the room.

'Ye husband 'll be more comfortable now, ma'am,' Mrs. Hayward had said as she turned from the bed.

'He is not my husband,' Kamala had replied, feeling the idea involved a great number of complications, 'he . . . he is my brother.'

She did not know why she lied. It was in fact instinctive to save herself from explanations.

How could she possibly tell these people that she had never set eyes on the man until a short while ago, that they had only exchanged two sentences and then had started to gallop off after the hounds on an unaccountable impulse.

The Farmer and his wife would never understand, and what was more they would be extremely shocked at a lady nursing a man who was no relation.

'Oh ye brother!' Mrs. Hayward exclaimed. 'That be who he be. A' wonder why ye were not a wearing a wedding-ring.'

The woman might be old but she missed nothing, Kamala thought.

'Then ye 'll be wanting a separate bedroom, Miss,' Mrs. Hayward went on.

'Yes, please.'

Already it was dark and Kamala had no wish to ride further that evening, whether she had a patient to attend to or not.

The Stranger was delirious that night, and she knew that had she not been there to calm him down and prevent him from throwing himself about, his collar-bone would have slipped out of place and her work would have been in vain.

There was no question of her going the next day or the day after, she had to stay and look after him.

One thing was very certain, Uncle Marcus would not be searching for her in an isolated farm. Besides she had taken other precautions.

'May Oi ask ye name, Miss?' Mrs. Hayward enquired.

'Yes of course,' Kamala answered, 'my name is Lind. . . .'

She stopped suddenly. Supposing Uncle Marcus was making enquiries as to her whereabouts. It was stupid to give her own name.

'. . Lindham,' she had finished.

She knew now she must explain to the Stranger the part he had to play. She felt suddenly nervous at the thought.

There was something in the direct gaze of his eyes— dark eyes which seemed very penetrating. It made her feel he was a man who would dislike subterfuge and dishonesty.

Before she could begin her story he asked:

'Is there anyone here who could fetch the things that were attached to my horse's saddle, or have you already had them brought upstairs?'

'They are here,' Kamala answered.

The Stranger put his hand up to his chin.

'I want a shave and I expect I need a wash.'

'You have been washed.'

'I have?'

Kamala blushed.

'I . . . I washed your face and your arms,' she said, 'and of course, owing to all your bandages, there was not a . . . great deal to do.'

'I am beginning to think I am dreaming,' the Stranger said. 'When I first came to consciousness I thought for a moment I must be in Heaven and there was an angel looking after me. Now I am convinced I was right. But you appear to be a very practical little angel.'

'I only hope that your collar-bone will knit correctly,' Kamala said.

'I have broken it before,' the Stranger replied carelessly, 'and I cannot believe that you are not a great deal more skilful than the Able Seaman who last time set it in place with considerable roughness.'

'You are a sailor!' Kamala exclaimed. 'I thought you must be.'

'Why did you guess that?' he asked.

'Your tattoo marks,' Kamala replied a little shyly.

The Stranger smiled.

'I had forgotten them.'

'Papa told me that tattooing is an art in India and China,' Kamala said, 'and that it has been brought back to Europe by sailors. Have you been to the East?'

'I have been to both India and China,' the Stranger replied, 'but the tattooing on my arms was actually done in Borneo.'

Kamala walked across the room to collect a leather box of razors from a drawer in the washhand-stand.

'Your razors are here,' she said. 'I will fetch you some hot water. Do you think you can manage with one hand?'

'I am sure I can,' the Stranger replied, 'if you get someone to hold a mirror for me.'

'I will hold it for you.'

'I cannot expect you to wait on me hand and foot,' the Stranger said almost sharply. 'There must be someone else in this place.'

'There is only Mrs. Hayward, at the moment,' Kamala said, 'and she will be getting ready the meal for the men when they come in from the fields. I do not like to ask her, she has done so much already.'

She came back to the bedside as she spoke carrying the razors in her hand.

'Fred, the youngest boy, will be up later,' she went on. 'He is willing to do anything you wish.'

'I still feel rather mutton-headed,' the Stranger said looking at her. 'I suppose there must be some good explanation as to why you are looking after me, and why having got me safely to this farm you have not gone on your way.'

'I think you have talked enough for now,' Kamala re-replied. 'You are tired. Can we leave our explanations until you have had another sleep?'

She saw as she spoke that his eyelids were dropping, and she knew that even their short conversation had proved over-fatiguing.

It was not only natural tiredness; her Father had always impressed on her how important it was for a man with a broken collar-bone to keep as still and quiet as possible so that the bone would have a chance to knit.

She had therefore found to her delight that Mrs. Hayward had a little laudanum in a cupboard in the kitchen.

'Th' Doctor g've's it to Mr. Hayward when he had ter have one of his toes amputated,' she explained. '‘T'was poisoned by a rusty nail. In agony he were.

' "Give him as much rum as he'll drink, Mrs. Hayward," the Doctor says, "and put a couple o' teaspoonfuls o' this in it."

' 'T'made him drowsy while th' operation were a taking place and Oi keeps him unconscious for th' next two nights. Oi could never have kept him still otherwise. Not with th' pain he were in.'

'I can well believe it,' Kamala replied, thinking that her Father would have saved the toe without amputating it.

But what was left of the laudanum was useful where the Stranger was concerned. The effect would linger a little,

40

she thought, but now that his concussion was better there would be no need to give him any more.

She watched him fall asleep, and putting down the razors by the bedside went downstairs to the kitchen.

'My brother is better, Mrs. Hayward,' she said, 'he was talking quite sensibly. May I make him some beef broth as you suggested?'

'Ye make what ye like, Miss,' Mrs. Hayward replied, 'ye 're a better cook than Oi be. And Oi've always believed in giving a man something nourishing when he comes a round, so to speak.'

'I am sure you are right,' Kamala said.

She made the broth and when the Stranger woke again, she fed him spoonful after spoonful.

'I was beginning to feel hungry,' he said, 'and it was rude of me to fall asleep when we were talking.'

'You could not help it,' Kamala said. I had to give you laudanum to keep you quiet. You were too big for me to manage alone.'

'Was I rough?' he asked quickly.

'Not with me, but with yourself.'

'Did I talk?'

'You muttered a great deal about money. It seemed to be worrying you.'

'Money is always an infernal worry,' he said. 'Have you not found that?'

'Indeed I have,' Kamala answered.

She thought of how her parents had struggled against poverty and how, to obtain enough money to run away from her Uncle, she had been forced to take twenty-five pounds from her Aunt's desk.

She still felt ashamed, even though she kept telling herself it was not stealing. But it was pleasant to know that she would be able to pay Mrs. Hayward for her board and lodging.

The Stranger had some money of his own. Without pry-

41

ing, she had noticed as she emptied the pockets of his coat before brushing it clean that he had a purse and a wallet which she felt sure must contain some bank-notes.

It had been impossible not to wonder who he was and where he was going.

In his saddle-bag he had a change of linen, his razors, and a hairbrush. While rolled up and attached to the saddle, as Kamala had attached her things, there was a heavy riding-coat.

His clothes were well cut, his boots well made, but there was not much other evidence of wealth and his horse, though a large and sturdy animal, was not noticeably well-bred.

Kamala put the last spoonful of nourishing beef broth into her patient's mouth and rose from the side of the bed on which she had been sitting.

'You can have something to eat later, if you are hungry.'

'I am beginning to feel very hungry,' he said, 'but I still want to shave myself. I do not like your seeing me like this.'

'I will go and get you some hot water.'

Kamala's hand was on the door before she turned back.

'By the way, just in case anyone should mention it, I have told Mrs. Hayward that we are ... brother and sister.'

She saw his eyebrows go up and added:

'Our name is ... Lindham.'

She slipped out of the room before he could reply. When she came back she saw that he had pushed himself still further up on his pillows.

He did not say anything and she brought him the basin, set it in front of him, together with an enamel jug filled with hot water, a cake of soap and a towel.

'I have a mirror in my bedroom next door,' she said. 'I will fetch it.'

She brought it, and again sitting on the side of the bed held it in position so that he could see himself.

He looked at his reflection and grinned.

'I look a pretty rough rogue! I am surprised that you are prepared to claim me as a relation!'

'You must forgive me if it seems ... presumptuous,' Kamala said nervously, 'but they thought at first we were ... husband and wife, and I could not explain that we were ... strangers—not unless I was prepared to leave you and go away.'

'I have already asked you why you did not do so,' the Stranger replied, applying the soap to his chin.

'You were not in a fit state to be left.'

'It was not your fault I was such a fool.'

'No, but Papa would never have left anyone who was sick or injured. So I felt I had to look after you.'

The Stranger did not speak until he had finished shaving himself very carefully. Then as he wiped his square chin with a towel he said:

'If you are determined to minister to me, would it be asking too much if I might have my hairbrush.'

Kamala took away the basin and the jug. It was impossible for the Stranger to wipe his razor-blade clean with one hand. She cleaned it for him and put the razor back into the box.

Then she fetched the hairbrush, noticing it was quite a plain cheap one, and handed it to him, again holding the mirror so that he could see himself.

With the dark stubble shaved from his chin and upper lip he was very handsome.

He had a straight nose, a firm mouth with a slightly cynical twist at the corners and deep-set eyes in a sunburnt face.

When he was asleep he had looked younger. Now that he was awake, there was, Kamala thought, something very authoritative and commanding about him.

He brushed his thick dark hair into some semblance of

order, and then when she had put the brush back into its place on the dressing-table he said:

'Now, Miss Lindham, I want to hear about you. Who are you and where are you going?'

'Yes . . . of course, . . . I will explain,' Kamala said a little nervously.

She brought a hard cane chair, set it down beside the bed, and folding her hands in her lap rather like a child who is about to begin a lesson she began:

'My name is Lind . . . ham. Kamala Lind. . . .'

'Kamala?' the Stranger interrupted. 'That means lotus.'

'How did you know that?'

'I told you I have been in India. It is a strange name for an English girl to have.'

'My Father was deeply interested in Sanskrit, the Vedas, and in Eastern religions. Above anything else in the world, he always wished that he could have had the good fortune to visit India.'

'It is a very beautiful place,' the Stranger said, 'as beautiful as your name and you.'

For a moment Kamala glanced at him as if she had not heard him right, and then at the look in his eyes, she dropped her own. Her lashes were very dark against her cheeks which were suddenly suffused with colour.

'How old are you?' the Stranger asked.

'Eighteen.'

'Why are you riding alone?'

'I was on my way to Southampton,' Kamala said. 'I am going to . . . France.'

She glanced up, and seeing the expression in the Stranger's eyes she added quickly:

'To stay with . . . my Aunt.'

'And your Parents allowed you to go on this journey unaccompanied?'

'My Parents are dead.'

'Then whoever is responsible for you?'

44

'I shall be quite ... all right,' Kamala said. 'I understand there are Paddle-Steamers that go from Southampton to Le Havre every day.'

'There are,' the Stranger replied, 'but you should not be travelling without a maid or a companion. It is a long way to Southampton.'

'It will not take me many days,' Kamala said, 'and Rollo ... that is my horse ... is strong.'

'It is still a journey that a girl should not take unchaperoned,' the Stranger said almost severely, 'especially one who looks like you!'

'What have my looks to do with it?' Kamala enquired innocently.

'A great deal!' he replied. 'And now perhaps you will tell me the truth.'

'The truth?' Kamala ejaculated.

'As to why you are alone,' he said. 'I do not believe that anyone in their senses would permit it. If their permission was—asked!'

Kamala looked confused.

Without realising she was doing so, she had put out her hands and started plaiting together the wool fringe on the bed-cover.

She did not speak and after a moment the Stranger said:

'I am waiting.'

She glanced up at him for a moment and then looked away again. It should be of no interest to him, she thought. She had done him a kindness, but that gave him no right to question her.

No right to look so severe. Then somehow it was hard to bear the silence.

'I have ... run away,' she said at length in a low voice.

'I thought so,' he said quietly. 'From whom?'

'My Guardian.'

'Was that not rather foolish?'

45

'I had to go ... you do not ... understand. Besides it is no ... business of ... yours.'

She got up as she spoke, and walking towards the fire stood with her back to him.

'I think you have made it my business,' the man in the bed said. 'You had your opportunity to run away from me when I was unconscious, but you did not go. Instead you stayed and said I was your brother. That means that I am involved morally if not legally.'

'All I want to ... do is to reach ... Southampton.'

'That will not be difficult, but it would make things easier if you would tell me why you are so anxious to leave your home or wherever it is you have been living.'

There was silence and then at length, almost as if she were compelled against her will to answer him, Kamala said :

'I have been living with my Uncle. He told me that I had to ... marry someone of his ... choice.'

'Surely if you do not wish to marry the man in question, you could have persuaded your Uncle to see reason, rather than run away in such a reprehensible manner.'

'There was no possibility of ... reasoning with ... him.'

'Why not?'

'He did not ask for my ... consent, he merely told me I had to marry this man who frightens me.'

'Why does he frighten you?'

'He is old for one thing, nearly sixty, and ... cruel. Crueller even than ... my Uncle. It is said that he beat his first wife to ... death.'

'Your Uncle really wanted you to marry such a brute?'

'He wished to be rid of me. His daughter ... my cousin ... is to marry a nobleman and she was afraid that if I was at home ...'

Kamala's voice faded away.

She had forgotten the man in the bed, she was remembering that scene in the Breakfast Room and Sophie saying

'I hate you! I hate you!' and slapping her across the face.

'What you are saying,' the man in the bed interrupted her thoughts, 'is that your cousin was jealous of you. She did not trust her nobleman not to prefer you to her.'

'What is the point of . . . talking about it?' Kamala asked. 'I have run away, I have left them all . . . behind, I want to . . . forget.'

'I think you should go back,' the man in the bed said. 'By now your Uncle will be disturbed by your disappearance and I am sure you can persuade him to listen to you. He could not really expect you—at eighteen, to marry a man of sixty.'

'He not only expects it, he will insist on it!' Kamala cried. 'If I had stayed I would . . . have had to do as he wished. He would have beaten me until I . . . agreed.'

'Beaten you!'

The words were almost like a pistol-shot.

'Do you know what it is like to be . . . whipped until you can no longer . . . think?' Kamala asked, 'until the pain is so . . . agonising you would agree to . . . anything, . . . anything, rather than . . . endure any more? That is why I ran away! That is why I can never go back . . . never . . .'

Her voice broke on a sob, but her words, passionate with fear, seemed still to echo round the small room.

There was silence and then the man in the bed said:

'Come here.'

Because she was used to obeying orders, Kamala turned towards him.

She walked to the bed and stood looking down at him, her eyes dark with anxiety, her lips trembling a little with the intensity of her feelings.

He put out his hand. Her fingers fluttered as she felt the strength and warmth of his.

'Look at me,' he said in his deep voice, 'look at me, Kamala.'

She obeyed him and looked down into his dark eyes

47

which seemed to be searching deep beneath the surface, into her very heart.

'Is what you have told me true?'

'It is . . . true.'

'Your Uncle has really beaten you? Is there a man alive who would beat anything so small and so—lovely?'

'He was always beating me,' Kamala answered. 'I told you he dislikes me.'

'Then you are right to leave him, you are right to go to your Aunt. But you must not go alone, I will take you to her.'

Just for a moment Kamala's eyes were held by his. Then she looked away.

'If you will take me as far as Southampton,' she said in a whisper. 'I would be very grateful . . . I am only afraid that my Uncle will catch up with me and take me . . . back.'

'He shall not do that,' the Stranger promised, 'though I can hardly credit that you are not exaggerating his brutality.'

'I swear to you it is the truth,' Kamala said. 'He despised my Father because he had no money, and my Mother because she married him. I have been so . . . miserable these past three years.'

'And now?' the Stranger asked still holding her hand.

'I am happy and free! Everything feels different. Even looking after you has been a joy. A happiness I have not known since Mama and Papa were drowned.'

'How were they drowned?'

'At sea coming back from Italy,' Kamala replied. 'They could afford the holiday because of an advance on one of Papa's books. They were so happy, they called it a second honeymoon, but they never . . . came back.'

'So you had to go to live with your Uncle?'

Kamala shivered at the memory, the expression on her face was very eloquent.

48

'Forget it!' the man in the bed said sharply. 'Forget the past and think about the future. You will love France: it is a very beautiful country, almost as beautiful as Italy.'

'You have been there?'

'I have been to many places,' he answered. 'But just for the moment let us sort out our immediate problems. If you have told Mrs. Hayward that your name is Lindham, —I presume I also have a new surname?'

'I am sorry, but you were not in a position to answer me when I asked you who you were!' Kamala said with a smile.

'My name is Veryan,' he answered, 'Conrad Veryan, though for the moment I must be Conrad Lindham.'

'I like the name Conrad, it suits you.'

'Just as yours suits you, little Lotus.'

She flushed at his tone. Then before she could speak they heard Mrs. Hayward coming up the stairs. She pushed open the door and came in carrying a tray.

'Oi've brought ye a bite of somew'at more substantial to eat, Sir,' she said. 'If Oi knows th' appetite of a young man, as well Oi should, with four of me own to feed. Now ye're back in the land of th' living, ye'll be hungry.'

'You are quite right, Mrs. Hayward,' Conrad Veryan said, 'and I am very grateful to you for all the trouble that you have been put to since I have been ill. My—my sister has been telling me of your kindness.'

'Has been a pleasure, Sir. Though we've been worrie't about ye.'

'It was my own stupidity for jumping a gate when my horse was tired.'

Mrs. Hayward set the tray down in front of him and took the cover off a plate heaped with eggs, ham and roast potatoes.

' 'Tisn't really a gentleman's meal, Sir,' she said apologetically, 'but Oi dare say ye won't find it unpalatable.'

'I will not indeed,' Conrad Veryan replied with a smile, 'and I promise you I will do justice to it.'

'And Oi were a wondering, Sir, whether ye'd be fancying a glass of cider or maybe a mug of ale? Mr. Hayward has a small barrel of each in th' house left over from th' harvesting.'

'I am sure your ale is excellent,' Conrad Veryan replied.

'I will fetch it,' Kamala said. 'You must not come up these stairs again, Mrs. Hayward. I know your legs are aching from standing so long in the kitchen.'

'That's true, Miss, though Oi should not be a bothering ye.'

'We have given you far too much trouble as it is.'

Kamala followed the Farmer's wife down the stairs. When she brought back the ale it was to find that Conrad Veryan had finished all that was on the plate.

'Now I am feeling stronger,' he said, 'we will leave tomorrow.'

'We should give it another two days,' Kamala answered, 'three if possible.'

'I think you are fussing over me like a mother-hen!'

'You will find it uncomfortable to ride,' Kamala prophesied.

He finally agreed he would wait and see what he felt like in the morning. It was already getting dark and a chill wind was blowing up which rattled the windows.

Kamala drew the curtains and put several more logs on the fire. The candles were cheap and spluttered from time to time, giving a very small light in the room.

But the flames leapt up, and lying against his pillows Conrad Veryan watched the firelight on Kamala's face.

'She is lovely,' he thought to himself.

So lovely it was absurd to think of her travelling about the countryside alone or being subjected to the brutality of her Uncle.

Could she be lying to him? He had looked into her eyes and he could not believe it was possible.

There was something so honest and straightforward about her—a child's eyes with a child's innocent trust of the unknown.

Because they seemed so close in the small room he spoke his thoughts aloud.

'You will have to marry sooner or later.'

She glanced up at him nervously.

'Why do you say that?'

'Because a woman, especially one as attractive as you, needs a husband to look after her.'

'I will never marry unless I am . . . in love.'

'Are you sure of that? Most women marry for security, comfort, position.'

'I suppose we all want those things,' Kamala said, 'but at the same time to be married . . . is to be so intimate . . . so much a part of a man! I could not marry unless I . . . loved him and he . . . loved me.'

'Are you sure of that?'

'Completely and absolutely sure. My cousin is to marry for his title, someone she has never seen. Can you imagine what a travesty it will be of everything that is beautiful and sacred?'

Kamala paused for a moment and then she went on:

'It is just a sale between . . . two people. He will sell himself for her money, she will sell herself for his rank in society. The whole idea is . . . crude and . . . horrible.'

'And yet in the East marriages are arranged without the bride and bridegroom ever meeting each other,' Conrad Veryan said.

'And they are happy?'

'They appear to be,' he answered. 'The woman is grateful because she has someone to protect her and to give her his name. The man needs someone to care for him, to give him children.'

51

'That is the East,' Kamala said, 'and I know too it happens in England. Parents and Guardians choose what they consider a suitable bridegroom and the girl is forced to the altar whether she wishes it or not. But Papa always said it was barbaric. He promised me that unless I loved a man as he and Mama loved each other, that I need not marry.'

'But you would not wish to be an old maid? Not that it is likely!'

'I would rather be an old maid than a slave to a man of sixty who ... desires me only because he wants to have an ... heir.'

'Do you really think that is his only motive?'

As Conrad Veryan spoke, Kamala remembered the glint in the General's eyes when he had told her that a lotus was sweet to the touch. She had seen a smile on his thin lips, heard a note in his voice which made her afraid.

'I do not think I understand all that ... marriage entails,' she said slowly. 'I do not know, ... because Mama never told me, ... exactly how a man and a woman make ... love to each other. But I am sure ... utterly sure ... that unless the woman ... loved her husband ... really loved him ... anything he did to her would be frightening and somehow ... obscene.'

Her voice quivered into silence. Then Conrad Veryan said very quietly:

'You are right, Kamala! You must not marry until you fall in love.'

3

It was five days before they finally set off for Southampton.

Conrad insisted on trying to ride before that, but after trotting round the fields for half an hour or so he returned white and shaking and was obviously relieved to be able to slip back into bed.

'I told you it was too soon!' Kamala said in a scolding voice.

'You sound regrettably like a Nurse I had when I was six,' Conrad replied. 'Invariably she was right and she never omitted "I told you so!"'

'You must give your bones a chance to become as strong as you feel yourself,' Kamala admonished.

She saw he was in considerable pain, and insisted on undoing his bandages to find out if the ride had done any serious harm.

Everything was in place, and then he felt her small fingers massaging his shoulder gently but skilfully.

'I believe you have green fingers,' he said, 'or whatever is the equivalent term when it is applied to the body rather than the soil.'

'I wish it were true, because that is what people always said about Papa,' Kamala replied. 'As soon as he touched them they began to get better.'

'Do you think you have the same power?'

'I pray to have it,' she answered. 'When I am massaging a patient, setting their bones or even trying to soothe them to sleep, I pray that a Divine power shall pass through me to them.'

'You are a very remarkable person,' Conrad said quietly.

He slept after Kamala had finished massaging him. When he woke he found it was evening and once again she was sitting by the fire and he could watch her in the candlelight.

Kamala looked up and saw he was awake.

'Do you feel better?'

'Much better,' he answered. 'I think you really have some special magic, but I will not test it too hard. I will bow to your skilful judgment and we will wait another three days before we start our journey to Southampton.'

'Are you bored?' Kamala asked.

'Here in this quiet farmhouse,' he answered. 'I have seldom been more interested and—intrigued.'

'By . . . me?'

'You are a very intriguing person!'

'In what way?'

'I have never met anyone like you!'

'I am glad I do not resemble . . . the girls you must have met in . . . every port.'

'If they had been like you perhaps I would not have sailed for home.'

Kamala looked at him uncertainly. He had spoken in a dry, rather cynical tone, which made her unsure whether he was mocking her or not.

She had the feeling that at times, he forced himself to a brusqueness and an indifference he did not really feel.

It was almost as if he deliberately set her on one side, at a distance from him.

'Tell me more about France,' she suggested to change the subject.

'I do not know it as well as I know Italy,' Conrad answered, 'but you will enjoy Paris if you go there.'

'In what way?' Kamala asked.

'It has a beauty of its own for one thing,' he replied, 'and its people are charming. They have natural good manners, they are courteous, anxious to please and perhaps enjoy good living more than any other people on earth.'

'I thought all that was lost with the Revolution,' Kamala said.

'Revolutions may depose Kings,' Conrad answered, 'but they do not alter the essential character of the people.'

'No, I suppose that has been proved true all through history,' Kamala agreed.

It was extraordinary, he thought, how intelligent she was and how much knowledge she had of the customs and the character of nations all over the world.

'How do you know so much?' he asked her once when they were discussing the East and he found she had quite a comprehensive grasp of Buddhism.

Kamala smiled.

'Papa always said if we cannot travel with our bodies, there is no restriction on our minds.'

'You must have read a great deal.'

'I read whenever I get a chance,' Kamala answered.

There was a touch of bitterness in her voice when she thought how Uncle Marcus had denied her books, and told her continually that, if she had any spare time on her hands she should sew.

As if he understood her resentment, Conrad said:

'Now you are free of your Uncle, you will be able to read whenever you wish. Do you think your Aunt will have a large library?'

Kamala turned to look into the fire.

'I do not . . know.'

'At least she will not prevent—your reading.'

'I hope . . . not.'

'You sound uncertain. Perhaps you have not seen this Aunt for some years?'

'N . . . no.'

'And if you are not happy with her, what will you do then?'

'I am sure everything will be all right once I get to France,' Kamala replied.

She longed to admit to him that she had no Aunt. But he had been so shocked at her travelling alone that she was afraid that if he learnt that in fact she knew no-one in France and had nowhere to go once she arrived at Le Havre, he might insist on her going back to her Uncle.

That was the only reasonable and sensible course he could take, and therefore whatever happened she must not tell him the truth.

She would say goodbye to him at Southampton and he would assume that she would be in good hands once she reached the other side of the Channel.

All the same she hated any form of deception. He had been so kind, so understanding, and she knew that she could trust him.

He flattered her once, he had told her she was lovely, but in a manner which did not make her afraid, and she was only glad that he should think of her in such a way.

'I am lucky! Very lucky!' Kamala said to herself almost every night when she went to bed.

She was not so innocent that she did not realise that speaking as she had to a stranger, she might have found herself in difficult, if not unpleasant circumstances.

As it was, no-one could have been more considerate or more gentle with her than Conrad Veryan had been.

She had known few men, as those who had sought her out at the Castle had either been embarrassing or repellent.

She thought of General Warrington. She could imagine what his behaviour would have been in similar circumstances.

She knew little of such things, but she realised that to many men a woman was a plaything, a sport, a creature to be hunted as one might hunt a fox.

Conrad Veryan was different. He was very much a man,

no one could deny his masculinity. Yet he could be gentle and understanding, considerate and kind.

'He is rather a wonderful person,' Kamala whispered to herself.

When finally Conrad declared that he would wait no longer and that they must start their journey southwards, it was a cold and windy day with grey clouds and a promise of rain.

Kamala came into the yard as Conrad was saddling the horses.

He saw that she carried the rolled shawl in her hands which contained everything she possessed and was wearing a blue riding-habit with a thin muslin blouse.

'Have you no cloak?' he asked.

She shook her head.

'It was impossible for me to bring one.'

'Then we must stop and buy one in the first town we come to,' he said almost sharply.

'I shall be all right.'

Kamala was thinking of the expense knowing that she had already parted with some of her precious sovereigns to Mrs. Hayward.

She had an argument about it with Conrad.

'I will pay what is owed,' he said the night before.

'I will pay for myself,' Kamala replied.

'I cannot allow you to do that, considering that you have stayed here entirely on my account,' he answered. 'If I had not been laid up, you would have reached Southampton before now.'

'All the same,' Kamala said, 'I could not permit you, a stranger, to pay for my food and lodging.'

'You sound very conventional,' he said with a smile. 'Surely it is a little late in the day to be strait-laced when we have been staying here as brother and sister. Besides,

Mrs. Hayward will think it strange if we separately settle our obligations.'

Kamala could see the point of that.

'Then I will give you what I owe and you can pay her for us both.'

'Must you humiliate me?' Conrad asked. 'A man should always pay for a woman, or should I say a Gentleman for a Lady?'

Kamala looked at him for a moment and then she said:

'When you reach Southampton, what do you intend to do?'

'I must find myself a ship.'

'Because you need the money?'

'If you want to know,' he replied, 'I have to find employment and quickly.'

'I rather suspected that,' Kamala said. 'Therefore, because we are both poor, you will forget your pride and I will pay for myself.'

He laughed before he asked:

'Tell me honestly, Kamala, have you enough money with which to reach France?'

'I have twenty-five pounds,' Kamala answered, 'and when I reach Southampton I shall have to sell Rollo.'

'Then you are certainly not penniless,' Conrad said with a note of relief in his voice.

He therefore took the two sovereigns Kamala gave him.

'I do not think we can give Mrs. Hayward less,' she said hesitatingly, 'or do you think it is not enough?'

'I think she will be delighted if we give her four guineas for the time we have stayed here,' Conrad replied and he was not mistaken.

Mrs. Hayward was overwhelmed at receiving such a generous sum and they left the farmhouse with her blessings ringing in their ears.

'You will need a cloak not only for the ride,' Conrad said as a blustery wind whipped Kamala's fair hair across her cheeks, 'but also for crossing the Channel. It will be extremely cold and maybe very rough. Are you a good sailor?'

'I have never been on the sea,' Kamala answered, 'so I can only hope that I shall not be seasick. Are you ever ill?'

'Like Nelson, if the ship pitches or rolls abnormally, I sometimes feel a little queasy when I first go abroad,' Conrad replied. 'But usually when there is a storm one is too busy. There are sails to be taken down and a hundred things to be done, so that one has no time to think of one's self.'

'Not to think about it, is perhaps the answer to most illnesses,' Kamala said. 'Which is why children recover so much quicker than grown-ups.'

It was difficult to talk as Conrad was in a hurry to reach the nearest town.

It was not a large place but he found the way to an Emporium for Ladies and insisted that Kamala should buy a heavy cloak of thick wool with a hood that could cover her head.

She was disappointed that there was not much choice and the only cloak that was heavy and warm enough to please Conrad was black. She would have liked to purchase one in blue or even red, which she felt would brighten up the winter's day.

But Conrad dismissed them as too light and not serviceable enough for her requirements. She therefore had to bow to his choice and wrap herself in the black cloak.

'I look like something from the Spanish Inquisition,' she said laughingly when once more she was back in the saddle.

She had no idea that the dark cloak enhanced her beauty, making her skin look very white and her eyes vividly blue.

'I think the tortures you will inflict on your victims might be worse,' Conrad said dryly, but she did not quite understand what he meant.

They rode for several hours after luncheon until Kamala

could see that he was getting tired. His face was drawn and early in the afternoon she insisted they stop at a small wayside Inn.

'You are too big for me to pick up if you fall off your horse,' she said. 'Besides I too am tired. I have had so little exercise this past week.'

'Very well, Nurse,' Conrad said meekly. 'Better a hard bed than a scolding tongue!'

Kamala laughed.

'You always have the last word,' she said accusingly. 'I thought that at least was a woman's prerogative.'

The Inn was not as comfortable as the farmhouse, but it was comparatively clean. There were two bedrooms they could hire and good stabling for the horses.

'We will now use my name,' Conrad had said firmly before they entered the Inn.

'Of course, if you prefer it,' Kamala agreed.

'I shall certainly feel more at ease, than having to remember to be Mr. Lindham,' he replied.

Kamala could not help wondering what he would say if he knew that Lindham was not her name either.

'So many subterfuges!' she sighed to herself. 'I wish we could be truthful.'

Conrad had unsaddled the horses and seen that they were fed. But when he came into the small parlour where the Landlord said they could sit and where a meal would be served for them, Kamala saw how desperately tired he was.

'You have done too much,' she said softly.

He sat down in an armchair and she fetched a footstool on which he could rest his feet.

'I am ashamed that I should be so weak,' he murmured.

'You had a bad concussion,' she answered, 'and I know that your shoulder must be aching. When we go upstairs I will massage it for you.'

They had a simple and not particularly palatable meal and went upstairs immediately afterwards. Conrad had ordered a fire in both bedrooms and this time he insisted on Kamala taking the larger of the two.

'It is time I ceased playing the invalid,' he said. 'I have been cosseted for too long.'

'I think you really enjoy being cosseted,' Kamala smiled. 'Take off your coat and sit down in this low chair.'

She thought for a moment he was going to refuse and then because he was tired he obeyed.

He undid his shirt and she pulled it off his left shoulder and started to massage him as she had done before.

'That is better—much better,' he said.

She continued working on him praying as she did so that he might soon be strong and well.

She was not thinking of herself, and it was therefore with surprise that she suddenly felt Conrad reach up and put his hand over hers.

'Have I ever thanked you for what you have done for me?' he asked.

'Many times,' she replied. 'Is your shoulder better now?'

'I am no longer in pain.'

'Then it is time you went to bed. We will be able to ride further tomorrow.'

He lifted her hand from his shoulder as she spoke and turning his head touched it with his lips.

For a moment Kamala was startled. Then because his mouth was warm, firm and somehow possessive, she felt the colour rise in her cheeks.

She made a little movement to be free and immediately he released her and rose to his feet.

'Hurry into bed, Kamala,' he said, 'and sleep well.'

'I shall do that,' she replied, 'the wind is very tiring. Good-night, Conrad.'

'Good-night, Kamala.'

She did not look at him, feeling shy because he had kissed her hand. Then as he reached the door she heard him say :

'I wish I could thank you, but there are no words and I have no poetry.'

When she was in bed, she could not sleep. What did he mean, she wondered, by saying—'I have no poetry?' Had he thought that poetry was particularly applicable to her?

She would like him to think of her as a lovely ethereal nymph rising from a lake in the morning mist, or dancing in the light of full moon.

She sighed: real life was so practical, so commonplace. She had to arrange for his shirts to be washed, she had ironed them as she had brushed his coat, muddy from his fall.

His boots were not polished to her liking. He was continually sending her to see that the horses were properly fed.

What would he think of her if he saw her in an elegant evening gown with flowers in her hair?

She wished now she had worn one of her more elaborate dresses under her riding-habit; the one she had chosen was very plain.

'I have no poetry!'

She could hear his voice saying the words again and again as she fell asleep. Tomorrow they would be together and perhaps she would be brave enough to ask him what he had meant.

The morrow was unfortunately a wet day. It was very cold when they started and before mid-day, when they had ridden less than ten miles, the rain came down—a rain which gradually turned to sleet.

Conrad had put on his heavy riding-coat and Kamala was thankful that he had insisted on her buying the black cloak.

She pulled the hood low over her face so that all that showed was the tip of her little nose, but despite its thickness and the fact that it was almost rainproof she was still cold.

They stopped at a wayside Inn for lunch. Conrad persuaded the Innkeeper's wife to cook them eggs and ham which was a great deal more warming than the cheese and pickles which was the fare usually provided for travellers.

He also insisted on Kamala drinking some home-brewed cider, and when they set off again she found it was so strong that she was almost light-headed. But at least she was warmer.

It was, however, a warmth that did not last. The sleet was blowing hard in their faces, and this slowed the horses down and made them disinclined to press on at reasonable speed.

It was also growing steadily colder, and after two hours Kamala felt as if her very bones were frozen.

After a time it was almost impossible to see, but she realised they were in a wild, apparently uninhabited part of the country.

There seemed to be no houses, no farms, and, while they had kept clear of the main highways, not even any country roads.

'Damn it all,' she heard Conrad say, 'we cannot go on like this! We will have to find somewhere where we can shelter.'

'Surely there ... should be an ... Inn,' Kamala said faintly, feeling as she spoke the wind whistling the very words away from her cold lips.

'We have not seen a hamlet for the last five miles,' Conrad replied, 'and then it was only a few scattered cottages.'

The force of the wind driving the sleet seemed to increase.

Kamala was almost too cold to keep in the saddle, too cold to speak or ask that they should rest.

Then Conrad bent forward and taking hold of Rollo's bridle, turned him sharply to the right.

63

'I can see something over there,' he said. 'We will find out what it is.'

What he had seen was an old barn, broken down and dilapidated. When Conrad pulled open the doors, which were half off their hinges to bring the horses out of the sleet, they found it still half full of hay.

'This is better than nothing,' Conrad said grudgingly, and his voice seemed to echo eerily round the rafters.

There was an opening at the far end and he walked across to it. He was out of sight for a moment, and then Kamala heard him shout.

'Come and look! We are in luck!'

Walking stiffly because her legs could hardly obey her, Kamala moved towards him.

She found herself in what must once have been a farm cottage no bigger than a hut, consisting only of one room. The two windows were boarded up and the outside door was locked.

But there were the rough remains of a stone fire-place, powdered ashes and some dry pieces of wood lying about, as if the place had been used by other travellers, perhaps tramps.

'I will get a fire going,' Conrad said. 'Are you very cold?'

'Free ... zing,' Kamala managed to say through chattering teeth.

She was too cold even to remove her wet cloak. Her hands did not feel as if they belonged to her.

She went back into the barn so that she could sit down on the hay.

She knew she ought to do something to help, but for the moment she was too numb to think what was required.

The horses had made themselves at home and were eating the hay at the other end of the barn.

Kamala shut her eyes.

When she opened them again it was to feel Conrad pulling her to her feet.

'Come along,' he said, 'I have a fire going.'

She was so stiff that he had almost to carry her to the fire-side. She saw he had also moved into the room a mound of hay so that there was somewhere for her to sit.

'We must be careful the hay does not catch fire,' he cautioned, 'or we will be in trouble. I am not so concerned with the interests of the owner, as the fact that it will mean that we have no roof over our heads.'

'I cannot ... go any ... further,' Kamala murmured.

'I have no intention of asking you to do so,' he replied. 'I should have stopped an hour ago. Forgive me, Kamala, I was thinking of my own capabilities, not yours.'

'I shall be ... all right,' she said.

Realising she was too exhausted to do it herself, he pulled her wet gloves from her hands. Then he felt her cloak and the sleeve of her riding-jacket.

'You must take off your cloak,' he said, 'it is too wet.'

He touched the bottom of her skirt.

'This is soaked too,' he said. 'Take it off and I will hang it by the fire.'

He drew her cloak from her shoulders as he spoke, then realised that Kamala was staring at him in shocked surprise.

'I ... I cannot take off my skirt,' she said, 'not ... not with you here.'

'You have petticoats underneath,' he replied, 'remember, Kamala, I am your brother.'

She did not answer and after a moment he continued:

'You have seen me partially naked, washed me and you have massaged my shoulder. Is it really so reprehensible for me to ask you to remove a wet skirt which will undoubtedly give you a cold, if nothing worse, unless I dry it.'

'It seems ... different somehow,' Kamala said in a low voice.

He smiled at her as if she were a small child.

'I will not look, and I will bring in some more hay. When you have divested yourself as modestly as possible, I suggest you sit down and cover yourself with it.'

There was laughter in his voice and Kamala asked:

'Do you ... think I am ... very prudish?'

'I think that when you are so cold it is hard to think sensibly,' he replied. 'I cannot have you ill! Remember I am not in any way as skilful a nurse as you. What is more I have an aversion to sickness!'

Kamala gave a little choking laugh and then, as he turned his back arranging her cloak and his own riding-coat in front of the fire, she slipped off her riding-skirt.

It was only wet as far as her knees, but she knew that Conrad was right: if she kept it on all night the damp would undoubtedly give her a cold if not a fever.

Fortunately her riding-boots buttoned neatly to the ankle had kept her feet dry.

She put the wet skirt on the floor, sat down in the hay and pulled an armful over her white petticoats.

'Are you decent?' Conrad asked.

'Yes,' Kamala answered. 'Are you ... laughing at me?'

'I would never laugh at you unkindly,' he said in his deep voice.

He turned as he spoke and she looked up into his dark eyes.

'I know ... you think ... I am ... very foolish.'

'One day I will tell you what I think,' he answered '—but not now. We are both too cold and unpleasantly hungry.'

As he spoke of it, Kamala realised that she was indeed very hungry.

'If I had any sense,' Conrad went on in an irritated tone, 'I would have bought something to eat when we stopped for luncheon, but I imagined we would find an Inn quite easily. I had no idea the weather would become so rough.'

He walked back into the barn as he spoke and a few seconds later returned with something in his hands.

'It may not be a feast of Lucullus,' he said, 'but I have found a few potatoes! We will bake them in front of the fire, at least they will stop the more acute pangs of an empty stomach.'

'When I was a child I used to bake potatoes in a bonfire on Guy Fawkes day,' Kamala said. 'They always tasted delicious.'

'We are a few days too late to celebrate that particular festival,' Conrad said, 'but let us hope the potatoes taste as good.'

Because they were so hungry the potatoes seemed even more delicious than Kamala had remembered.

There were several bad ones amongst those Conrad had collected, but there were enough good ones to blunt their hunger and take away the empty feeling which had been accentuated by the cold.

'I should also have brought some brandy with me,' Conrad said lying back against the mound of hay at Kamala's side.

'If you make a list of all the things we might have brought it would fill a book,' she answered. 'I have been remembering dozens of necessities I omitted to pack when I ran away.'

'Like what?' he enquired.

'Extra handkerchiefs, a scarf, thicker stockings! Oh there are hundreds of them! But, as my Nurse used to say, "What can't be cured, must be endured!"'

Conrad laughed and rose to make up the fire.

'We should count our blessings,' he said. 'If this wood had not been here I should have had to go outside and collect some. I am only hoping there is enough to last the night.'

He looked at it doubtfully then gave an exclamation.

He went to the barn and came back with a big oak beam, which had once supported the roof but had fallen down.

'I noticed this as we came in,' Conrad said. 'It will burn slowly and keep us warm while we are asleep.'

'It seems to be getting colder.'

Kamala shivered as she spoke and Conrad reached out to feel her cloak and see if it was now dry. But the sleet had penetrated deep into the wool.

He went into the barn to fetch more hay, stacking it round her so that she was almost covered in it.

'Not a very decorative quilt,' he said, 'but I think you will find it quite effective.'

'I am sure . . . I will be all . . . right,' she said bravely.

The wind seemed to increase and was now blowing so hard and so noisily that she was half afraid the roof would blow off.

But the little house must have stood many storms, and although at one end of the room the rain was dripping through the roof onto the flagged floor, where they were sitting was quite dry.

Conrad made up the fire, then he came and sat down again next to Kamala. As he did so a gust of wind seemed nearly to lift the whole place off the ground.

'We are fortunate not to be out in that.'

'Very fortunate,' Kamala agreed.

He saw her shiver and realised that she was still cold.

'Let me feel your hands.'

He took them in his and found that the warmth she had engendered for a short time by holding the hot potatoes had disappeared.

'We shall have to get close to each other,' he said. 'Once when I was at sea in the Arctic regions, we found the only way to prevent us from getting frostbite, was to sleep as near to each other as we could—man to man. Body heat is more effective than any fire.'

68

He put his arm round Kamala as he spoke and drew her to him.

'I want you to put your left hand inside your jacket against your breast,' he said.

A little bewildered, she did as he asked.

'Keep it there,' he said. 'Now give me your right hand.'

She did as she was told and to her surprise he thrust it inside his jacket against his shirt. Then pulling her still closer until her head was against his shoulder, with his free hand he covered them both up to their necks with hay.

Kamala was stiff with embarrassment. There was something strange and even a little frightening in being closer to a man than she had ever been before.

She could feel Conrad's heart beating beneath her fingers and she was acutely conscious of his arms round her, her cheek against his riding-coat.

'Relax,' Conrad said softly above her head, 'and if you are shocked at being so close to me, remember it will be no consolation to your prudery if you are covered in ice in the morning and stiff as a board.'

Realising that he was teasing her, she gave a little laugh and found she was in fact no longer shocked.

'That is better!' he said. 'I had begun to think I had gone to bed with a broomstick.'

'I wonder what . . . people would think if they could . . . see us.'

'They would think and say a lot of very unpleasant things,' Conrad answered, 'but as they are never likely to know what has occurred it is not of any particular consequence. What is much more important is whether we feel we are doing wrong. Do you think it is wrong of me, little Kamala, to save you from being an icicle in the morning?'

'No, of course not,' Kamala answered.

Then after a moment she added :

'If I was really your sister, would you be upset if you knew I was . . . close to a man . . . like this?'

Conrad thought before he replied:

'In similar circumstances it would of course depend on the man—and the woman.'

'What could a woman do that was wrong?' Kamala asked in surprise.

'Nothing that you would understand,' Conrad replied.

She gave a little sigh.

'Am I very . . . ignorant?'

She felt his arms tighten as if involuntarily. Then he said gently:

'Go to sleep, Kamala. Tomorrow there will doubtless be another adventure. This is the sort of tale with which we can amuse our grandchildren! Yours and my adventures as we travel into the unknown.'

The words seemed to kindle Kamala's imagination.

This was an adventure, she thought, an adventure so exciting, so unexpected that she knew Conrad was right and she would remember it all her life.

Her hand against his chest was growing warmer and there was something secure and very pleasant about being in his arms.

She felt safe, safe from everything that frightened her. Safe from Uncle Marcus, safe for the moment, even from her fears of the future.

She gave a little sigh of relief and without realising it cuddled a little closer to him. Her eyes closed and very shortly she fell asleep.

But Conrad Veryan lay awake for a long time watching the flames from the fire throw strange shadows on the broken walls, while the wind outside wailed like a lost soul.

4

Kamala awoke to find she was alone.

At first she could not think where she was, until as she stared up at the rough beams overhead and down at the smouldering ashes of the fire, she remembered.

Where had Conrad gone?

For a moment she felt a sense of panic in case he had left her. Then she heard him whistling and realised he was in the barn attending to the horses.

Kamala rose to her feet, shook off the hay and saw that her velvet riding-skirt had been arranged neatly beside her.

'Conrad must have put it there,' she thought, and blushed that she should have lain in his arms all night wearing only her petticoats.

She quickly put on her riding-skirt and attempted to tidy her hair before she went into the barn, to see the horses already saddled, and Conrad opening the rickety doors.

'Good morning,' he said, 'may I enquire if Your Ladyship has slept well?'

'Extraordinarily well, thank you, Sir,' Kamala replied. 'I have never known a more comfortable bed or indeed more efficient service.'

'Unfortunately our Landlord has forgotten to provide us with breakfast,' Conrad said, 'and I suggest that as quickly as possible we repair the omission.'

'I am hungry too,' Kamala smiled, and picking up her dry cloak she put it round her shoulders.

It was a clear morning and, though the ground was still

wet from the night before, the air was crisp which made Kamala feel there might be sharp frost later on.

They set off at a good pace, the horses well rested, and half an hour later came to a black and white timbered Inn standing on a picturesque village green.

'We could have reached here last night,' Conrad remarked.

'It was not worth the risk,' Kamala replied. 'And after all, we should not complain. I, personally, was very comfortable.'

'So was—I.'

He looked at her as he spoke, and although there was nothing exceptional about his words, Kamala suddenly felt confused by the expression in his eyes.

She felt he was remembering how closely they had lain together. She had never been in a man's arms before, but Conrad had not made her feel afraid.

He could not have been kinder, he could not have made the whole episode seem more reasonable and inevitable in the circumstances.

'I want to thank you,' she said impulsively.

'What for?' he asked and then added so she knew he understood, 'there is nothing for which you have to thank me. You were very sensible and—brave.'

They were able to wash, Conrad to shave and both ate an enormous breakfast in the small Inn before they set off once more towards the coast.

The horses made good progress and when finally they stopped for the night, Kamala knew that the following day they would reach Southampton.

When she retired that night on a small hard bed it was with a feeling of deep depression. She had so little time left with Conrad.

It was almost impossible to realise that after tomorrow she would have to go on without him, and they might never meet again.

She had not realised until now how comforting it was to be with a man, to leave him to make the decisions, to know that she was secure.

In addition to that, she had never before known such comradeship. There seemed to be so much to talk about, so much to discuss.

They argued, they disagreed and then would find themselves completely in accord on subjects on which Kamala had never expected a man to be interested.

Conrad was well read and well educated, in a way that surprised her.

She had thought that sailors were only concerned with physical achievements and would have no use for literature and the rather obscure subjects which had delighted her Father and on which she had grown extremely knowledgeable.

But Conrad had not only visited strange countries, he had also learnt about their people, and their politics. He had understood their ambitions and their difficuties.

'For ordinary people in every country in the world the problems are the same,' he remarked. 'How to stay alive, how to find work, how to have enough food.'

'And for the others?' Kamala inquired.

'All the pleasures that money can buy, the comforts and the concubines!'

He spoke bitterly.

'Must one be rich to enjoy life?' Kamala asked.

He did not answer for a moment. Then he said in a different tone:

'That is a pertinent question, Kamala, and one which does not deserve a flippant reply— No, money does not bring enjoyment of the real gifts of life, only the superficial ones!'

He paused and went on:

'There is always sunshine, beauty and of course—love, for those who can raise their eyes from the flesh-pots.'

He did not say any more. Kamala longed to ask him if he had found love and what it had meant to him. But she thought he might think that she was impertinently curious.

For Kamala the hours sped by so quickly but when at last they reached the outskirts of Southampton her heart sank and she felt depressed to the point of tears because tomorrow they would separate.

'Shall I ever see him again?' she wondered.

She realised that while they had talked so much of so many things, he had told her very little about himself.

All she knew was that he was a sailor, and that once he had seen her safely on to the Paddle-Steamer he would find himself a new ship and set off in search of new horizons.

She had a wild impulse to ask him to take her with him.

Then she knew that if she even suggested such a thing, he would not only refuse her but might insist, however much she protested, on sending her back to her Uncle.

There was nothing else he could do under the circumstances, she told herself logically.

She was only a stranger he had befriended. He had escorted her to Southampton where he was going himself and he was grateful to her because she had set his collarbone and nursed him back to health.

Conrad had, in fact, recovered almost completely from the accident. His shoulder still ached a little, but every day he admitted to feeling it less, and judging by his appetite there was nothing wrong with him otherwise.

'I know of a small Inn which is clean and respectable where I have stayed before,' he told Kamala just before they reached Southampton.

The Inn was near the quay and as they rode towards it, Kamala looked at the sea, grey in the afternoon light, and felt a little shiver of fear that tomorrow she would be crossing the Channel, leaving behind everything that was familiar.

'What lies ahead of me,' she wondered. 'What troubles, what difficulties? Can I ever manage on my own?'

There was one consolation in knowing that she would have some money.

Even if Conrad could not obtain seventy pounds for Rollo whatever he fetched added to what she had already, would keep her for many months until she found employment.

'I will call at the schools in Le Havre and ask if they want a teacher,' Kamala told herself.

She could speak French fluently and could read it without any difficulty.

She was glad now to think how much French literature she knew and was grateful that her Father had insisted on her being proficient in French grammar.

'You are very serious,' Conrad said when he came into the small parlour of 'Drake's Drum' and found her sitting staring at the fire.

'I was waiting for you,' Kamala said quickly.

'I have already made enquiries about selling the horses. The Landlord knows a dealer who will give us an honest price. He has sent a boy to ask him to come down to the Inn as soon as he can.'

'And the Paddle-Steamer?' Kamala faltered.

'It crosses every day at noon,' Conrad answered. 'Of course it does not always set out in very rough weather, so we will have to wait for the morning to be quite certain that you can embark.'

'We can see what the sea is like from the windows,' she murmured.

He sat down on the other side of the fire-place.

'You will be all right?'

It was a statement rather than a question.

'Yes.'

'Does your Aunt know you are coming?'

'No.'

'Then how are you certain she is there? You told me you had not seen her for some time.'

'My ... my Father ... has ... had letters from her,' Kamala replied, not daring to look at Conrad in case he should realise she was lying.

'That must have been over three years ago, as your parents were drowned in 1836.'

'Y ... Yes.'

'Are you not taking rather a chance in going to Le Havre without being completely certain she is still living there?'

'I am ... sure it will be ... all ... right.'

It seemed as if Conrad was going to say something then changed his mind.

Kamala thought, although she might have been mistaken, that his hand went out towards her, but unexpectedly he got to his feet.

'I am just going to walk as far as the harbour and see what ships are in,' he said abruptly. 'I will not be long. The Landlord says that he will not be able to serve us with supper for at least an hour.'

He was gone from the room without waiting for her reply.

'I am not at all hungry,' Kamala thought miserably.

After a little while she went upstairs to her bedroom and changed from her riding-habit into her only gown.

As she put it on she suddenly wished she had something different to wear this last night. Something beautiful! An evening dress of blue tulle with a full skirt and a low décolletage which would reveal her neck and the tops of her white shoulders.

Conrad had never seen her like that. If he did would he admire her, would he think she was pretty ... or even lovely?

She had once worn a blue dress which she knew made her look her best. It had belonged to her Mother and when she was living at Castle Bray she altered it to fit herself.

She had gone down to dinner in it, happy because it reminded her of the gay, laughter filled days at home. The full skirt and the little puff sleeves trimmed with lace and white and pink velvet bows made her feel romantic—a fairy-tale Princess.

'Why are you dressed up like a circus horse?'

Her Uncle's coarse, ugly, voice brought her back to reality.

'This was one of Mama's gowns, Uncle Marcus!'

'It was doubtless suitably frivolous for your—Mother.'

The tone in which he spoke was insulting.

'How d . . .' Kamala bit back the angry words from her lips. She knew her Uncle was deliberately provoking her.

'Did you wish to say anything?'

'No . . . no, Uncle Marcus!'

Only silence could deprive him of an excuse to beat her for impertinence.

'Then go and change immediately! I shall give orders that the gown is to be burnt. The rubbish-dump is the right place for it!'

For a moment Kamala looked at him, her eyes blazing with anger. Then as he waited expectantly, a cruel smile on his lips, she turned away.

He hated her because she was pretty, because he knew that while he could browbeat her into outward subservience, there was some spark of pride and rebelliousness within her he could never subdue. Conrad was different, so very different in every way.

Kamala took immense pains in arranging her hair and yet when finally she was ready to go downstairs she still felt dissatisfied.

She wanted him to remember her, she wanted him to think of her when she was gone. But was it likely when he was setting off on a new adventure himself?

There would be a ship waiting for him in the harbour. A ship going to India, China, the West Indies or South

Africa. What did it matter where he went if she could not go with him and must be left behind?

She felt that never again in her life would she be as happy as she had been these last days.

Perhaps never as happy as she had been the night when he had held her in his arms because she was cold. They had eaten baked potatoes in a leaking broken-down hut, and incredibly it had been a wonderful experience.

Slowly Kamala went down the narrow oak staircase into the parlour.

She thought to find Conrad there but the room was empty. And with a disproportionate sense of loneliness she sat down again in front of the fire.

Then her heart leapt with an irrepressible excitement because she heard his voice in the passage.

He came into the room pulling off his overcoat.

'It is bitterly cold outside,' he said. 'I would not be surprised if we have a black frost.'

'Did you find a ship?'

Her voice sounded unfamiliar.

'I found several,' he answered. 'You need not worry about me, Kamala. I have a wide choice, and the Paddle-Steamers are not full at this time of year, so there will be no difficulty in your obtaining a passage tomorrow.'

It seemed to her that his voice was hard and indifferent. He sat down in the chair opposite her and smoothed out a newspaper he had carried in under his arm.

'*The Times!*' Kamala exclaimed. 'Has anything exciting happened? I feel as if we have been away a long time from civilisation.'

It was true. They might have been in some far off foreign land this past week.

Out of touch with everything except themselves, the outside world had not encroached upon them and, as far as Kamala was concerned, they had not been curious.

'There appears to be nothing but eulogies about the

78

charm of Prince Albert of Saxe-Coburg and Gotha and pictures of the Queen,' Conrad said turning the pages. 'She obviously intends to marry him, and if there is one thing which the people of every country in the world enjoy more than anything else, it is a Royal wedding.'

'I should like to see the Queen,' Kamala said. 'She is so young and pretty! I hope Prince Albert will be kind to her.'

'I am sure he will be,' Conrad replied. 'He appears to be a decent fellow in spite of the fact that he is a German.'

'You do not like Germans?' Kamala asked.

'I find them stiff and formal if they are aristocrats and aggressive if they are not.'

'Then you must not sail on a German ship.'

'I have no intention of doing so.'

'Tell me what ships you found in the harbour.'

He did not reply and she looked at him in surprise. He appeared to be deeply intent on reading something in the newspaper.

Because it was their last night together she felt annoyed at his preoccupaton with anything rather than herself.

'I asked you . . .' she began.

Then suddenly he folded the newspaper in half and held it out to her pointing to an item low down on the page.

'Perhaps you will explain this,' he said in a voice she had never heard from him before.

She took the paper from him, read the head-line and felt her heart miss a beat. Slowly because she was so afraid she read:

'WEALTHY LANDOWNER'S LOST NIECE

Mr. Marcus Pleyton, of Castle Bray in the County of Berkshire, asks that anyone who has seen his niece by marriage, Miss Kamala Lindsey, should communicate with him immediately. Miss Lindsey, an attractive girl of eighteen, was last seen riding towards the village of Little Bray on a roan horse with the name of Rollo.

Aged eighteen, with fair hair and blue eyes, Miss Lindsey has made her home at the Castle since the death of her parents, Mr. & Mrs. Andrew Lindsey, in 1836 when they were drowned at sea.

Mr. Marcus Pleyton, who is deeply distressed at the disappearance of his niece, fears this may prove to be a matter for the police. He offers a reward of one hundred pounds for any information which finally leads to the discovery of her whereabouts.'

As Kamala finished reading the paragraph she sprang to her feet.

'He is trying to find me!' she cried. 'He has offered a reward for me! Someone will inform on me and then he will ... drag me back! I must leave for France tonight! Perhaps he is having the Paddle-Steamers watched! Find me another sort of ship, a boat, anything! Once I get to France I can hide ... it is a big country ... and he will not be able to ... discover me. I cannot go back! I cannot!'

She dropped the newspaper on the floor and without realising what she was doing threw herself against Conrad who had risen to his feet and held on to him frantically.

'Save me ... save me!' she begged. 'I cannot go back ... I cannot!'

He held her for a moment.

Then gently he pushed her back into the chair she had just vacated.

'It is all right, Kamala,' he said quietly, 'you are safe, he will not find you.'

'He will ... he will ... he always wins! I cannot escape him.'

Conrad, still holding her hand, drew his own chair nearer to her. He sat down and said quietly:

'Suppose now you tell me the truth. Your name is Lindsey and you have no Aunt in France!'

Kamala was trembling and her breath was coming in frightened gasps between her lips.

'N . . . no.'

'Why did you not tell me so?'

'Because . . . I did not wish to be a . . . further encumbrance . . . on you.'

'You knew I would not let you go to France alone,' his voice was stern.

'Yes . . . I knew . . . that.'

Conrad released her hand and sat back in his chair. Kamala looked up at him with terrified eyes.

'You will help me . . . you will not make me . . . return to . . . Uncle Marcus? You will help me . . . to escape him?'

'I will not make you return to your Uncle,' Conrad agreed, 'but, Kamala, we must be sensible about this.'

'There is nothing sensible we can do,' she answered. 'If I am in England, he will find me! Someone will be glad to earn a hundred pounds! I have to go to France! Can you not see it is the only place I will be . . . free of him?'

'You cannot go to France alone,' Conrad answered. 'Use your brains, Kamala. You are little more than a child and you are very pretty. What do you think will happen to you?'

'I will find work,' Kamala replied. 'I thought I would ask at the schools if they require an English teacher. I can take private pupils. I might even become a governess to a French family.'

'And do you think that such positions will be open to you without a reference?'

She was silent.

'Then what can I . . . do?' she asked at length. 'I would rather . . . die than marry . . . General Warrington.'

Again there was silence. After a moment Conrad pushed back his chair and walked across the room.

He stood with his back to Kamala and because she knew he was worried and perturbed she said hesitatingly:

81

'This is not your ... problem. Forget me! I will manage ... somehow. God will look ... after me.'

'And do you think God will be able to protect you from the sort of men who will never leave you alone?' Conrad asked harshly.

'Perhaps I could make ... myself look ... ugly,' Kamala faltered.

He laughed, it was a bitter sound.

'You are so young!' he said. 'You do not understand what the world is like or what you are up against. I have to do something for you. God alone knows what!'

'Why must you?' Kamala asked. 'You do not know me, we have just met by accident. You have no obligation whatever towards me. Just go on with your own life! Do what you were going to do before you met me.'

'Do you really think that is possible?' Conrad asked.

There was something in his voice, and in the expression in his eyes, which made her feel strangely excited. Then in a very different tone he said :

'I have never told you, Kamala, about myself and now I am going to do so. I am the youngest of three sons. My parents lived in Cornwall.'

'Of course, your name is Cornish!' Kamala interrupted. 'I thought I must have heard it somewhere. Veryan Bay was marked in the Atlas I used as a child.'

'My family name occurs frequently in the history of Cornwall,' Conrad said. 'But blue blood and deeds of gallantry do not ensure a comfortable bank balance! Because we had very little money, I went off adventuring when I left school at the age of eighteen.'

'As a sailor?' Kamala asked.

'I went to sea in a Schooner,' Conrad replied. 'I came home at intervals to find my Father growing very frail and my Mother in ill-health. But my brothers were looking after them and as there was little I could do I went back to sea.'

He paused as if he was recalling a sequence of events.

'After my last voyage which had been to India,' he continued, 'I returned with what seemed to me to be quite a considerable sum of money—over a thousand pounds. I intended to give the greater part of it to my parents and spend the rest on riotous living.'

There was a short silence before he said:

'I am not pretending, Kamala, that I have lived anything but a full life. I am an adventurer and I have enjoyed my adventuring.

'It never struck me that I might save for my old age or worry where the next penny was coming from. There seemed to be enough when I needed it.'

He walked towards the door and back again before he continued.

'When I arrived home three weeks ago I found things had changed drastically. My brothers had both been drowned while attempting to save the lives of some seamen whose ship had run ashore on the rocks.

'There was a high sea and the boat in which they put out overturned and eventually no-one was saved!'

'How terrible!' Kamala cried.

'What is more,' Conrad went on, 'I found that my Father had died and my Mother was very weak. After my brothers' death, nothing had been done in the house or on the estate. The servants had not been paid, the place had not been farmed because the workers had left, and the family was in fact deeply in debt.'

Conrad took a deep breath as if he was remembering what a shock it had all been.

'I fortunately had enough money to pay the outstanding wages and to keep the pensioners my Father had always saved from starvation. But I realised that I must have more money and within a short space of time. My Mother's life hangs on a thread and only by the greatest care and attention can she be kept alive.'

Kamala drew a deep breath.

'So that is why you were going to Southampton to ... find a ship?'

'Yes—that is why,' Conrad agreed.

'But how will you get enough money to support your Mother and all the other people?' Kamala asked.

'There are ways of making money quickly at sea,' he answered, 'and when I went down to the harbour tonight I knew the way was waiting for me.'

'Tell me about it.'

'There is a clipper in the harbour belonging to a man called Van Wyck. He is half Dutch, half English. He is an extremely rich, extremely astute man, and his wealth comes from the cargoes which he runs between country and country. Mostly they are things which are not free for export or import.'

'You mean he is a smuggler?' Kamala asked.

'Not exactly,' Conrad answered. 'Yet perhaps that is the right word on a very grand scale. I was in the harbour only a short time, but I discovered that Van Wyck is now taking his clipper to Mexico.'

'And what will he collect from there?'

'Gold or silver,' Conrad answered. 'Since their independence in 1821, Mexico has forbidden the export of both metals except by the Government. But I do not imagine that Van Wyck's cargo will have a government stamp on it.'

'And you will go with him,' Kamala asked.

'I have not asked him yet,' Conrad answered. 'But not many men have my experience of such cargoes and most owners are only too eager to engage someone like myself.'

'I am sure ... that Van Wyck would wish to ... have you,' Kamala said in a low voice.

'But what am I to do about you?' Conrad asked.

'F ... forget me.'

'And if I tell you that that is impossible?'

84

Their eyes met across the room and Kamala suddenly found it was hard to breathe.

She felt as if something magnetic passed between them, something inescapable and wonderful, which made her tremble.

She could not take her eyes from his. Her lips parted and she thought for one wild moment that she must rise from her chair and run into his arms.

Then he turned away from her and broke the spell.

He walked to the window, drew back the curtains and opened the casement as if in need of air. The cold came surging into the room like a tidal wave.

Conrad stood looking out into the darkness. Then he said harshly!

'Damn you! Damn all women!'

Kamala felt as if he had struck her. She wanted to apologise, wanted to ask his forgiveness, but her voice seemed caught in her throat.

After some minutes when the temperature in the room had dropped almost to freezing, Conrad shut the window with a bang.

There was something aggressive in the manner in which he walked back to the fire. He was frowning and his eyes were hard.

Kamala did not look at him, she was staring into the flames. But she was acutely conscious of him, conscious that he was angry.

A tear ran down her cheek. She did not wipe it away, because she hoped he would not notice it.

He did not speak, only stood beside her so large and overpowering that she felt hopelessly small and insignificant. Why should he worry about her?

Another tear followed the first.

'For God's sake do not cry,' he said sharply. 'If there is one thing I cannot stand it is a woman in tears.'

'I ... I am not c ... crying,' Kamala murmured.

In answer he threw his handkerchief into her lap.

She picked it up, then realising that the irritation in his voice had sapped the last remnants of her control, she rose to her feet.

'I . . . I am s . . sorry,' she whispered and ran from the room.

Upstairs in her bedroom she fought against an overwhelming desire to throw herself on the bed and burst into a tempest of weeping.

Instead she washed her face in cold water.

'I am tired and hungry,' she thought, 'that is what is wrong with me. I must not spoil our last evening together by upsetting him.'

The thought of it being their last evening was a stab in her heart, but she forced herself to go downstairs, apprehensive in case he should still be angry.

When she reached the parlour it was to find the Landlord bringing in their supper and her return was therefore saved from any awkwardness.

Although Conrad made no comment at her reappearance she had the feeling that he was ashamed of his bad temper.

They made desultory conversation on unimportant subjects while they were eating and being waited on by the Landlord and his daughter. She was a young woman who cast admiring glances at Conrad although he did not appear to notice her.

'Conrad has the indefinable quality,' Kamala thought, 'which makes one realise at first sight that he is of consequence. Father had had it too.'

It had nothing to do with money or expensive well-cut clothes and luxurious surroundings. Marcus Pleyton had all these in abundance and yet he remained unimpressive, a man of no real account.

'Women will always be attracted to Conrad,' Kamala thought, 'he is handsome and has so much presence. It

86

would be impossible for him to be ignored in any company, however grand.'

Finally dinner was finished, the table was cleared and they were alone.

'You are tired tonight,' Conrad said. 'I suggest we leave our problems until the morning.'

Kamala wanted to say that she would be unable to sleep when her whole future lay in the balance, but she was afraid it might annoy him.

'Yes ... of course. Perhaps we shall find a solution in our ... dreams!'

'My dreams are seldom so helpful,' Conrad said dryly.

Because he seemed to expect it of her, Kamala rose to her feet. She did not wish to leave him, she wanted to stay.

This was their last night and it was an agony to go to bed thinking he was still incensed with her.

'Good night, Kamala.'

His voice was stern without the warmth and the kindliness she had grown to expect.

'G ... good-night.'

She hesitated. She wanted to tell him once again how sorry she was to be such a nuisance, but before she could speak the Landlord entered the room.

'The Horsedealer has arrived, Sir. He's looking at the horses.'

'I will come to the stables,' Conrad replied. 'Good-night, Kamala.'

There was nothing more she could say, she thought despairingly. He walked away down the passage and she climbed the staircase to her bedroom.

She stood looking at the narrow bed, the worn carpet, the cheap scratched furniture, and shuddered. She knew she could no longer impose on Conrad.

He had told her that he had stayed in this Inn before, and it could only have been because he could not afford anything better.

He had his Mother and his dependants to support. How could she increase his commitments and perhaps prevent him from sailing to Mexico?

Kamala made up her mind. There was no alternative.

Slowly but deliberately she forced herself to change back into her riding-habit. It was much warmer than her gown and too cumbersome to carry.

She put all her small belongings and the discarded gown into her shawl, made it into a bundle and laid it on the bed. Then she waited.

It was nearly an hour later that she heard Conrad come upstairs.

He paused on the landing outside her room and she held her breath in case he should knock on her door.

But he must have thought she was asleep, because after a second or so he went into his own bedroom. She could hear him moving about and thought he must be undressing.

'Goodbye,' she whispered, 'God keep you and watch over you.'

She could not pray any more, it made her feel like crying. She put on her cloak and picked up the bundle from the bed.

It would be better to creep out now. Later she thought it might be difficult to find other accommodation for the night.

Vaguely Kamala remembered hearing that Inns would often refuse to serve an unaccompanied woman. She wondered why.

She felt a sudden fear of going out on her own into the streets of Southampton. Supposing there were drunkards about, supposing men spoke to her? She had no idea which way to go or where to find a respectable lodging. Then she told herself severely:

'I have to learn to look after myself!'

When she reached France it would be even more difficult!

But she had chosen to be independent, and she could not be a coward or cling to a man who did not want her.

'Please God . . . help me!'

She picked up her bundle, as she did there was a knock on the door.

She stood paralysed into immobility.

The knock came again, and then as she did not answer the door opened and Conrad still fully dressed walked into the room.

Kamala's heart seemed to turn a somersault and stop beating. Her face was very pale as she faced him, her black cloak covering her habit, the bundle in her arms.

'I felt you might be doing something like this,' he said. 'Where the devil do you think you are going?'

The question seemed to vibrate between them and then there was a silence.

She tried to meet the anger in his eyes, the fierceness of his expression, and failed.

'Where were you going?' he asked the question again.

'A . away!'

'That is obvious!'

'I . . . I do not want to b . bother . . . you.'

'You are thinking of me? Kamala, how can you be so foolish?'

His voice was suddenly kind, she felt the tears well into her eyes—the tears he despised and which irritated him.

She turned her head aside.

'Let m . me . . . go. I m . must not be an encumbrance . . . you have . . . so many people for whom you must . . . provide. I am of no i . importance in your l . life.'

'Did you really think I would let you leave me?'

There was a tone in his voice which made her look up into his face, and then without meaning to do so, instinctively, without conscious thought, she moved towards him.

His arms went round her and she hid her face against his shoulder.

'I am sorry .. I wanted to d . do what is r .. right.'

'I will decide that.'

She felt as if she were a ship that had reached harbour after a rough voyage. She could put herself into his hands! She was safe! Safe when she had thought to be alone and helpless.

He put her gently but firmly away from him.

'Let us have no more self-sacrificing gestures or mad impulsive actions of this sort.'

His voice was serious but he was not angry. He took her cloak from her shoulders.

'Can I trust you, or shall I keep this in my room? You would not last long in the cold outside without it.'

'I will not . . . run away.'

'Can I be sure of that?'

'I will give you my . . . word of honour.'

'And that of course I must accept,' he said with laughter in his voice. 'Go to bed, Kamala. Heroics are invariably fatiguing.'

She looked up at him uncertainly, her eyes in the candle-light dark with anxiety.

'We must think of where I can . . . go early tomorrow. If you do not . . . see Mr. Van Wyck he might . . . sail without . . . you.'

'There will be other ships,' Conrad said lightly.

'If only I could come with . . . you,' Kamala said wistfully, 'as cabin boy, or even as a . stowaway.'

Conrad looked at her little pointed face, big blue eyes and her hair shining in the firelight.

'Do you really think anyone would take you for a boy?' he smiled.

Then suddenly he was still.

'I have an—idea,' he said very slowly. 'It seems impossible, yet we might—we might just pull it off!'

5

'We have won! We have succeeded!'

Kamala said the words to herself as lying in the darkness she felt the Clipper begin to move.

There was the noise of men running on the deck overhead, the slap of the sails in the wind, the soft lap of the water against the sides.

They were moving! The wind was taking them slowly out of harbour and soon they would be on the open sea.

Kamala felt every muscle in her body relax and she knew then how tensed and strained she had been while they waited.

'If they find us before we are at sea,' Conrad had said, 'then we will have failed and there is nothing we can do about it.'

But they had succeeded. Succeeded against what had seemed almost impossible odds! Conrad's fantastic gamble had come off!

He had worked out and explained everything down to the last detail, and Kamala knew now that lying on the floor beside her he must be feeling almost as elated as she was.

But, she thought, she had more to gain than he had. He would have gone to sea anyway.

He would have been aboard the *Aphrodite* while she would have been left behind unless as he said in his own words they could—'pull it off'.

When he had first told her of his plan, she had thought he must be crazy.

Then as he explained exactly what he intended to do, she

felt a strange, sweet excitement creep over her knowing that not only could she be with him, but that he wanted her.

She could hear his voice saying :

'Do you really think I would leave you?' and she knew that from that moment her fear and depression had gone and she was no longer desperate and afraid.

Conrad would not abandon her, she would not be alone, she did not have to face a strange and frightening world without him.

There were shouts overhead and a sudden crack almost like a cannon shot as the wind swept out the foresails. The whole Clipper seemed to quiver and the sound of the waves slapping against the sides and breaking in spray over the deck seemed to intensify. They were gathering speed.

There was something exhilarating in thinking of the tapering white Clipper with its three tall masts skimming over the grey waves on the early morning tide.

'This is the greatest adventure I have ever undertaken!' Kamala thought to herself.

She longed to speak to Conrad and learn if he was as excited as she was.

It seemed so strange to think of him lying on the floor closely bound by the ropes she had wound around him and gagged with a handkerchief tied tightly behind his neck.

He had gagged her first. They had rehearsed at the Inn exactly how they could manage both to be bound when they would be discovered in the cabin.

'We have to make it convincing,' Conrad said over and over again. 'Not for one moment must they suspect. Van Wyck is a clever man. If he had the slightest idea that this was a put-up job to get you aboard, then I would hate to think of the consequences.'

'What could he do?' Kamala asked curiously.

'Do not let us even discuss it,' Conrad said. 'But make

no mistake, Kamala, we cannot afford to make a slip, how-ever small, which might arouse his suspicions.'

'I will be careful ... very careful,' Kamala promised.

She would have promised Conrad anything because she was so happy at the thought of being with him. Yet the plot they had arranged between them had not seemed real.

It was a charade, a theatrical performance in which they were taking the leading parts rather than an action which was vitally important because on it depended their whole future.

Conrad had sat down on the little narrow bed in Kamala's room at the Inn, and as he talked of what they should do the pieces fell into place like a jig-saw puzzle.

'We are brother and sister,' he said slowly, 'people of importance, who have come down to the Quay out of curiosity. You must be wearing an evening gown and that, Kamala, is all you will be able to take with you.'

She looked at him wide-eyed and he repeated:

'You will have what you stand up in, nothing else. Your jewels, your money and of course mine will all have been taken by the ruffians who assaulted us.'

'What ruffians?' she asked.

'Four of them, against whom I could not defend myself, who robbed us and then, having rendered us insensible, tied us up and shanghaied us aboard the Clipper.'

It took a little while for Kamala to grasp exactly what was involved, but when she did and she realised that if his plan succeeded she would be able to go with Conrad to Mexico her face was radiant.

'I may be doing the wrong thing,' Conrad said as he looked down into her eyes shining with excitement, 'but I can think of no alternative.'

'All that matters is that I can be with you,' Kamala said.

She paused and then she said in a very small voice:

'You are quite ... sure that you want to take me with you? You would not rather ... leave me behind?'

'I think we have already proved that is impossible,' he said dryly.

She was not certain whether he was really pleased or whether she had forced herself upon him.

Now with her feet bound and her hands held back by a rope which she herself had passed round her legs and round her waist, she felt so happy that she wanted to cry with joy.

'We are together! Together on a new adventure!' she told herself. 'Whatever happens, I must never let him regret it.'

Early in the morning Conrad had taken her into the smartest street in Southampton to buy an evening gown. He had insisted on choosing it for her and she had found that his taste was excellent.

It was a very pretty gown of white taffeta trimmed with lace which he finally decided became her better than any of the others. And he also bought her an evening cloak of black velvet trimmed with white swansdown.

The hood of it framed her face, making her, he thought to himself, look even more like a small angel that had dropped out of Heaven by mistake, than she had appeared when he was first returned to consciousness.

From the Emporium which catered for Kamala they went to a Gentleman's outfitters.

Kamala thought that Conrad had never looked more handsome than in a cutaway evening coat with long tails, white frilled evening shirt and a high cravat with the points of his collar reaching above his square chin.

Their purchases made a hole in the money which Conrad had obtained for the horses, but nevertheless there was quite a lot left and Kamala gave him what remained of her twenty-five pounds.

'I will bank it for you,' he said.

'No,' she answered, 'send it to your home with your own money.'

He hesitated for a moment and she knew he disliked the thought of taking money from her.

'If when you return you are rich,' she said, 'you can give it back to me. It will do no good sitting in the Bank and you know even better than I do that you need it for your Mother.'

'Are you sure?' he asked.

'Quite sure,' she answered. 'It would be very foolish of you not to see the good sense of what I suggest.'

'Very well, Kamala,' he said, 'and thank you.'

He lifted her hand for a moment to his lips and she felt herself thrill because his mouth touched her skin.

It was the only expression of affection he had shown her since they had risen in the morning.

He had returned, she thought, to his manner of seeming a little apart from her, almost as if he was determined to keep their relationship on a not too intimate footing.

But now she did not feel perturbed even when an indifferent note crept into his voice. He wanted her to go with him on the voyage, that was all that mattered!

She had been half afraid when she woke after only a few hours' sleep that he might have changed his mind. She sat up in bed with a sudden terror that he might have decided that she was after all an encumbrance and gone on his way without her.

Supposing he had already left the Inn? Supposing he had gone down to the harbour, and found a ship that was sailing that very morning and had gone aboard?

She was torturing herself with a thousand fears, when she heard the Landlord come heavily up the stairs, knock on the door next to hers and heard Conrad's voice say:

'Come in.'

She had known then that she was being childish. Yet all the same she had risen hurriedly and dressed herself so as to be downstairs before Conrad appeared. She was taking no chances!

But as the day wore on she had found that he really was in earnest. He schooled her in everything she must say and do.

'There is not a great deal you have to know about me. I am your elder brother and I have been away from home for years on end. You do not know Cornwall, so do not be inveigled into discussing the county, in case anyone on board knows it better than you.'

He thought for a moment, then added:

'You have been staying away with relations since you have grown up because our family thought life in such an obscure part of England was rather dull for you.'

'I am trying to remember everything you tell me,' Kamala said.

'Well, do not forget your name is Veryan,' Conrad said with a smile.

'You will not change my Christian name?' Kamala asked.

'No, it suits you too well,' he replied, and she thought there was a faint warmth in his voice.

They went back to the Inn and on the way Conrad bought the ropes with which they were to be bound. He was wise enough, again thinking of detail, not to purchase new ones.

'Thieves would not be so extravagant,' he said, 'they would have stolen old ones lying about on the quay for their nefarious purposes.'

Conrad also bought two rough cotton handkerchiefs such as sailors and workmen wore round their necks.

'They ought by rights to be dirty,' he said, 'but I think in these circumstances we will cheat a little. Instead we will make them wet and allow them to dry rough and crumpled.'

'What are they for?' Kamala asked.

'They are gags,' Conrad said. 'You will wear one, I the other.'

'Gags?'

Kamala's voice was incredulous.

'If you were not gagged would you not cry for help? In which case someone might hear you before the ship leaves the harbour.'

How right Conrad had been, Kamala thought, because just before the boat sailed a man had come down the companionway and entered one of the other cabins in the stern.

Kamala had heard his footsteps approaching and felt her heart almost stand still with fear. She could hardly breathe.

Supposing he entered the cabin? Supposing he saw her lying on the bed and Conrad on the floor? There was still time for them to be freed and put ashore.

Conrad had chosen the cabin in which they lay.

'Everything depends on timing,' he had said to Kamala when they had gone down to the harbour. 'Timing and of course inevitably on a touch of good luck.'

'I am sure we shall have that,' Kamala said. 'It was luck that I met you, luck that Mr. Van Wyck's ship is in harbour, luck that you should have had such a clever idea!'

'Do not tempt the fates by speaking too soon,' Conrad smiled.

They had walked down to the Quay after supper at the Inn. They had paid their bill, told the Landlord they were leaving to stay with friends and had asked him to keep their luggage as they might not require it for some weeks.

The Landlord had not seemed curious, he was used to the comings and goings of sailors and he had known Conrad for some years.

'Everything will be safe with me, Sir,' he replied.

When they had reached the harbour, the Clipper *Aphrodite* looked, Kamala thought, very beautiful with its lights glowing in the darkness and its high elegant masts silhouetted against the sky.

The harbour was full of other ships. Their lights reflected

in the water had a magic quality along with the salt on the wind and the cry of the gulls. It all seemed to Kamala to be in tune with her own excitement.

'How are we going to get aboard?' she had asked Conrad before they left.

'I have discovered,' he replied, 'that Van Wyck is dining ashore, and if my calculations are right, he should not be returning until a short while before they sail.'

'And what about the sailors?' Kamala asked.

'If I know anything of seamen in port, they will not come aboard until the last moment,' he replied. 'But they will of course have left two guards on the Clipper.'

'Will they not see us?' Kamala asked apprehensively.

'Not if we are clever,' Conrad answered.

As they walked along the Quay, which seemed almost deserted, Kamala felt that every footstep they took must draw the attention of the guards or the seamen aboard the other vessels.

Conrad however seemed very much at his ease moving with an assurance which proclaimed no anxiety, and looking extremely smart with a black evening cloak lined with red satin floating from his broad shoulders.

When they were opposite the Clipper, Conrad drew Kamala swiftly into the dark shadows of an open wharf.

'You must wait here,' he said, 'and when I tell you to move—move very quickly!'

'What is going to happen?' she asked.

She could see the Clipper directly in front of them and as her eyes grew accustomed to the darkness, she could see two men sitting together on the deck.

'Those must be the guards,' she thought.

She realised it would be impossible for her and Conrad to step across the narrow gang-way onto the deck and down the companionway without being seen.

She wanted to point out the impossibility of such a move

to Conrad, but when she began to speak he hushed her into silence.

Then suddenly there was a noise of exploding fireworks in the harbour.

It was only a small dinghy sailing down between the Schooners and the other ships with fireworks bursting from it and, more dangerous, some rags and straw on board it were already on fire.

There was a rush from every ship to the side of the deck nearest the harbour to see what was happening.

There was a sound of men shouting and cursing, as some broad oaths echoed across the water as the dinghy seemed likely to bump against the sides of the ships and perhaps set them on fire.

Conrad took Kamala by the hand.

With almost incredible speed he pulled her across the gang-way down the companionway and into the depths of the Clipper.

She had one glance as she went at the backs of two sea-men who were guarding the ship as they leant over the gunwale staring at the commotion in the harbour.

Down below there were candle-lanterns to guide them and in the stern there were the doors of four cabins in a row. Conrad opened the first. There was a light burning inside and Kamala could see men's clothes lying about. The cabin was obviously being used.

Conrad opened another door. That too had a man's coat lying over the chair, a brush and other toilet accessories on a high chest of drawers.

Conrad opened the third door and this cabin was in darkness. He drew Kamala inside, but left the door open so that she could see the outlines of a bed, a chair and other furniture.

The cabin was, she noted, luxuriously fitted out, the carpet beneath her feet was thick, and the bed, when finally she lay on it, was extremely comfortable.

For a moment however, she could only try to remember feverishly everything Conrad had told her to do.

'We have at least got aboard,' he said, his voice steady and quiet.

'The fireworks . . . were they your idea?'

'Quite an expensive one, but it worked!'

He handed her one of the cotton handkerchiefs.

'Do not be frightened. Just pray that all goes well.'

'I . . . will,' Kamala whispered.

She could not see his face, but she felt herself quiver because she was so near him. Then he put the handkerchief across his mouth and turned his head so she could tie it tight.

'Does that hurt?' she asked.

He shook his head, then pulled the second handkerchief over her lips, and tied it over her hair but not too tightly.

Kamala had a wild impulse to hold on to him, to pull him close to her, so that he must take her in his arms as he had done before. But already Conrad had finished with her and was tying the rope tightly around his ankles.

Handing the end to Kamala she wound it round him until it reached his wrists. He had taught her at the Inn how to make some rather complicated knots to hold his hands together.

She encircled his shoulders and then fastened the rope at his back.

As soon as she had finished he dropped down onto the floor lying on the carpet as if he had been thrown there. Then obedient to the nod of his head and the instruction in his eyes, Kamala closed the door.

She had to grope her way back to the bed and lying on it she pulled the rope with its noose knot, which Conrad had prepared for her, over her ankles.

She then wound it over her full skirts and finally after two twists round her waist, slipped her hands together through another noose with which the rope ended.

The tighter she pulled, the tighter the rope became and now all she had to do was to lie back against the pillows and wait.

'Perhaps,' Kamala thought, 'this is the most difficult part of all!'

To wait thinking they might be discovered! Knowing that if they were, their whole plan would be ruined and it would be hard to think of an alternative.

Conrad had told her to pray. She tried, but she found her thoughts continually wandering to him, hoping he was not too uncomfortable. Should she take the rope off her own hands and loosen his?

She knew that if she did so Conrad would be annoyed. He had told her they must not make a slip which could arouse suspicion. No! she had done what she had been told to do. Now she must wait and pray—

'Please, God, do not let us be discovered too soon! Let us reach Mexico ... together. And let Conrad make all the money he requires ... please God!'

She found herself going over everything they had said and done since Conrad had fallen following the hounds. How strange and exciting it had been! How much he had changed her life since she had known him.

'Thank You, God, for Conrad,' she said in her heart. 'Thank You ... thank You.'

It was an hour later that the seamen came aboard. There must have been a large number of them and they were very merry.

One of them was singing a bawdy song but their quarters were in the bows and there was no fear of their entering the Master cabins.

The real fear of discovery came later when someone entered one of the occupied cabins next door and just before midnight when the owner and another man came aboard.

They were talking English and Kamala heard them say something about a fine night but the chance of a strong wind later.

They must have come to their cabins, Kamala thought, to collect more suitable clothing for seeing the ship leave harbour, because they went up on deck after spending only a few moments below.

It was then she waited tense and terrified in case something should prevent the ship from leaving. Supposing the wind fell? Supposing the owner changed his mind? So many things might happen!

But her fears were unnecessary. They were leaving! They were at sea! The ship was running before the wind. There was no roar or thunder from the sea, only a long sibilant hiss.

Kamala had been through so much all day and had hardly slept the night before. So that without supposing such a thing was possible, she fell asleep.

The bed was comfortable, the ropes did not chafe her ankles or her wrists as she had feared Conrad's might, and she slept dreamlessly.

When she awoke without feeling frightened it was to find the grey light of a wet morning coming through the portholes.

She drew a deep breath and turned so she could see Conrad was still there.

He was lying uncomfortably on the carpet, but his eyes were smiling as he looked up at her. It was then she heard someone opening the door of one of the cabins.

Conrad gave a little nod and she knew what she must do.

'Help!' she cried through the gag. 'Help!'

It was not a very loud sound, but Conrad picked up his bound feet and beat with them on the ground.

'Help!' Kamala cried again. 'Help!'

She realised that a man who had been walking down the alley had turned back and was listening. Conrad beat with his feet again and Kamala tried to shout louder against the cotton handkerchief.

Suddenly the door was opened. A man stood in the aperture and Kamala guessed it was Mr. Van Wyck.

He was tall and his skin was tanned to the colour of leather. He had grey hair at the temples and not undistinguished features. He stared at them in complete astonishment and then moving towards the bed undid the gag at the back of Kamala's head.

'Who are you? What are you doing here?'

His voice had just a touch of a foreign accent. He began to take the rope from her wrists.

'I can hardly remember what . . . happened. Oh my brother! Is he all . . . right?'

Mr. Van Wyck looked down at the floor and then with an exclamation knelt to undo Conrad's gag.

He took it from his mouth and began to untie the complicated knots with which Kamala had bound him.

'Thank you,' Conrad said hoarsely. 'Where are we?'

'Aboard my ship,' Mr. Van Wyck replied, 'the Clipper *Aphrodite*.'

'The *Aphrodite*! I do not believe it!' Conrad ejaculated.

'Why such surprise?' Mr. Van Wyck enquired.

Conrad put his free hand to the ground and pushed himself into a sitting position. Then he put his fingers to his head as if it hurt him.

'I am trying to remember what happened,' he said. 'Yes, of course, someone hit me on the head! There were four of them—four rough brutes and there was little I could do about it!'

He put his hand as he spoke in his waistcoat pocket.

'My watch! my cravat pin, both gone!' he exclaimed, 'and I presume my money as well! Damn it! I was carrying a large sum!'

'They have taken my . . . necklace,' Kamala said from

the bed, 'and the bracelet which belonged to ... Mama.'

'I cannot think how they got away with it,' Mr. Van Wyck exclaimed, 'and how did they get you aboard? and why?'

'I have no idea,' Conrad said in bewilderment. 'I suppose they must have thought we would inform on them.'

'That is likely,' Mr. Van Wyck agreed. 'I remember reading recently that some footpads who robbed a traveller were caught when they tried to dispose of a gold watch engraved with a coronet.'

'I cannot aspire to a coronet,' Conrad replied, 'but my watch was certainly engraved with my crest.'

He smiled and added, 'At least we should be grateful that our assailants did not push us into the sea.'

Kamala gave a little cry.

'Had they done so we should have ... died of cold,' she faltered.

'They would have drowned us,' Conrad said grimly. 'Are you sure you are all right, my dear?'

'Yes, I think so,' Kamala answered. 'I must have fainted when I saw you fighting with those horrible men ... I do not remember anything until I found myself here on the bed ... gagged!'

She paused to draw breath, then cried:

'Your head! Oh Conrad, did they hurt you? I ... saw one of the men ... strike you with a cudgel!'

Conrad touched his head again tentatively.

'I do not think the skin is broken, but it is very tender. Luckily my hair is thick.'

'I was so frightened,' Kamala faltered.

'It must have been most alarming!' Mr. Van Wyck said sympathetically.

'I was afraid too when I found we were ... here that we would not be able to attract anyone's attention.'

'It is lucky I heard you,' Mr. Van Wyck replied. 'This cabin was not in use.'

He had finished untying Conrad who rose stiffly to his feet, rubbing his wrists to restore the circulation.

'Whoever the thieves were they at least knew how to tie a sailor's knot,' Mr. Van Wyck said. 'It would have been impossible for you to free yourself.'

'I guessed that,' Conrad replied, 'and thank you very much. I imagine your name is Van Wyck.'

Mr. Van Wyck smiled.

'I presume you have heard of the *Aphrodite*.'

'And of you,' Conrad answered. 'You have a great reputation.'

'And may I know your name?'

'I am Conrad Veryan—Sir Conrad Veryan,' Conrad replied to Kamala's surprise, 'and this is my sister, Kamala.'

Mr. Van Wyck made Kamala a courtly if somewhat exaggerated bow.

'I am honoured, Miss Veryan.'

'But what are we to do?' Kamala asked in a voice of distress. 'How can we get ashore?'

'That is a question I can answer quite simply,' Mr. Van Wyck replied, 'it is impossible! We are already past the Lizard and heading for the open sea. Even if I was prepared to put about, in this north-east wind it would be a very dangerous operation.'

'Then what can we do?'

'I am afraid, Miss Veryan, you have no choice but to be my guest.'

Kamala looked at Conrad as if for confirmation.

'As a seaman,' he said, 'I know, my dear, Mr. Van Wyck is speaking the truth. There is nothing he can do about our predicament, and we must therefore accept his hospitality.'

'You are a seaman?' Mr. Van Wyck asked.

'I am indeed,' Conrad answered. 'Until quite recently I was Captain of the *Norma*.'

'The *Norma*!' Mr. Van Wyck exclaimed. 'Then I am very glad to make your acquaintance, Sir Conrad. Tales of your escapades against the pirates off the coast of Africa are already being sung in Amsterdam.'

'I am honoured!' Conrad said modestly.

'You sank one of their ships and crippled another, and managed to get away!'

'We had the advantage of being a far faster ship,' Conrad said lightly.

'It was a very notable feat,' Mr. Van Wyck exclaimed. 'You must tell me all about it.'

'I shall be delighted to do so,' Conrad said, 'and I have an idea, Sir, there will be plenty of time.'

'That will certainly not be in short supply,' Mr. Van Wyck smiled. 'But I know you of all people will not mind being at sea.'

'Indeed, no, although I had planned to be at home for the next few months,' Conrad replied. 'I was in fact hoping next year to buy my own ship. I found on my return from India that my Father had died and I had inherited.'

'Then you could afford a Clipper,' Mr. Van Wyck smiled.

'I would certainly be proud to own a boat as fine as the *Aphrodite*,' Conrad said truthfully.

'I will show you over it,' Mr. Van Wyck promised proudly. 'But our immediate problem after breakfast, and I should think you are both hungry, will be to find you some clothes.'

He looked at Conrad and added:

'You and I are about the same size, but I am wondering what we are going to do about your sister.'

Kamala looked down at her pretty white silk and lace gown.

'I cannot think this is very suitable for a sea voyage,' she said.

'You look very beautiful in it,' Mr. Van Wyck remarked, 'but at the same time I am afraid even with your cloak you will be cold until we reach the Gulf Stream.'

He saw Kamala's face of dismay and added quickly:

'Do not perturb yourself, Spider will find something. His ingenuity is inexhaustible.'

'And who is Spider?' Conrad asked.

'He is my valet, and his name is appropriate because he is so industrious with his needle.'

He went to the door and raising his voice shouted:

'Spider! Spider!'

There was the sound of someone running and a very small man, middle-aged with a bald head, came to Mr. Van Wyck's side.

'You wanted me, Sir?'

'I do indeed, Spider. This lady and gentleman have been shanghaied, robbed and thrown aboard the ship. I am delighted at the thought of their company, but at the same time they have nothing to wear except what they stand up in.'

'That should not be too difficult, Sir,' Spider said with an assurance that was almost amusing.

'Now let me see,' Mr. Van Wyck said, 'Miss Veryan should have this cabin, it is the larger of the two available, and Sir Conrad can be next door.'

'We are indeed extremely sorry to impose on you like this,' Conrad said.

'I assure you it is no imposition,' Mr. Van Wyck replied and he looked at Kamala as he spoke.

They went to breakfast in the Saloon which was furnished more luxuriously than anything Conrad had seen at sea before. Waiting there was a slightly older man whom Mr. Van Wyck introduced as Señor Adalid Quintero, and explained their unexpected appearance.

'The Señor is an old friend of mine,' he went on. 'He knows Mexico well and is also extremely knowledgeable on metals.'

He glanced at Conrad as he spoke.

'I imagine, Sir Conrad, you have some idea as to why I am making this voyage.'

'I know of course that you carry many valuable cargoes,' Conrad replied. 'Would I be right in thinking that on this occasion it will be a commodity which appeals to everyone and which none of us can do without.'

'You would be right,' Mr. Van Wyck said with a smile, 'gold is something we all need! And Señor Quintero has another idea.'

'Indeed! And what is that?' Conrad asked.

'I suppose,' Mr. Van Wyck said addressing his Spanish friend, 'that we must let our new guests into our secret. After all they cannot go ashore and inform on us, nor can they reveal our intentions to anyone but ourselves.'

Both the Spaniard and Mr. Van Wyck laughed almost uproariously at his joke.

'What we intend to bring back from Mexico,' Mr. Van Wyck said leaning across the table, 'is a cargo which will be of great interest to Miss Veryan.'

'Of interest to me?' Kamala exclaimed, 'I cannot think what it might be.'

'It is something which all women crave,' Mr. Van Wyck said tantalisingly. 'Now what does a lovely lady like you want more than anything else?'

Kamala considered for a moment. She knew that what she really wanted was love. But that was hardly likely to be a cargo Mr. Van Wyck would carry on the Clipper!

She tried to think of what he would find in Mexico except gold or silver.

'I cannot imagine what it is,' she answered.

'It would become you greatly,' Mr. Van Wyck said, 'not that you need any enhancement of your beauty.'

There was something in the way he spoke which made her feel that he was being over-familiar, and she turned away from the boldness of his eyes to Conrad.

'Can you not guess the answer?' she asked. 'I am sure you are cleverer than I am at such puzzles.'

'I ought to be able to solve the problem,' he said. 'But

I must say that my head still feels rather numb after the blow I received last night, so I have an excuse for not being as alert as I might be.'

'You have indeed,' Mr. Van Wyck said. 'You are lucky you do not have a bad concussion. These rogues strike hard.'

'It certainly annoys me to think that we cannot apprehend them and hand them over to the police,' Conrad said in exasperated tones. 'I know now it was crazy of me to take Kamala to see the ships, but she was so anxious to do so as she was leaving Southampton early this morning. I gave in to her pleadings and now we are both paying for it.'

'But not too painfully, I hope,' Mr. Van Wyck smiled.

'No indeed,' Conrad replied. 'We both realise how fortunate we are. And now please tell us your secret.'

'What we hope, the Señor and I, to find and bring back to Europe in large quantities,' Mr. Van Wyck replied, 'are diamonds.'

'Diamonds!' Kamala exclaimed. 'How exciting!'

'I thought you would think so,' Mr. Van Wyck answered. 'Tell them, Adalid, what you have told me.'

'There are indeed almost unbelievable quantities of diamonds in Mexico today,' the Spanish Señor answered. 'You will be astonished when you see that every Mexican lady literally glitters with them. She wears them round her neck, in her ears, on her wrists, and no man above the rank of a *lépero* would dream of being married without presenting his bride with a pair of diamond ear-rings and a pearl necklace with a diamond clasp.'

'How fascinating!' Kamala exclaimed. 'But what is a *lépero*?'

'A beggar!' the Señor smiled. 'But truthfully diamonds are so plentiful that even children wear them, and no rich Dowager dies in peace until she has bequeathed to the

Church her largest diamond or her richest pearl necklace.'

'Are the pearls valuable?' Conrad asked.

'They are mostly pear-shaped,' the Señor answered, 'but some are round and those, of course, are the most sought after. A necklace of really large round pearls is worth something like two hundred thousand dollars, and they, like diamonds, are considered by Mexican society, which of course includes the Spaniards who are the real aristocrats, a necessity of life quite as much as their shoes and stockings.'

'I am extremely interested by all this,' Conrad said. 'And of course jewels are easy to carry.'

'That is what was in my mind,' Mr. Van Wyck replied.

'Do the Mexicans have rubies and emeralds as well?' Kamala asked.

'Strangely enough,' the Spaniard answered, 'their diamonds are always worn plain or with pearls. Coloured stones are considered trash, which I think is a pity. But diamonds are a sign of prestige and of social status.'

He saw Kamala was interested and went on.

'The whole of Texataxo belonged before the revolution to a Count Regla, who was so wealthy that when his son was christened the whole party walked from the house to the Church upon ingots of silver. And his wife, the Countess, when she quarrelled with the Queen of Spain sent her as a token of reconciliation a white satin slipper entirely covered with large diamonds.'

'Only one?' Kamala questioned.

'I hardly think the Queen was intended to wear it!' the Spaniard replied.

'I can see you have a new and very profitable idea,' Conrad said in a quiet voice to Mr. Van Wyck.

'That is what I thought,' he replied. 'Brazilian diamonds at the moment are fetching enormous prices, but no-one has thought to bring Mexican diamonds to Europe. That is an omission I intend to repair.'

'I hope you will allow me to assist you.'

'We must talk about that,' Mr. Van Wyck answered. 'In the meantime, may I say what a pleasure it is to have you with me, and your sister will, I know, enliven what might have proved a very dull voyage not only with her beauty, but with her charm and her conversation.'

Kamala was sitting beside him at the table. As he spoke he took her hand and raised it to his lips. It was not entirely a conventional gesture.

She felt his mouth against her bare skin and unexpectedly it made her shudder.

She did not know why, but at that moment she decided that Mr. Van Wyck was not as genial or indeed as pleasant as he appeared.

6

The next few days although the sea was rough Kamala was delighted to find that she was not affected by it.

In fact she felt a strange exhilaration at the noise of the waves, the slap of the sails, the creak of the masts, the scent of tar, cordage and brine, and the busy life of the seamen.

She would watch the men high up the masts calling to one another as they released the topsails, and she would look towards the grey horizon in the West and feel that the adventure of discovery was just beginning.

They had an easterly wind far out into the Atlantic.

Even apart from the interest in watching and trying to understand all that was being done on the ship, Kamala found that her days seemed to be filled from the moment she got up in the morning, until she went to bed.

First of all everything was slower than it was ashore. It was more difficult to dress and it took far longer when the ship was rolling or pitching.

When she went on deck she had to be very careful not only to prevent herself from being swept overboard, but also to avoid being soaked by the spray or from getting her feet wet in the wash of the waves when they swept onto the deck.

It seemed unnecessary with so much water provided by the sea that the deck should also require washing. But every morning Kamala was awoken by the seamen banging down their heavy wooden buckets and scrubbing the decks to the accompaniment of harsh orders from the Mate.

The first two days Kamala felt it was too cold to leave the warm and comfortable Saloon for the sharp November wind and sleet outside. But to her amazement by the evening Spider had made her a gown.

'Where did you get the material?' she asked in surprise.

He had brought her the wide-skirted elegant dress of a thick green silk with a faint pattern woven into it. The tight bodice was buttoned up the front with small pearl buttons, and the collar and the cuffs were edged with what appeared to be white lace.

'It's one of the bed-spreads, Miss,' Spider answered.

'A bed-spread!' Kamala exclaimed and then added anxiously, 'Do you think Mr. Van Wyck will mind?'

'He won't mind, Miss,' Spider replied confidently. 'We always have more on board than we need, and just as the Master 'll not miss the clothes he's lent Sir Conrad, so you can rest assured he has no idea he even possessed a bed-spread this colour.'

Kamala laughed.

'Well, I am very grateful for it because it certainly makes a beautiful gown. But where did you get the lace?'

'It's not lace, Miss,' Spider answered, 'it's mosquito netting. The Master buys the finest obtainable and we have a great roll of it aboard.'

He scratched his few remaining hairs and then he said slowly :

'I was just thinking, Miss, that I could make you a nice thin dress of it. It'll be hot when we reaches the Azores and, though I hopes to get some material there for other gowns, you'll need something cool as soon as we hits the Gulf Stream.'

'It sounds delightful,' Kamala smiled.

But it was too soon to think of the warm days ahead. Spider produced a large square of fringed wool embroidered in bright colours which he told Kamala was a tablecloth and which folded into a triangle made her a pretty shawl.

She wore it round her shoulders until he produced, rather as a Conjuror might produce a rabbit from a hat, a jacket of black satin which buttoned from her neck to her waist and had long warm sleeves.

'Where did this come from?' she enquired.

'I was sure, Miss, that Sir Conrad would not be requiring his evening cloak on this trip.'

'His evening cloak!' Kamala exclaimed.

She found the little jacket not only warm and comfortable, but with her white skin and fair hair very becoming. It was exactly what she needed to wear over her silk gown.

At the same time she could not help feeling it was extremely extravagant when she remembered how much Conrad had been obliged to pay for the cloak he had only worn once, when he escorted her down the Quay.

It was however no use worrying at this moment about extravagances. They had no money and therefore they could spend none and she could only pray that somehow Conrad would be able to share in the wealth that awaited Mr. Van Wyck when they reached Mexico.

The two men had long discussions on where they should land, how they should obtain a cargo of gold, and who would find for them the diamonds and the pearls which Mr. Van Wyck was determined to take back to Amsterdam.

He was of course relying on his friend Señor Quintero to do the bargaining.

'I have a little Spanish,' he said, 'but not enough for such important negotiations. I am relying upon you, Adalid.'

'I hope I will not fail you,' the Señor replied.

The conversation gave Kamala an idea. As soon as Mr. Van Wyck and Conrad had gone up on deck and she was alone in the saloon with the Spaniard, she said to him:

'I wonder, Señor, if I might ask a very great favour.'

'But of course, Miss Veryan,' he replied. 'If there is anything I can do for you, I am at your service.'

'I was wondering,' Kamala said hesitatingly, 'if you
will be so obliging as to teach me Spanish. I know a few
words, but I am quite proficient in French and I have
enough Italian to be able to understand the Operas.'

'Both these languages will be a great help,' the Señor
replied.

He became very enthusiastic when he discovered how
quickly Kamala understood what he was trying to teach
her and how eager she was to learn.

As soon as Mr. Van Wyck and Conrad were out of the
Saloon after breakfast each morning they settled down to
Kamala's lessons.

In a very short while she was finding it comparatively
easy to read one of the Señor's books that he had brought
with him.

Of course it was impossible not to talk to him about
Mexico and the Mexicans.

'If you will not think it a rude question,' she said, 'is it
not true that the Spanish were extremely cruel when they
conquered the country?'

'I do not think it rude,' the Señor replied. 'My father
left Spain because he was too much a liberal to tolerate
the authority of the Church. He settled in Amsterdam and
my mother is Dutch. I can therefore answer your question
quite truthfully and say the Spanish were monstrously
cruel.'

'But surely things are much better now?' Kamala said.

'The brutality of the conquerors and the horrors of the
Inquisition will never be forgotten,' the Señor replied.

'The Church, as set up by the Spanish, still owns one
half of the real property of Mexico and half the capital of
the country. Besides there are many Spaniards still living
there.'

The Señor thought for a moment.

'The European-born Spaniards, called Gachupines, are not so many in number, but they are the real aristocrats and are still acknowledged to be the most important people in the whole country. There are also a great many Creoles, or American-born Spaniards, and everyone else is subservient to them.'

'Of what do the others consist?' Kamala asked. 'I hope you do not mind answering my questions, but I am so curious to know about Mexico.'

'I think you are very wise,' the Señor answered. 'It is always of importance to learn about new peoples and try to understand them. But to answer your question, Indians make up 50 per cent of the population. There are too the Negroes who were originally imported from Africa, and there are those they call Sambos who are half Negro and half Indian, besides Mulattos who are half Negro and half European.'

'I must try and remember all this,' Kamala said.

'And,' the Señor continued, 'there are the Mestizos, a mixture of Indian and European. Some of their women are very lovely.'

'I am longing to see Mexico,' Kamala said, 'because I understand it is exceedingly beautiful.'

'I shall be disappointed if you do not think so,' the Señor replied. 'This is my third visit and five years ago I stayed for two years moving about seeing the silver mines, the excavations for gold, and learning a great deal about its people.'

'Men are so lucky!' Kamala said with a sigh. 'They can travel all over the world while women have to stay behind.

She was thinking of Conrad as she spoke, realising that to him this was just another voyage, while to her it was a thrilling experience she had never dreamt of undertaking.

As the days passed by she found it impossible to be alone with Conrad.

Mr. Van Wyck seemed to expect him to assist him in the running of the ship, and when the two men returned to the Saloon, Señor Quintero was always there.

They would play cards in the evening. Kamala, who was proficient at piquet, soon learnt whist and several other games of chance at which Conrad and Mr. Van Wyck gambled inordinately. But only on paper, because Conrad had no money with him.

'When this voyage is over, if I am not careful I shall be owing you a fortune,' Conrad said one evening when he had had a run of bad luck. 'When I reach Mexico I shall have to take to pearl-diving so as not to be in your debt.'

'I will show you an easier way of making money than that,' Mr. Van Wyck said.

But although Kamala saw a sudden glint of interest in Conrad's eyes, the Dutchman said no more.

She was well aware, and it made her very uncomfortable, that Mr. Van Wyck's interest in her was increasing day by day.

It was not so much what he said, although he paid her flowery and extravagant compliments which were so foreign to her ears, that she did not take them seriously.

But she knew from the way he would make an excuse to touch her as the ship rolled, the frequency with which he kissed her hand and indeed the manner in which he looked at her with bold eyes, that he was attracted to her.

She was not really afraid, she was only on her guard and felt that if they were ever alone he might make advances to her.

She wanted to discuss it with Conrad, but he appeared to go out of his way to treat her with the kind and easy indifference of a brother to his sister.

He was polite, he asked after her wellbeing, but never for one moment was his voice anything but cool and friendly.

Never did he show her any demonstration of affection

that he would not have shown had they in truth been related.

Sometimes at night Kamala thought frantically she would
never again know the closeness and the companionship she
had enjoyed on their ride to Southampton.

She would recall how she had lain in Conrad's arms in the
broken-down farm hut, and how he had held her close
when she had been terrified at the thought of Uncle Marcus
discovering her whereabouts.

But the Conrad who had told her she was lovely, and
who had said that he had no poetry, had vanished and in his
place was a pleasant but distant man who treated her as a
sister!

He was only acting, Kamala told herself over and over
again; yet she could not prevent a strange ache within herself because he seemed no longer to care about her.

She had discovered one thing which was faintly comforting. When she had hung the gown that Spider had made
up for her in the oak cupboard in her cabin, she had noticed there was a streak of light at the back of it.

Curious, she pushed her gown on one side and saw that
the cupboard was joined to the panelled wall of the cabin.
In the centre the panelling had obviously been cut or
wrenched away and did not fit firmly in place.

On closer inspection Kamala found that the light in fact
came from Conrad's cabin which adjoined hers.

She pulled at the carved oak which faced into the cupboard and realised she could easily move it.

Obviously the panelling in Conrad's cabin could also
be lifted from its place.

At some time the occupants of the two cabins must
have wished to communicate with each other without having to go outside their own doors.

It was amusing to speculate who could have contrived
the secret opening.

Had the Clipper at some time carried two secret lovers

and had they crept into each other's cabins without their host being aware of it.

She longed to find out who it could have been, but when she tentatively asked Spider who had been aboard the Clipper on other voyages, she received an answer she did not expect.

'These are such fine cabins,' she said. 'I am sure Mr. Van Wyck must often have important guests aboard.'

'Not when he is on what we might call, Miss, his business trips,' Spider answered.

'So these lovely cabins remain empty,' Kamala said looking round as she spoke and noting the expensive furnishings, the carved bed-head and dressing-table of rosewood.

'Well as it happens, Miss,' Spider replied, 'this is the best cabin of the lot. The Master Suite one might say. But Mr. Van Wyck likes to sleep on the starboard side of the ship, so he changed into the one next door.'

'So this was Mr. Van Wyck's cabin,' Kamala said reflectively.

'Yes, Miss, the Master used it for years,' Spider replied.

He then started to talk once again of her gowns, which Kamala knew was to him an absorbing subject.

'I always thought, Miss,' Spider said to her once, 'that if I'd had the chance, I could have set up my own dressmaking establishment. I was an apprentice to a tailor when I was only seven years old. A skilful cutter he was and he taught me a great deal. But I'd rather design for a lady any day. Her gowns can be an inspiration, 'tis almost like listening to music.'

'He is an artist in his own way,' Kamala thought.

She found it was for him a sheer delight to design her clothes, making them out of all sorts of unexpected materials.

And he admired her appearance so wholeheartedly that she could not find it impertinent.

He fashioned a night-gown for her out of two of Mr. Van Wyck's silk shirts. With the long sleeves edged with lace and the lace-edged collar with which it fastened at the neck, it was warm and she loved the feel of the soft silk next to her skin.

'You will need muslin, Miss, when it gets hot,' Spider told her, 'and that 'll be easy to buy in the Azores. Why in Mexico all the dark-skinned señoritas trail about in white muslin! And it is not nearly so becoming to them as the gay colours which they think too native.'

Spider's greatest achievement was when he fashioned for Kamala a pair of slippers.

'These satin ones are not going to last long, Miss,' he said.

To her astonishment he managed to make slippers of suède from one of Mr. Van Wyck's waistcoats with soles of unplaited rope. They were very comfortable and she kept her satin slippers to wear in the evenings.

When the sea was not too rough they all changed for dinner.

Sometimes as they sat round the table in the Saloon enjoying an excellent meal with delicious wines, Kamala felt it was all a dream and they were not travelling to another country but being carried in a magic ship to the stars.

She spoke her thoughts aloud.

'I have a feeling,' she said, 'that we shall not land in Mexico, but on the moon or perhaps Mars.'

'Venus would be more appropriate,' Mr. Van Wyck said watching the sparkle in her eyes.

'Perhaps I am being too imaginative. I am sure from all the Señor has told me, Mexico will be a Paradise.'

'It certainly looks like one at this time of the year,' Señor Quintero said.

'And when we reach Paradise,' Mr. Van Wyck said insistently, 'who will play Adam to your Eve?'

'You are confusing Paradise with the Garden of Eden,' Kamala said quietly.

'Then let me tell you that either place would seem like Heaven with you.'

There was a depth in Mr. Van Wyck's voice which made Kamala feel uncomfortable.

She longed to look at Conrad as if for protection, but then she felt that might be dangerous. Had he not warned her to be careful?

'Have you been telling my sister that Mexico is Paradise?' Conrad said in a joking voice to the Señor. 'If you have, she will undoubtedly be disappointed when she sees the abject poverty, the beggars and the down-trodden Indians who are little better than slaves.'

'I see no reason,' Mr. Van Wyck said almost aggressively, 'why your sister should see any of those things. I will show her the beauty of the countryside. She will hear the song of the multi-coloured birds and I will deck her with diamonds whose brilliance will pale in comparison with her eyes.'

'I think we are all talking a lot of nonsense,' Kamala said, in what she hoped was a matter-of-fact voice. 'What about a game of cards?'

She spoke quickly so as to divert Mr. Van Wyck's attention from herself but she was not successful.

'I want to find you a necklace of perfect pearls,' he said in a low voice. 'They must have the soft lustre of your skin.'

'It is very kind of you,' Kamala replied, 'but you know I could not accept such a present.'

'You will change your mind,' he replied, 'when you see what I have to offer.'

She shook her head.

'I am grateful for your kindness, just as I am grateful for the delightful gowns which you have permitted Spider

121

to make for me. But as my brother will explain to you, we cannot be any further in your debt.'

She glanced at Conrad as she spoke, feeling she must have his support.

To her surprise and consternation, she found he was talking intimately with Señor Quintero and not attending to anything that Mr. Van Wyck was saying to her.

'He is not so proud,' Mr. Van Wyck said following her eyes. Then he added quietly:

'Your brother is ambitious. He wishes to become my partner.'

'Then I hope you will be generous enough to offer him the position,' Kamala said.

There was a pause and, almost despite her resolution not to do so, she found herself looking up into Mr. Van Wyck's face.

He was staring down at her with an expression that she could not fail to understand.

There was a glimmer of fire in the darkness of his eyes and she felt a little tremor of fear before she looked away, her lashes dark against her cheeks.

'It depends entirely upon you,' Mr. Van Wyck said softly.

'On me?' Kamala faltered, 'I do not. . . think I know what you . . . mean.'

'I think you do,' he said. 'And if you are fond of your brother, you will wish to help him.'

Kamala felt herself tremble. For the last few days she had realised that Mr. Van Wyck was stalking her as a sportsman might stalk an elusive stag. Now he had come into the open and she was afraid.

To her relief, before she could reply, Conrad rose to his feet.

'I feel like a turn on deck,' he said. 'What about coming with me, Van Wyck?'

'Yes, of course,' the Dutchman replied.

His eyes flickered over Kamala's pale face and there was a faint smile on his lips as if he knew that he had disturbed her.

Then he rose and followed Conrad from the Saloon.

Kamala found her breath coming unevenly. She was afraid, not for herself, but for Conrad.

The Señor had apparently noticed nothing unusual. He picked up the Spanish book which he and Kamala had been reading together.

'Shall we continue?' he asked.

'Yes, of course,' she replied in a rather breathless voice.

'Or better still, I will read you a conversation in Spanish,' he said. 'You must try to be more flowery in your language, Miss Veryan. You will find that the Mexicans in particular speak in a most exaggerated manner to each other, using terms of affection which would certainly not be countenanced in Europe.'

'Spanish politeness is proverbial,' Kamala said.

'Add that to the Mexican type and you get a confection not unlike an over-rich wedding-cake,' the Señor said.

Kamala managed to laugh. As she did so the Saloon door was suddenly flung open and Mr. Van Wyck burst into the cabin.

He ignored his guests and went across the room to a cupboard set in the wall at the far end.

'There has been an accident,' he said briefly.

'An accident!'

Kamala made the words a cry of sheer horror.

'Conrad! Is he hurt?'

She felt as she spoke as if an iron hand clamped down on her heart and a century seemed to pass before Mr. Van Wyck replied:

'It is not your brother who is injured. One of the seamen has broken an arm. It is of no consequence, but I need a bandage.

He went from the room and Kamala sank back again

in the chair from which she had half risen, her face ashen with the shock. For a moment she had imagined that Conrad had been hurt.

Conrad whom she loved!

She knew then in a moment of revelation that she had loved him from the very beginning. She had not realised it!

She had not known that the feeling she had for him was not affection or the need for his protection, but because she loved him as a woman loves a man.

She must have loved him, she thought, from the moment she saw him lying on the muddy ground when his horse had fallen at the gate. She had loved him when she had set his collar-bone, and had been determined for it to heal even though he was a stranger!

Love! What was love? A desire to be close to a man, to belong to him, and to know that it would be impossible to live without him!

That was what she had been feeling for Conrad although in her foolishness and because she was so ignorant she had not known it for what it was.

But now she knew! It had come to her like a flash of lightning because she had been afraid for him.

She felt her heart start beating again, but she knew that while her colour returned to normal and she was no longer trembling with shock, she herself had changed.

She was in love! She was not a girl afraid of her independence, afraid of setting off alone on the unknown, but a woman who had been striving instinctively for the love which was within her and which suffused her whole being.

'I love him! I love him! I love him!' she told herself.

She wondered if he was aware of her love or if it was as much of a secret to him as it had been to herself?

'I love him!'

Even to think of him made her breath come quicker and

made her feel as if the Saloon was touched with a golden glow of joy and happiness.

Then she remembered she must be careful.

'We must not make a single slip,' Conrad had said.

To reveal that her feelings for him were not that of a sister for a brother might not be a slip but a catastrophe!

She had to be careful. She had, above all else, to keep Mr. Van Wyck from knowing they were not what they appeared to be.

'It will be difficult to deceive him,' Kamala thought. 'Very difficult! He is growing more possessive! I can almost feel his hands going out towards me ... attempting to draw me to him.'

She felt suddenly sick at the thought that another man should touch her. It was Conrad whom she loved, Conrad who made her quiver with an exciting awareness whenever he was near.

Why had she not realised that this was love?

Why had she not known, when he held her to him in the hut and they lay together covered with hay, that what she felt was not only security and comfort, but love?

Conrad! Conrad! She felt her whole being cry out to him and realised that Señor Quintero had read her a long passage from one of his books and she had not heard a word of it.

When Conrad and Mr. Van Wyck returned, their hair blown in the wind, their faces wet with the spray of the waves, she was glad that it was time to go to bed.

'Is the seaman all right?' Kamala asked.

'The Mate set his arm quite skilfully,' Conrad replied, 'otherwise we might have asked for your assistance.'

'Your sister understands the setting of bones?' Mr. Van Wyck asked in surprise.

'Indeed, she is very proficient at it,' Conrad answered. 'She recently set my collar-bone when I had a fall out hunting. She did it better than any doctor.'

'If you are interested in healing,' the Señor exclaimed excitedly, 'then you will be thrilled, Miss Veryan, with the many medicines and herbs that you can find in Mexico. There is a profusion of them.'

'I seem to remember,' Conrad said, 'that Spanish historians who wrote about the Conquest of Mexico all mentioned the tremendous knowledge the Mexican physicians had of herbs.'

'That is true,' the Señor replied, 'and in every street market today you can find innumerable infusions, decoctions, ointments, plasters and oils for sale.'

'I am deeply interested in herbs,' Kamala said.

'Then one of the first things I will do when we arrive in Mexico is to take you to a market,' Mr. Van Wyck interposed.

It was obvious it was an invitation for Kamala alone, but she turned to the Señor and said:

'Please do not forget to tell me more tomorrow. It will be interesting to find out how much knowledge there is in Mexico that is not known to our own English herbalists.'

'I have a book on the subject somewhere,' the Señor answered. 'I will find it and we will study it together.'

'That is a promise,' Kamala said with a smile. 'Good night, Señor.'

She dropped him a curtsey and then curtseyed to Mr. Van Wyck. She did not extend her hand but he held out his and waited until reluctantly she gave him hers. He raised it to his lips and held it there, his eyes looking at hers as he did so.

'Good-night, beautiful little Lady,' he said caressingly. 'There is so much for us both to do in the Paradise that lies ahead.'

Kamala drew her hand sharply from his hold.

'Good-night, Conrad,' she said with a little quiver in her voice and went from the Saloon.

In her cabin she undressed slowly, her eyes troubled as she thought of Mr. Van Wyck.

She wondered if it would be possible for Conrad to find them another ship when they reached the Azores and then she knew that however apprehensive she might be, she could not ask him to give up his dreams of wealth for her sake.

Fortunately the following day they ran into rough weather.

The ship pitched and tossed, the topsails had to be furled and great waves crashed over the bulwarks to the roar of a blasting wind.

It was far too dangerous for Kamala to go on deck although Conrad and Mr. Van Wyck spent most of their time there.

When they did come below they were too tired and too buffeted by the elements to do anything but eat, snatch a few hours' rest in their cabins and go above again.

Kamala did not feel sick, but the lack of air and the effort it cost to prevent herself from being thrown from side to side gave her a headache.

Like everyone else she was relieved when suddenly the wind dropped and the sea gradually subsided.

'It will be warmer from now on, Miss,' Spider said.

His unimpaired cheerfulness made her smile as he brought her the gown he had fashioned from mosquito netting.

'Oh it is pretty, Spider! Very pretty!' Kamala exclaimed, seeing the full skirts which she could wear over her silk petticoats and the tight bodice which revealed the young curves of her figure.

There were short puff sleeves, rouched cleverly so that they appeared at a distance to be made of lace.

'It is quite the prettiest gown I have ever had,' she said in all truthfulness.

'I'm glad you are pleased, Miss,' Spider said, 'but wait

until we reach Santa Cruz de Gracia in the Azores, I intend to make you quite a trousseau.'

'Please keep an account of everything you spend,' Kamala said. 'Once my brother has some money, I know he will wish to reimburse Mr. Van Wyck for everything which he has expended on our behalf.'

'Don't you worry about that, Miss,' Spider answered. 'The Master is used to extravagance where ladies are concerned. And I mean real extravagance! Why those that have been on this boat have cost him a fortune one way or another.'

Kamala's eyes widened, and as if Spider realised he had said too much, he coughed apologetically and went quickly from the cabin.

It was nice to feel they were moving smoothly and with only a faint breeze over the calmer water. The sunshine was warm and golden, so that Kamala could now go on deck without wearing her cloak.

She stood looking out to sea, the wind making her fair hair curl round her oval forehead.

'Tomorrow we shall reach the Azores,' Conrad's voice said.

She had not heard him approach and as she looked round her heart leapt at the sight of him. They were alone on their part of the deck.

'I want to talk to you,' she said softly.

'It is impossible,' he said not looking at her but staring out to sea. 'There will be a chance when we are in port, but be careful, Kamala, until then be—very careful.'

Kamala looked at him enquiringly, but his face was turned away from her, his handsome features silhouetted against the blue sky.

'I love you,' she told herself.

She wondered what he would say if she said her thoughts aloud.

He did not love her, she knew that, but she thought he must have some affection for her.

Or was he only being chivalrous because she had attached herself to him like a small lost dog, and it was not in him to be cruel enough to leave her behind?

'I love you! I love you!' her heart whispered.

Then she heard Mr. Van Wyck calling him and realised their moment alone was over.

When she changed for dinner she hung her gown up in the cupboard, she looked longingly at the panel that communicated with Conrad's cabin.

Supposing she went in to speak to him late at night? What would he think?

She felt her cheeks burn at the thought. She had been in his bedroom at the farmhouse and he had come into hers at the Inn. But then they had been living a strange life which seemed to have nothing to do with the conventions.

Now they were back in the ordinary world and she felt Conrad might think it forward and immodest of her if she went to his cabin.

Perhaps he would think she was pursuing him! Perhaps he would find her importunate, a woman who would not leave him alone! There must have been many of those in his life, she thought.

And then she realised that she could not sink to Mr. Van Wyck's level.

There must have been some reason why he had a special entrance into the cabin next door. Had his passenger been perhaps a married woman, whose husband was sleeping elsewhere?

There were innumerable possibilities as to why there was this secret access from his cabin into the one next door, and all of them were ... unpleasant.

'If Conrad wishes to speak to me, he will find a way to do so!' Kamala told herself.

But she knew despondently that somehow he had grown

so far away from her that she no longer knew what he felt or thought.

They played whist that evening and she found that Mr. Van Wyck made every excuse to touch her hand when they were passing cards to each other.

She even had the suspicion that he tried to press her knee under the table, but she turned sideways in her chair moving herself so far away from him that if it had been intentional he was not able to do so again.

He paid her compliments. He told her a dozen times she was beautiful, that she was beguiling, enchanting. a goddess on whose shrine he worshipped, a woman who had no reason to seek Paradise because she could only have come from it.

It seemed to Kamala that he was like a rough sea sweeping over her, subduing her by his ardour, and that she could not escape him.

At last the game ended and she was able to go to bed.

Again Mr. Van Wyck kissed her hand lingeringly. She thought too there was some insistent pressure in the touch of his fingers.

In her own cabin she gave a sigh of relief. She only wished they were reaching Mexico tomorrow and not the Azores. She had a feeling that as the weather grew hotter and Mr. Van Wyck had less to do on deck, he would have more time to devote himself to her.

She hung up her gown, took off her voluminous petticoats and found lying on the bed the thin night-gown that Spider had promised her.

He had found that her evening gown had a chiffon lining. It was not necessary, as he had pointed out, but only an extra extravagance on the part of the dressmaker.

Spider had removed the chiffon and made a very lovely night-gown of it. The top was draped in the Grecian fashion over Kamala's small pointed breasts and caught on each shoulder with a love knot.

The skirt was full but transparent, and when Kamala looked at herself in the mirror, she could see clearly the outline of her exquisite figure with its tiny waist and narrow hips.

'Would Conrad think I look pretty?' she asked herself. Then blushed at the immodesty of such a thought.

She remembered that she had forgotten to lock her door and walked across the cabin to do so. When she reached it she stared unbelievingly at the lock. There was no key!

She thought she must be mistaken. She imagined the key might have fallen to the ground, but it was not there.

It had been there every night, and now it was gone!

'Perhaps Spider has taken it,' she thought.

But it was unlikely that he should suddenly remove the key of her cabin and if so for what reason?

She looked around and taking a chair from the wall she brought it to the door and fixed it firmly under the handle.

It was fortunate, she thought, that Mr. Van Wyck had been extravagant in building the Clipper and had ornamented the doors in the Master Suite with gold handles that were not only expensive but strong and beautifully chased.

The chair fitted firmly.

'I am being nonsensical,' Kamala told herself. 'No-one is likely to come to my cabin. No-one has attempted to do so before.'

She lifted the candle-lantern from the hook in the ceiling and set it down beside her bed. Now that their passage was comparatively smooth she could read before she went to sleep.

She opened a Spanish book which the Señor had lent her.

It was a novel which she found very interesting. It taught her a great deal about Spanish customs and Spanish conversation.

She turned the pages, but after a little while she realised she was not taking in a single word. She was thinking about

Conrad and wondering how they could contrive to be together when they reached the Azores.

There was so much she wanted to say to him, so much she wanted to hear.

When they were alone would he drop the indifference he had been showing towards her? Would he become again the man she loved and with whom she had been so overwhelmingly happy, although at the time she had not understood the depth and strength of her own feelings.

A small sound startled her!

It was different from the creak of the ship and the whistle of the wind. Almost instinctively she glanced towards the door.

She could see it quite clearly in the light of the candle which was beside her bed. Then as she looked she saw the handle turn, slowly but unmistakably.

Kamala's heart seemed to leap in her throat. She wondered for a moment if it was Conrad who was outside. Could he be coming to see her, to talk to her as she wished?

The handle turned again and now there was pressure on the door, but the sturdy oak chair she had placed there held its position.

She felt suddenly frightened. There was something sinister and ominous about the turn of the handle and the movement of the door against the chair.

She felt herself begin to tremble. She wanted to scream but some caution within herself prevented her from doing so, and anyway her voice seemed choked within her throat.

She sprang out of bed and moved swiftly across the room. She opened the cupboard and pulled the door close behind her. For a moment she was in darkness, then she saw the slight streak of light.

She found the rough edge of the panel with the tips of her fingers, and pulled!

For a moment she thought she must have been mistaken. There was no opening concealed there!

Then as she pulled it harder still there was the sound of wood splintering as if it had been held in place by gum or some other device. The broken panel tipped forward into the cupboard. She dropped it down and pushed hard at the panel which faced into Conrad's cabin. It fell with a crash and Kamala stepped over it.

Conrad was not in bed but sitting at a table in his shirt sleeves inspecting some maps. He looked round in astonishment. When he saw who it was he jumped to his feet.

'Kamala! What has happened?'

She put her fingers to her lips and then trembling because she was so frightened she whispered:

'There is . . . someone at my . . . door.'

He looked at her searchingly before he said:

'Wait here! I will see to it.'

Opening the door of his cabin he went out, closing it behind him.

Kamala felt she could hardly breathe as she listened.

'Oh there you are, Van Wyck!' she heard Conrad say, 'I was just coming in search of you. My sister is frightened because she swears there is a rat in her cabin.'

'A rat!' Mr. Van Wyck's voice exclaimed. 'Then we must certainly do something about it.'

'We must indeed,' Conrad said, with a hint of laughter in his voice. 'Women are all the same, they will face a typhoon or an earthquake, but a rat or a mouse sends them into hysterics!'

'We must certainly prevent your sister being hysterical,' Mr. Van Wyck said. 'I will have the cabin searched thoroughly in the morning. Can you calm her fears for to-night?'

'I expect so,' Conrad replied in a bored voice.

'Then I must leave her in your tender care,' Mr. Van Wyck said. 'Good-night!'

'Good-night,' Conrad replied.

He came back into his cabin. Kamala had moved just

behind the door so she could listen to what was being said.

Now without thinking what she was doing or remembering that she was wearing nothing except the soft transparent night-gown which Spider had made for her, she moved instinctively towards Conrad, her face upturned to his.

His arms went round her and his lips found hers.

Just for a moment she was still in sheer surprise; then like quicksilver a sudden ecstasy shot through her and her mouth clung to his.

She had not realised that a kiss could be like this, a moment of rapture, a moment so exquisite, so wonderful that the whole world seemed suffused with light.

Then as suddenly as he had taken her Conrad set her free. He walked away from her to stand the other side of the cabin with his back turned.

'Forgive me!' he said, in a strange voice. 'It is because I have been so long without a woman—any woman!'

There was silence until as if he could not help himself he turned round and saw Kamala's stricken face.

Her expression was one of numb bewilderment as if she had been mortally wounded when she least expected it.

In one stride he was at her side again and he swept her back into his arms.

'No, darling! No! For God's sake do not look like that! I did not mean it! Oh my sweet, I did not mean it.'

He was kissing her again wildly, passionately, possessively, and she felt as if he lifted her from the depths of dark despair up into the sun where the two of them were alone together in a wonder that was beyond words.

He took his lips from her mouth to kiss her eyes, her cheeks, her neck and then as he lingered on the round softness of it, and she trembled with happiness, he realised how little she wore.

He lifted her up, carried her to the bed, set her down

amongst the pillows, and pulled the silk quilt over her.

'Oh, Conrad!'

It was the first words Kamala had been able to speak.

She was looking up into his eyes, her own wide and shining with a radiance and wonder he had never before seen in any woman's face.

'My darling, my precious, my little love!'

He kissed her again and now she put her arms round his neck and drew him closer. . . .

Time stood still until at last with an almost superhuman effort, Conrad took his mouth from Kamala's to sit looking down at her lips soft and warm from his kisses, her hair golden against the pillows.

'You tried me too hard,' he said unsteadily.

'Do you . . . love me?'

'I have loved you since the first moment I saw you,' he answered.

'As I loved . . . you,' she whispered, 'but I did not . . . realise it was love.'

'When did you know that you loved me?'

'I have . . . known it for . . . days.'

Her hands fluttered towards him as if she would draw him down to her again, but gently he took them in his and laid them on the quilt over her breasts.

'This is madness!'

'Is it?'

'Of course it is,' he answered. 'I have nothing to offer you, nothing.'

'I am not asking for anything,' Kamala said in a soft voice.

'I told you that my family were poor,' Conrad said and there was an indefinable pain in his voice. 'But it is worse than that. They are poverty stricken—on the edge of starvation!

'When I returned home with fortunately enough money to keep them for the next four or five months, I knew that they are my responsibility and that my whole life must be dedicated to them.'

He drew a deep breath as if remembering the hardship of what he had undertaken.

'Even if my Mother dies, which is very likely,' he went on, 'there are the pensioners and ancient employees whose whole life has been spent in the service of my parents. How can I turn them off to die in a hedgerow?

'They have no savings. They had subsisted until I returned on the charity of the local trades-people and a loan from a friend in London. That has to be repaid.'

'And your house?' Kamala asked.

'That is not mine to sell even if I wished to do so,' he answered. 'It has been in my family for over 500 years. It is entailed on the son whom I shall never be able to afford.'

He looked down at her and she saw the agony in his eyes.

'Can you not understand what I am saying to you?' he asked. 'I love you, but I must not play with fire.'

'You mean it is . . . wrong to . . . love me?'

'It is not wrong, my darling,' he answered, 'it is only impossible, because I cannot marry you.'

'I am not asking you to do so,' Kamala replied. 'I am content as long as I can be . . . close to you . . . as long as I know you . . . love me.'

'Do you think it is possible for me to be close to you and not make you mine?' Conrad asked. 'It has been hard enough already!'

She heard the agony behind the hoarseness of his voice.

'Hard?' she questioned.

'My darling, you are so young, so innocent,' he said. 'You do not know what it is like to love a woman as I love you and know that you dare not touch her.'

'Why . . . why must you not . . . touch me?' Kamala asked.

'Because, my sweet, it would be so easy to hurt you, to ruin your life, if I could not keep my love under control.'

'I do not understand,' Kamala said piteously. 'I just want to . . . be with you.'

He bent forward and kissed her very gently.

'I love you,' he said, 'and because I love you I have to protect you. Tonight I lost my head because you came in here so unexpectedly and because I was afraid, as you were afraid, of another man.'

'There will never be anyone but . . . you,' Kamala said. 'I love you with all my heart, there is no-one in the whole world but . . . you.'

Conrad gave a little sound that was half a groan and put his fingers on her lips.

'You must not say such things to me,' he said. 'Can you not understand, my darling, because I love you so madly, all I want to do is to make you love me? I want to tell you of my love, not once, but a million times! But it is dangerous for both of us.'

'Dangerous?' Kamala asked thinking of Mr. Van Wyck.

'Dangerous because, my sweet, I am only a man and I love you almost unbearably. My whole body aches for you and if I lose my head, if I make you mine, then I might give you a baby.'

Kamala was very still then she said softly:

'Now I understand why Mama said I must never . . . marry anyone unless I loved them. I love you and it would be . . . very wonderful to have your . . . child.'

'Oh, Kamala! Kamala!' Conrad murmured.

Once again his lips were on hers and he kissed her until she was unable to breathe.

After a long, long time, he set her free and rose from the bed to walk across the cabin.

'I have to make you understand,' he said, 'that this situation is dangerous not only because I love you. That is something I should be able to control, although I do not pretend for one moment it will be easy, but there are other dangers.'

His voice had changed and Kamala knew instinctively what he meant.

'Mr. Van Wyck,' she whispered.

'Exactly.'

He sat down on the bed again and took her hands in his.

'I did not wish you to know this, darling, but now I have to tell you. He is infatuated with you and I am not quite certain what we can do about it.'

'Has he mentioned it to you?' Kamala asked.

'He has hinted so broadly that I could not be mistaken,' Conrad replied, 'that if I wish to have a participating share in his cargo, to be in fact a partner—if only a junior partner in this enterprise—you are part of the deal!'

'He has already said something like that to ... me,' Kamala said.

'Blast him! Why did we ever trust him?' Conrad asked angrily. 'I had heard that he was a hard man but clever and adventurous. I did not realise that he was also cruel and a bad master to his crew. This is not a happy ship.'

Kamala did not speak and he went on :

'From the conversations I have had with him, I realise too that he is a womaniser of the worst sort. He has a wife in Amsterdam who is very rich, but they do not get on together.'

'He has a wife!' Kamala exclaimed in surprise. 'But I thought ...'

'I have said he is infatuated with you,' Conrad said quietly, 'but he does not intend to marry you.'

'I would not marry him if he was the last man in the world. But what he is asking is ...'

Her voice died away as she realised the full implication of what Mr. Van Wyck had intended when he tried to enter her cabin.

Then she gave a little cry of fear and reached out her arms to Conrad.

'You will not let him ... you will not let him ... touch me ... will you?' she begged. 'I am ... frightened of him! I have seen the look in his eyes and I am ... afraid.'

'Oh, my sweet! my darling! my precious one! I should never have brought you with me!' Conrad said. 'I am such a fool! I should have known that there would be men who would want you. Men who would lust after you and that this sort of situation could be really dangerous.'

'In what way?' Kamala asked.

'I am convinced,' Conrad replied speaking slowly, 'that Van Wyck will stick at nothing to get his own way, and only I stand between you and him.'

'Do you ... mean,' Kamala questioned, 'that he might ... hurt you?'

'It is easy at sea for a man to fall overboard and be lost,' Conrad replied.

He looked down into Kamala's eyes as he spoke and she gave a cry of sheer horror.

'No! no! no! it must not happen! Rather than that I will do ... anything he wants.'

Conrad held her so close in his arms she could hardly breathe.

'That is something that will never happen,' he said. 'But we have to be clever, my darling. I have got you into this mess and somehow I have to get you out of it.'

'But how?' Kamala asked.

'God alone knows the answer to that!' Conrad replied.

7

'It is lovely! I had never imagined anything could be so beautiful!' Kamala exclaimed.

She was slightly breathless, as was Conrad; for they had climbed one of the steep heights behind the port and now they could look over a vast vista.

The sea was vividly blue as the robe of a Madonna, stretching towards an indefinable misty horizon, the mountains perched high into the sky, the pretty Portuguese houses nestling round the harbour had red roofs, and everywhere there was a profusion of flowers.

There were flowers crimson, blue, yellow and white bestrewing the sides of the mountains clustering in the shelter of the dark ravines and round the mango groves. Their colour was almost blinding in the hot sunshine, their fragrance scenting the air.

'Say it is beautiful,' Kamala pleaded.

'Very beautiful!' Conrad agreed, but he was looking at Kamala and not at the view.

She sank down on the soft ground and lay back, her eyes shining, her hair vividly gold. A sheer rock rising above them shadowed her face from the strength of the sun.

'At last we are alone,' Conrad said in a deep voice.

He stretched himself down beside her as he spoke.

'I was afraid we would never get away,' Kamala said with a little quiver in her voice.

Then apprehensively, as if she was half afraid that even so high above the *Aphrodite* they were not safe, she asked:

'Where is . . . Mr. Van Wyck?'

'If his conversation before you came to breakfast is anything to go by,' Conrad said, 'he is in a bawdy house.'

'What is that?' Kamala asked.

'A place I should not have mentioned to you.'

'Are there . . . pretty women there?'

'Inevitably!'

'Then why did . . . you not go with him?'

'You know the answer to that.'

There was a silence for a moment and then Kamala said in a hesitating voice:

'I would not . . . wish you to feel . . . constrained because of . . . me.'

She was staring up at the sky as she spoke and now Conrad turned towards her, supporting himself on his elbow so that he looked down on her.

Her head was encircled by flowers, the skirts of her white dress made of mosquito netting seemed to float away from her tiny waist, as if they were as insubstantial as the white crests of the waves.

His eyes examined her face for a long time until at last, a little shy under his scrutiny, she asked:

'Why are you . . . . looking at me like . . . that?'

'I am looking for some flaw,' he replied. 'I cannot believe it is possible to find anyone as perfect as you.'

'Please do not look too hard,' she pleaded.

'I do not only love you for your beauty,' he said slowly, 'I love you because you are everything that a man dreams he might find in a woman. You are kind and sweet, intelligent, brave, and above all utterly and overwhelmingly desirable.'

Kamala felt herself thrill to the sudden throb of passion in his voice.

'I swore to myself last night,' he went on, 'that I would not kiss you again, but now there is nothing else in the world so important as your lips.'

Her eyes met his and something so wonderful, so

ecstatic, passed between them that it was as if they were already part of each other, a man and a woman indivisibly united by love.

Then as Conrad saw that Kamala was trembling and he knew that she too was excited, he bent forward very slowly and his mouth found hers.

There was not the same passionate and insistent desire in his kiss as there had been the night before, but instead there was something almost sacred and so spiritual that it was near to the divine.

'Darling, darling,' he whispered, 'I love you, dear God, how I love you!'

He kissed her again, until as if the rapture was too intense for him to bear, he turned away from her to lie looking up at the sky, his breath coming quickly, his heart beating wildly.

'I love you,' he said at length, 'but, my sweet, this is the last time I must tell you so until we reach Mexico.'

'I know that,' Kamala replied, 'and I will be careful. I swear to you I will do nothing to jeopardise your chances of sharing the cargo with Mr. Van Wyck.'

'I have no wish to share a cargo with him,' Conrad said. 'If I had a few pounds in my pocket I would leave the *Aphrodite* immediately and we would wait for another ship.'

He sighed before he continued:

'I even looked round the harbour this morning in case by any lucky chance there was a Schooner in port of which I had some knowledge or perhaps a Captain whom I had encountered in the past. But there are only a few Portuguese ships at anchor and we cannot live on air.'

He paused before he continued:

'If I had even half a brain in my head, I would have sewn some notes into my clothes so that they would be available in an emergency like this.'

'Spider might have found them,' Kamala said consolingly, 'and if he had told Mr. Van Wyck of his find, it would have looked extremely suspicious. Besides you know we needed all the money we had left to send to your home.'

'I am afraid for you,' Conrad said.

'I shall be all right,' Kamala affirmed with a confidence she was far from feeling. 'And once we reach Mexico perhaps we can somehow contrive to get away.'

'I hope so,' Conrad said with a sigh.

'I have a feeling,' Kamala replied in a soft voice, 'that we are being rather faint-hearted. Nothing we have undertaken has failed so far, and if we have faith I believe that somehow we shall find the wealth you seek. Perhaps then we will be able to love each other without being afraid.'

'I wish I could believe that was possible,' Conrad said.

'I do not think that a love such as ours could be lost or . . . wasted,' Kamala whispered.

Conrad raised himself once again to look down on her.

'It will never be lost,' he said, 'for I shall never love anyone else, my sweet dream, as I love you.'

It seemed to Kamala that the hours they spent on the mountainside were enchanted.

They were alone in a world where there was no danger, no fear, only love. A love so beautiful, so perfect, that she felt as if she was caught up into the golden heart of the sun and its glory became a part of herself.

Finally the shadows began to lengthen and they knew it was time to return.

They went down very quietly and without speaking through the fruit groves where the lemons and apricots hung golden on the trees and the pomegranate flowers were vividly pink against the green of their leaves.

Kamala picked an armful of flowers and Conrad wondered if any artist could do justice to the picture she made.

Only as they were nearing the town did he say to her:

'This is goodbye, my little love. Thank you for the most enchanting, magical hours I have ever spent.'

'They were perfect for me too,' Kamala said. 'Now I shall have something to remember, something to think about when we are back in the Clipper.'

'Do not look at me more than you can help,' Conrad commanded, 'and I must never look at you, or else our eyes will give away our secret.'

She stopped for a moment, her eyes, as he had just said, vividly expressive of her love.

'Believe,' she said, 'please, Conrad, believe that everything will come right for us! I shall pray for it, I will pray for it day and night, and I am sure deep in my heart that God will not fail us.'

He took her hand in his, turned it over and kissed the palm, a long lingering passionate kiss which made her quiver. Then he led her back to the ship.

Mr. Van Wyck did not come aboard until an hour after Kamala and Conrad had returned. Conrad met him on deck and realised, as he walked rather carefully up the gang-way, that he had been drinking.

'Oh, there you are, Sir Conrad!' he exclaimed. 'I was expecting you to join me. You missed the prettiest little soiled doves that I've seen for a long time. What's the matter with you? Not enough red blood in your veins?'

'My sister wished to see the flowers,' Conrad answered coldly. 'We went for a walk behind the town.'

'We should have changed places, that's what we should have done!' Mr. Van Wyck said with a leer.

Conrad turned aside so the Dutchman should not see the disgust he felt for him.

'Still I can tell you one thing,' Mr. van Wyck went on, 'I've not spent the day entirely on pleasure. I'm not saying that some of it was not enjoyable but I've also found another hand.'

'Do you really intend to leave the seaman who broke

his arm behind?' Conrad asked, a sharp note in his voice.

'Blast it, yes! What do you think I am? a charitable institution? The man will be no good for another three weeks. I've paid him off and found a replacement.'

Conrad felt it was a harsh decision which he as a Captain of a ship would never have made. But it was no use arguing with Van Wyck.

'I can tell you it is not easy to get a man who is any damn good in this place,' Mr. Van Wyck was saying. 'I heard there was an Englishman, the Mate of some Schooner which sailed without him, in the lower part of the town. I found the man. Of course he'd been drinking. He didn't make much sense, but I read his papers and he had the necessary qualifications.'

'So you signed him on,' Conrad said.

'I did a great deal more than that,' Mr. Van Wyck said with a loud laugh. 'I held his head under a pump to sober him and then told two of my men to frog-march him to the quay and onto the ship. He's down below, sleeping it off! Well he won't get much liquor afloat, and if we run into a strong sea before we reach Havana, we'll need able men, not cripples, aboard.'

'I hope he proves satisfactory,' Conrad said and left Mr. Van Wyck to give the orders for the sails to be hoisted.

Kamala came to breakfast the following morning determined that she would do everything in her power to make the voyage easy for Conrad.

They had not met at dinner the night before because he had been on deck helping Mr. Van Wyck to get the ship out on the evening tide, so she and the Señor had eaten alone.

The sea was comparatively calm and Kamala had retired to bed after dinner thinking she would read. But instead she had lain remembering the wonder and happiness of the afternoon, knowing that if she had loved Conrad before, she now loved him infinitely more.

'I love you! I love you!' she whispered to herself and fell asleep with a smile on her lips as she thought of all the things he had said to her.

She slept late, and when she entered the Saloon it was to find the Señor had finished his breakfast and was as usual deep in a book. He rose at her entrance and said eagerly:

'I have found some passages in this book on herbs which will be of great interest to you, Miss Veryan.'

'You must read them to me,' Kamala said. 'I am sure that my Spanish pronunciation is improving because I try to imitate yours.'

'You have such a beautiful voice,' the Señor replied gallantly, 'that anything you say, Señorita, is musical and pleasing to the ear.'

'Now tell me what I should reply to that?' Kamala laughed. 'You know I am far too English to find the right words.'

They were both laughing when the door of the Saloon opened and Conrad came in. Kamala looked at him and felt a sudden tremble of fear.

She had never seen him so stern and there was in fact an expression on his face that she could not understand.

He crossed the Saloon and sat down beside her on the sofa taking her hand in his.

'Tell me, Kamala,' he said, 'have you ever been vaccinated?'

There was a note almost of terror in his voice.

'Yes, I have,' Kamala replied. 'Papa was a great believer in it as he had met Dr. Jenner. My Father and Mother were therefore both vaccinated before they went to Italy, and Papa insisted that I should be done with them.'

Conrad gave a deep sigh that seemed to come from the

very depth of his being. His fingers tightened on Kamala's until they hurt.

'Thank God!'

'Why what has happened?' Kamala asked.

Conrad turned to the Spaniard.

'And you, Señor,' he asked, 'have you been vaccinated?'

'But of course,' the Señor replied, 'I would not travel as much as I do without taking such a very obvious precaution.'

'What is wrong?' Kamala asked quickly.

'The man whom Mr. Van Wyck engaged yesterday has smallpox,' Conrad replied. 'The other seamen reported that he had been sick all night and was delirious. As soon as I saw the dusky red eruptions all over his face, I knew what it was.'

'How could Van Wyck have thought the man was well enough to sail?' Señor Quintero asked angrily.

'Mr. Van Wyck told me that he had been drinking,' Conrad replied. 'But you know, Señor, that the fever which precedes the eruptions, the headache and the vomiting, might easily appear to the layman to be the result of alcohol.'

Conrad did not add that he felt in some ways it was a judgment on Van Wyck for having behaved so heartlessly towards the seaman who had broken his arm.

'As soon as I saw the man I was afraid for you,' he said to Kamala.

'Can I help him?' she asked.

'No, certainly not!' Conrad said sharply. 'You are to stay here and that is an order!'

'Surely most of the other seamen have been vaccinated?' Señor Quintero exclaimed. 'It is compulsory in a number of countries.'

'Not in England,' Conrad answered, 'nor in Holland.'

There was something in the way he said the last words which made the Señor glance at him sharply.

'You mean Van Wyck has not been vaccinated? Surely that is impossible?'

'He says he has always avoided doctors and their medicines,' Conrad said. 'But he has never been at close quarters to smallpox until now.'

He pressed Kamala's fingers and then rose and went from the Saloon. They did not see him again for some hours.

When he returned he had a list of everyone on the ship who had been vaccinated. The only Englishman was Spider.

He had been done the previous year in Denmark where vaccination was compulsory.

There were five Danish seamen aboard and like two Swedish they were immune. Two Bavarian sailors, although they had not been vaccinated for over ten years, were in Conrad's opinion a good risk.

But the English and the Dutch like Mr. Van Wyck had never availed themselves of the facilities which were obtainable in almost every port.

'It seems incredible,' Conrad said as they sat down to lunch, 'that England should not make vaccination compulsory when it was invented by an Englishman!'

'Papa has often spoken of Dr. Jenner,' Kamala said, 'and said how it is due to him that one of the greatest scourges in the world is gradually losing its terror.'

'Except to the English,' Conrad muttered angrily.

There was no doubt that Mr. Van Wyck was a frightened man.

He put on a big air of bravado, telling his guests over and over again how healthy he was, how smallpox came from dirt and disease and therefore there was not a chance in a million that he would catch it.

Yet Kamala realised that for the first time since she had been aboard the Clipper he was not interested in her.

She was no longer embarrassed at meeting the boldness of his eyes, there was no necessity for her to avoid the

148

touch of his hands or the close proximity of his body.

He decided that he was safest in the open air, and for the next ten days, while they all waited apprehensively to see who might develop the dreaded disease, they saw practically nothing of Mr. Van Wyck.

Kamala woke on the tenth day feeling afraid.

She knew how perturbed Conrad was and he, unlike the Master of the ship, made no pretence of dismissing the matter lightly or underestimating the dangerousness of the situation.

The man who had brought the smallpox aboard had died after three days, his body swollen so as to render his features unrecognisable.

The Señor had said a few prayers over him before the body had been cast into the sea, and it was Conrad who had insisted that everything below decks should be scrubbed out and disinfected.

'I think it would be a precaution at least,' he said to Van Wyck, 'if the men were issued with rather better food. We took on fruit and vegetables in Santa Cruz, but they are all finished. So is the meat.'

He dared not say openly that he was appalled by the manner in which Van Wyck treated his crew.

Food was short, the ship's biscuits that had come aboard in England were already full of maggots.

While the stern of the ship was furnished and fitted up in unbelievable luxury, the seamen's quarters in the bows were overcrowded, badly ventilated and with no comforts of any sort.

'Good God, Sir Conrad, you don't want to cosset seamen!' Mr. Van Wyck had thundered. 'Whatever you give them they will ask for more. I pay them well so if they want luxuries they can buy them for themselves.'

'There is not much that they can buy at the moment,' Conrad said dryly.

Mr. Van Wyck had however scoffed at him for trying

to mollycoddle the men and Conrad had been forced into silence.

'What will happen today?' Kamala asked herself.

She dressed and looked out through the porthole at a choppy sea under a cloudless sky. There was a strong wind and they were moving at a good speed.

'At this rate,' she thought with a sense of relief, 'we shall reach Mexico even sooner than we expect.'

She went into the Saloon to find as usual the Señor was there before her.

'Any news?' she asked and he knew to what she referred.

'I have seen no-one,' he replied.

As he spoke Spider came in with the coffee.

'Is everything all right, Spider?' Kamala enquired in a low voice.

'I am afraid not, Miss. Sir Conrad is for'ard at this moment; there are two men of whom he is suspicious.'

Kamala turned to the Señor.

'I am sure,' she said, 'they will be the two who helped the man aboard. They, if none of the others, have actually touched him.'

Conrad came into breakfast looking very serious and there was no need for Kamala and the Señor to ask him a question. They saw it in his eyes.

'Two men have a fever,' he said, 'and another has begun to vomit.'

Spider brought him his breakfast. He sat down and ate in silence.

'Please let me help!' Kamala pleaded.

'If there were anything you could do,' Conrad replied, 'I promise I would ask your assistance. I would not wish any woman to see the horrors of smallpox, but I know that as your Father's daughter you feel dedicated to assist those who are suffering. But I swear to you, Kamala, the men who have been vaccinated are doing everything they can to help the others.'

150

He left the Saloon as soon as he had finished.

There was no sign of Mr. Van Wyck and then, as Kamala picked up the Spanish book ready to start her lesson with Señor Quintero, Spider opened the door.

'It's the Master, Miss,' he said to Kamala, 'I don't like the look of him. Where is Sir Conrad?'

'He is not here,' Kamala answered, 'but I will come and see if there is anything I can do.'

Spider seemed so agitated that he made no protest and Kamala followed him into Mr. Van Wyck's cabin.

She saw as soon as she looked at the Dutchman that he was having a rigor and when she felt his pulse it was very quick. His temperature was obviously high and he did not recognise her. 'My head! my head!' he murmured.

When Kamala put her hand on his forehead, she could feel that the heat of his body was intense.

She told Spider to give his Master a cool drink and went on deck to find Conrad. He was just taking over the wheel from a man who was obviously collapsing at his post.

As he went across the deck to go below, he was suddenly violently sick and slumped against the side as if incapable of going further.

As two seamen went to his assistance, Kamala stood beside Conrad.

'Mr. Van Wyck has it,' she said in a quiet voice.

'Oh my God, not any more of them!' Conrad exclaimed.

'I am afraid there is no doubt about it,' Kamala answered. 'He has a very high temperature and is complaining of his head.'

'Will you keep away from him?' Conrad said angrily. 'I have said that I will not have you involved. Stay in your cabin or in the Saloon.'

'You cannot do everything yourself.'

'I can and I will,' Conrad retorted. 'And I will not have you concerned with this filth. You will obey me, Kamala!'

She looked up at him a little apprehensively, disturbed

by the anger in his voice and then as his eyes met hers his expression softened.

'I am trying to do what is best for everybody,' he said, 'even though you may not think so. It will only make it harder for me if you do not obey my orders!'

'I will obey you,' she said with a little sigh and went below.

Mr. Van Wyck died three days later and as Kamala watched his large body covered in a sheet being dropped into the sea, she tried to feel sorry.

She knew however she would be a hypocrite if she did not admit secretly to herself that she was glad she and Conrad no longer had to be afraid of him.

Ten other seamen including the Mate died one by one. There was no method of treating them, those who were well could do nothing but try to restrain them in their last restless delirium and then commit them to the waves.

The crew were now extremely short-handed. Conrad was now Captain of the ship, doing more than his fair share of duty. Kamala thought she had never seen him look so content and at peace with the world—it was the life he knew and understood.

Immediately he took over command he improved the food of the seamen and did away with a great deal of the harsh discipline which Mr. Van Wyck had thought essential.

Kamala would hear the men singing and whistling at their work, and she knew without being told that the *Aphrodite* was a happier ship than it had ever been before.

Only Spider mourned his Master, but he quickly transferred his allegiance to Conrad and even accepted grudgingly that the majority of things in Mr. Van Wyck's cabin must be cast overboard.

These included the mattress, the sheets, the hangings, and any of his clothes that he had worn after they reached the Azores.

'Seems a terrible waste, Miss!' Spider murmured to Kamala and she knew that the destruction of good materials meant more to him than the loss of life.

On Conrad's orders everything again was scrubbed and cleaned with disinfectant until Kamala complained it was now impossible to smell the sea.

Only once was Kamala alone with Conrad. She was sitting in the Saloon when he came in just before dinner. He stood in the doorway taking in the picture she made in her white dress.

Kamala's face lit up with joy at seeing him, and her eyes wide and deep with her love sought his.

'You are all right?' he asked.

'You can see I am.'

'You have no idea what a relief it is not to have to worry about you—not to be afraid.'

'Do you still . . . love me?'

She hardly breathed the words, but he heard them.

'One day I will tell you how much.'

He looked at her for a long moment. A sudden fire behind his eyes. Then he went from the Saloon closing the door behind him.

'We are clear now,' Conrad declared when five days had passed by after the last death and there were no more outbreaks of smallpox.

'At the same time I would not stop at Havana unless you are absolutely obliged to,' Señor Quintero said. 'They might insist on your being quarantined for three weeks or more, and I know of nothing more tantalising than to be anchored in a harbour and not to be allowed to go ashore.'

'I agree with you,' Conrad said. 'But we may all be on short rations long before we reach the coast of Mexico.'

Conrad told the men what he intended to do, taking them into his confidence in a manner which Mr. Van Wyck would have thought below his dignity.

The men responded, as Conrad knew they would, with a unanimous desire to reach Mexico as quickly as possible.

Actually the weather decided the question for them. They ran into a heavy storm and found themselves compelled to run before the wind and unable to make course for the harbours of Havana or any of the other islands.

It grew rougher and rougher and Conrad, afraid for the ship, was on deck by day and by night.

The decks were awash with white spume and the soaked sailors carried out their duties wearily but bravely.

It was after three days of buffeting, when the noise of the wind in the rigging and the creak of the plunging ship made Kamala fear that they might be going to the bottom, that Conrad came striding into the Saloon.

'We have reached the Gulf of Mexico!'

He looked desperately tired but there was a note of elation in his voice.

'Thank goodness for that!' the Señor exclaimed.

'It should be calmer from now on,' Conrad said. 'I have told Spider to cook us a good dinner tonight, I feel we all deserve it.'

'No-one,' Kamala thought, 'deserves it more than Conrad.'

He had seldom come down to meals at regular times, but had snatched something to eat and drink in between watches on deck. She had begun to wonder if he ever slept.

Now at last the storm was over—a storm which had shredded three of the sails, smashed a topmast and left the Clipper no longer looking smart as when it left the Azores.

Everything was white with salt, split sails littered the deck. The bulwarks had been carried away in places, and there was such a tangled medley of ropes everywhere that it seemed as if they could never be straight again.

But Conrad was smiling and so was his crew.

'The men say they have never served under a Captain

as fine as Sir Conrad,' Spider said, and Kamala felt a warm pride in her heart because he was appreciated.

'Have you no idea of where we are?' the Señor asked when Conrad had joined them at dinner.

'I found Van Wyck's maps are not very accurate,' Conrad answered. 'I imagine we shall soon be within sight of the coast, certainly by tomorrow morning. But the wind may have carried us north or south of the Gulf, I am not certain.'

'This coast has never been well charted,' the Señor replied. 'Although the Americans are trying their best, the Mexicans are still suspicious of strangers interfering and we all know that the Spanish have their own reasons for keeping the country backward.'

'But surely that will change now Mexico is independent?' Kamala asked.

The Señor shrugged his shoulders.

'I am told that shiploads of gold and silver are being conveyed to Spain,' he said. 'The Spanish aristocrats, I am quite certain, will be careful to feather their nests both here and in the old country. Many of them have seen the writing on the wall and have decided that if they leave Mexico they will certainly not go empty-handed.'

'Who shall blame them?' Conrad asked lightly. 'It is a land flowing with milk and honey, or rather with silver and gold.'

'I agree with you,' the Señor said. 'It has an inexhaustible wealth, but the Mexicans are lazy and do not like work, so it will be a brave and strong man who will finally exploit it.'

'And that should be you,' Kamala said softly to Conrad.

'You are asking too much,' he replied.

'After the way you have brought us here,' she told him, 'I believe you can do anything!'

Just for a moment he looked down into her eyes and then he rose to his feet.

'I must go back on deck,' he said. 'I would not like to

bring about an unhappy ending to the story by getting us all impaled on a rock.'

Kamala laughed, and she went to bed without worrying about anything except that Conrad was not having enough sleep.

Next day the sea was calm, and when Kamala went on deck it was to see the coast of Mexico just ahead of them.

'We are there! We have arrived!' she said to the Señor who was standing beside Conrad in the stern of the ship.

'I am longing to show you what I believe to be the most beautiful country in the world,' he said, 'especially at this time of year.'

'It is so hot!' she said. 'I can hardly believe it is January. Do you realise that Christmas Day passed and we never even remembered it.'

'It was not surprising,' the Señor remarked quietly.

Kamala recalled then that it was the day that Mr. Van Wyck had been committed to the ocean and half the ship's crew were down with smallpox.

All the same, she thought, she would have liked to wish Conrad a happy Christmas.

Then she turned her thoughts to the present.

'I want to see the cactus in bloom,' she said, 'and I want too to see the birds. I cannot really believe that one can actually see parrots, macaws and toucans perching in the trees. It seems unbelievable!'

'Wait and see,' the Señor said.

Kamala, seeing a smile in his usually rather sombre eyes, knew that he was as excited as she was at the thought of what lay ahead.

They had luncheon. Conrad came down to snatch a few mouthfuls of food and told them he was trying to find a harbour.

'The maps are hopeless,' he said, 'but I am sure there must be one somewhere. We are in vital need of food and water, we are running very short.'

It was the middle of the afternoon when Kamala, who had gone up on deck hoping for a closer sight of the land, saw two ships sailing towards them.

They were small but fast. Conrad called for a sailor to signal to them and asked the Señor to spell out the words 'Where are we?' in Spanish.

The seaman sent the signal. There was no reply. The ships came nearer.

'What do you make of them?' Conrad asked.

'I should think they are American built,' the Señor replied, 'they are certainly not Mexican.'

'They appear to be armed,' Conrad said looking through his telescope.

'That seems strange!'

'They are signalling,' Conrad said, 'it will be in Spanish. Can you read it for me?'

'Yes, of course,' the Señor answered.

He spelt out the letters and Kamala wrote them down.

'Go straight ahead,' she announced.

'What does that mean?' Conrad enquired. 'Is it an order or are they being helpful? Signal them that we are seeking a harbour and food and water.'

The seaman signalled the messages. A reply was received.

'It just says again go straight ahead,' the Señor translated.

'Then that is what we will do,' Conrad said. 'I imagine they are trying to be helpful.'

He looked at the ships through his telescope.

'The seamen are mostly Negroes,' he said, 'but they are well dressed. They carry quite heavy guns for such small vessels. They must be patrol ships of some sort.'

'The new Government must be surprisingly efficient,' the Señor said dryly.

One of the ships had turned in the wind and was now leading the Clipper towards the shore. The other came about and followed behind.

'Well, we are certainly being escorted in a Royal fashion,'

Conrad remarked. 'Let us hope our welcome will be as friendly.'

Kamala slipped down to the cabin and put on a new dress that Spider had made her since they left the Azores. He had only just finished it, having been too preoccupied with the smallpox epidemic to have time to sew.

He had draped fine white muslin very skilfully over a petticoat of pink satin so that on Kamala it had the glow and lustre of a pearl.

He had made a pink sash for her waist and there were tiny bows of pink ribbon to catch up the muslin and ornament the tiny sleeves.

She looked very young and very romantic in it, and having arranged her hair with a bow to match her dress, she came up to stand behind Conrad and watch the shore of Mexico grow nearer and nearer.

'I see there is something which looks like a Lagoon rather than a harbour ahead,' Conrad remarked to the Señor.

'I believe there are quite a number of Lagoons on the Gulf coast,' the Señor replied. 'I have never been in one, but they certainly offer a pleasant anchorage and are safe from the winds.'

They entered the Lagoon and Kamala saw it was comparatively small, and that it already contained quite a number of Schooners and fishing vessels.

The trees grew right down to the water's edge, and now at last behind them on the rising hills she could see the cacti with their yellow, red and purple flowers flaring exotically. Below the forest seemed to constitute an almost impenetrable jungle.

'It is lovely and mysterious,' Kamala murmured.

'Wait until you get away from the sea shore,' the Señor said. 'It is like stepping into a world of fantasy so primitive and yet so exciting one begins to forget that man himself is important.'

Kamala's eyes, however, were on the glory of the cacti.

She had never imagined it possible that there should be such fantastic colours.

Then ahead of them at the far end of the Lagoon they saw an enormous white building.

It had terraces and steps coming right down to the water's edge and standing waiting on the quay were a number of gorgeously arrayed personages. Even from the distance Kamala could see red coats, the glittering gold braid, the sparkle of epaulettes, the brilliance of decorations.

'We obviously have a reception party,' Conrad said dryly. 'What does this mean?'

'I have no idea,' the Señor answered.

The small ship in front gave a signal. The *Aphrodite* let go her anchor, the seamen began taking down sails.

'There is a boat coming out to us,' Kamala exclaimed. 'And the man aboard is very smart.'

'He is dark-skinned,' Conrad remarked in a low voice to the Señor.

The Señor waited until the boat got a little nearer before he said:

'He is a mulatto, I imagine a Major-Domo of some type. The house must be owned by some very wealthy grandee. Undoubtedly a Spaniard.'

He smiled as he spoke, but Kamala noticed that Conrad's eyes were a little wary.

'One thing,' the Señor said as the boat drew nearer, 'allow me to present you. To impress the Mexicans, and more especially the Spaniards, you must be of great importance.'

He glanced at Conrad and then at Kamala as he spoke and gave a chuckle.

'The lucky thing is that you both look very distinguished.'

'Let us hope they will think so,' Conrad remarked, 'as long as it means they will provide us with the stores that we need.'

'Leave it to me,' the Señor said.

The boat came alongside and Kamala saw that the gaudiest personage in a red uniform covered in gold was a mulatto, which the Señor had told her was the mixture of Negro and white.

As he came aboard they saw he was an enormous man, well over six feet tall. He drew his hat covered with rainbow-coloured feathers from his head and bowing with exaggerated politeness said in passable Spanish:

'Honoured Sirs and Madam, I bid you welcome in the name of His Supreme Excellency Don Miguel Moneda.'

Señor Quintero bowed and replied:

'We are indeed grateful for this greeting from His Supreme Excellency Don Miguel Moneda. Will you inform your Master that this ship is owned by a most distinguished nobleman from England who craves an audience with him.'

The flowery exchange of greetings continued for some time before finally Kamala, Conrad and the Señor found themselves being conveyed to shore in the boat.

Conrad gave some instructions to one of the seamen before he left and Kamala noticed that when he embarked he carried a small leather case in his hand.

As they drew nearer the house seemed even more large and grand and when they climbed the flight of white marble steps, Kamala was already extremely impressed.

The mulatto in his flamboyant uniform led them into the house.

Señor Quintero had already explained to Kamala how Mexican houses, large or small, were all built on the same pattern in a complete square.

In the centre was a courtyard with a fountain, and while all the rooms opened on to it, the most important were on the first or second floor.

Accordingly they climbed a staircase inside the courtyard which Kamala saw was made of silver. Then they were led into an enormous room running almost the whole length of the house and for a moment it took Kamala's breath away.

The walls were carved and decorated with gold, the floor was of a priceless marble and from the ceiling hung magnificent crystal and gold chandeliers which must have been brought from Spain.

There was gold everywhere. Gold tables, gold chairs, and seated at the far end of the room on what appeared to be a gold throne under a canopy of red velvet was His Supreme Excellency Don Miguel Moneda himself.

The mulatto approached him bowing almost to the ground and Kamala could not help feeling that because they had to walk the whole length of the room it somewhat exalted the Don's position and belittled theirs.

Señor Quintero greeted the Don and then presented Conrad and Kamala with such a glowing description of their importance that Kamala wanted to laugh.

The Don facing them listened gravely.

He had not risen at their approach but remained seated on his throne. Kamala saw that he had aristocratic features and dark hair above a high oval forehead.

He looked an autocrat, imperious and commanding. There was no doubt at all that he was a highly bred, proud and stiff-necked Spaniard.

In contrast to his servants he was dressed very austerely in black and only on his hand with his long thin tapering fingers was there a ring mounted with one enormous diamond. He listened carefully to all that the Señor said, and then as he finished rose slowly to his feet to come forward from his throne and walk down the steps to greet them.

'May I welcome you most warmly to Mexico, Sir Conrad Veryan,' he said to Conrad holding out his hand.

'We are delighted to be here, Your Supreme Excellency,' Conrad answered in English.

'I regret—I do not—speak your language—well,' the Don said slowly.

'How clever of you to speak any English at all!' Kamala exclaimed impulsively.

The Don turned to look at her as if surprised that she should have interrupted his conversation with Conrad. Slightly embarrassed, she curtsied.

He took her hand and raised it to his lips.

'I welcome you too, Señorita. My house and all in it, all I have belongs to you.'

'Muchsimas gracias, you are very gracious,' Kamala said in Spanish.

'You speak my language?'

'A little,' she replied, 'and I hope to be much more proficient before I leave Mexico.'

'Let us hope that will not be too soon.'

She smiled at him.

'A meal is being prepared for you,' he said. 'In the meantime will you honour me, Sir Conrad, by joining me in a glass of wine?'

'We should be delighted,' Conrad replied, 'and I must beg Your Supreme Excellency to be generous enough to supply my crew with food and drink.'

Señor Quintero translated what Conrad had said, but the Don merely made a gesture as if such a request was beneath his condescension.

'Arrangements have already been made.'

'Then I must thank you most sincerely,' Conrad remarked.

'We are indeed very grateful, Your Supreme Excellency,' Kamala interposed in Spanish. 'We encountered a very bad storm before we reached the sanctuary of the Gulf of Mexico and we are somewhat short-handed. So it has been a very strenuous voyage.'

She felt as she spoke that, while the Spaniard appeared to be listening to her, he was not particularly interested in their troubles or their adventures.

She did not know why, but she had the feeling that he

was preoccupied with his own thoughts; but that whatever they might be, they concerned them all.

They were however led into a magnificent Saloon almost as impressive as what Kamala called in her own mind, the 'throne room'.

Again there was a great deal of gold carving, but here there were also pictures, quite obviously of ancestors of their owner, and comfortable chairs and sofas.

Servants gorgeously apparelled appeared with wine. It was light and golden and Kamala found it quite delicious.

'I grow this myself,' the Don explained. 'Here in my Kingdom I am almost self-sufficient, I have everything.'

Kamala felt she had translated the word 'Kingdom' incorrectly. He must have meant a province, she thought. But the Don continued:

'I have everything. And here, as you will learn, I reign supreme. Those who serve me obey my commands and no-one opposes my will, for I am their King, their ruler and, to some of them, their god.'

Kamala looked in surprise and wondered if her Spanish was at fault. He spoke calmly without raising his voice and yet, surely, she thought, his words must be exaggerated.

Unexpectedly he rose to his feet.

'There are matters which require my attention,' he said. 'You will be shown to your rooms where you will rest. I invite you to dine with me at 9 o'clock. Muy buenos dias, Señorita.'

He went from the room before they could reply. Kamala looked at Señor Quintero.

'Did he really say this was his Kingdom and that he was a King?' she asked.

'Yes, he did, 'the Señor replied. 'I do not like it, Sir Conrad, there is something strange about that man.'

'That is what I thought,' Conrad agreed.

8

There was no time to say more because a man came hurrying into the room full of apologies.

'I am an Aide-de-camp to His Supreme Excellency,' he said in Spanish. 'I was out when you arrived. Please accept my most humble apologies and allow me to say I am at your service at all times.'

He kissed Kamala's hand and shook hands with Conrad and the Señor.

He was young and good-looking, but he too had that air of authority and condescension which Kamala had begun to think must be characteristic of all the pure-bred Spaniards in Mexico.

Their language might be fulsome and filled with compliments, but their eyes were hard and she could not help feeling there was a cruel twist to their lips.

'I would be grateful,' Conrad said quietly, 'if I could now go out to my ship and see that my men are being supplied with the food and water which His Supreme Excellency told me had already been arranged.'

'There is certainly no need for you to trouble yourself about them, Sir Conrad,' the Spaniard replied.

'As they are my responsibility, I must,' Conrad answered.

'If you will look from the window, Sir Conrad,' the Spaniard said, 'you will see they are already being brought ashore.'

Conrad, walking to the window which opened onto the balcony, stood in the sunshine and saw a boat full of seamen pulling away from the Clipper.

After a moment he said:

'It appears they are all leaving. There should be at least two men left behind.'

'That is also arranged,' the Spaniard said. 'Two of our own men will keep watch over your Clipper, while yours all come ashore to feast and enjoy themselves. Surely that is customary after a hard voyage?'

Kamala could see that Conrad was not pleased at his orders being changed. But it was difficult to find fault in the face of such geniality.

'I imagine my valet will be amongst those in the boat,' he said coldly after a moment's hesitation. 'I should wish him to attend to me.'

'But naturally,' the Spaniard agreed.

'And if we are to dine with His Supreme Excellency,' the Señor interposed, 'we would be grateful if our evening clothes could be brought ashore.'

'That is also being seen to,' the Spaniard informed him.

'Your hospitality is overwhelming,' Conrad remarked, but there was a touch of sarcasm in his voice.

'We must do our best to make you feel welcome,' the Spaniard replied.

He looked at the ornate French ormolu clock on the mantelshelf and said:

'I feel that you would now like to be shown your rooms and that you would wish to rest.'

'I think that would be an excellent idea,' Kamala said, thinking of Conrad and remembering how little sleep he had been able to have during the storm. 'Tomorrow I hope so much to see your wonderful cacti and the birds which the Señor has described to me. I believe they are very beautiful.'

'They are indeed,' the Spaniard smiled, 'and I hope that I may have the pleasure of escorting the Señorita round this rich and very fine Estate.'

He opened the door and Kamala walked out onto the balcony which encircled the courtyard.

It was built of marble and was cool, even though at this time of day the house, protected by the forests, seemed very hot and airless.

There was a sound of water rising iridescent in the centre of the courtyard and falling into a stone basin carved with life-size gods and goddesses, but before Kamala had time to look around, the Spaniard opened a door a little way along the balcony.

'This is a Sitting-room, Sir Conrad,' he said, 'which your party can use while you are staying here and where you can be entirely on your own. No-one will disturb you and you yourself can feel relaxed and at ease.'

'That is very gracious of you,' Kamala said before Conrad could speak.

She saw that the room was like the others: high ceilinged, luxuriously furnished and very comfortable.

'Your bedroom, Señorita,' the Spaniard went on, 'is next door and the two gentlemen are beyond you. There are maids to attend to you and you should find that your clothes have already arrived from the Clipper and been unpacked.'

It all seemed rather strange, Kamala thought, that they had not been asked what they wished to be brought, but it would have seemed churlish to complain and she could only thank the Spaniard again.

She walked into the bedroom with just a backward glance at Conrad hoping he would understand that she wanted to talk to him some time.

But he was not looking at her, and was saying something in a low voice to the Señor. So with a feeling that she was being rather deserted, Kamala heard the door close behind her.

Her bedroom was very grand, and again a great deal of gold had been employed in its decoration especially at the head and foot of the bed. Draped with mosquito curtains it was surmounted with a carved canopy of gold doves.

There were two Indian maids waiting to assist Kamala to undress.

They were pretty girls, dark-skinned with large eyes, beautiful teeth and long hair. They had small feet and little hands which were not very efficient. They moved slowly and spoke almost languorously.

They were both wearing what Kamala realised from the Señor's description was Mexican dress.

They had petticoats of yellow satin and the rest of the dress, which was of scarlet cashmere, was embroidered in gold and silver. The sleeves and body of the chemise was of cambric and trimmed with lace.

Kamala realised that it was modelled on a peasant's dress, but she thought that it must be very much finer than any Mexican peasant would be likely to wear.

The Indian girls spoke Spanish but in a dialect rather difficult to understand. Once she was undressed Kamala began to feel tired and it was too much effort to try to converse with them.

She lay down on top of the bed wearing the thin chiffon night-gown that Spider had made her. The maids put over her a very fine sheet of lawn then they pulled the mosquito curtains, lowered the sun-blinds and went from the room.

From behind the fine white curtains Kamala felt as if she were a nymph from the sea enveloped in mist.

It was almost as though she had been set apart and was alone in a world of her own. It gave her a strange feeling, and yet she was not really afraid.

Conrad was near, Conrad was next door, and she prayed that when they had both rested they would be able to talk together.

She fell asleep thinking of him, and she was not surprised several hours later to realise he was standing close to her bed just outside the mosquito-netting.

She could see his broad shoulders silhouetted in the light from the window.

He must have raised the sun-blinds because now the sun was sinking and it seemed to her that he was haloed in a blaze of glory.

She looked at him dreamily and he pulled aside the curtain.

It had been so hot that while she slept she had thrown aside the thin lawn sheet with which the maids covered her, and her body was naked save for her transparent chiffon night-gown.

For a moment Conrad was still, looking down at her.

'You are lovely,' he said at length hoarsely. 'More lovely even than I remembered you to be.'

She saw the sudden fire in his eyes and with a little cry, the colour flaring in her cheeks, she reached out to pull the sheet over her.

'I love you!' Conrad said and sat down on the edge of the bed.

'I wanted to see you,' Kamala said shyly. 'I hoped you would arrange that we could talk together.'

'It has not been altogether easy,' Conrad said with a smile. 'I had to climb from my balcony onto yours.'

She opened her eyes wide in surprise.

'But why?'

'Because the corridor is full of servants,' he said, 'and I thought that, even though we are supposed to be brother and sister, they might think it strange that I should visit you when you are not dressed.'

He paused and his eyes twinkled.

'Or very much undressed.'

Kamala blushed again.

'You have no right to come creeping in when I was not expecting you,' she said accusingly.

'You looked very beautiful,' he said.

Again there was that hoarse note in his voice and she

knew that she excited him. She put out her hands, but he drew further away.

'I dare not touch you,' he said. 'If I did, we might both forget where we are. We want all our wits about us, Kamala!'

'What do you mean by that?' Kamala enquired, realising he was speaking seriously.

'I do not know quite what is happening,' Conrad said. 'I wanted to go and talk to our seamen but the Spaniards have made it impossible. They have not actually forbidden me to do so, they have just put every obstacle in the way, telling me the men were being entertained, saying they were far from the house, everything with a courtesy which it is difficult to combat.'

'I do not understand their attitude,' Kamala said.

'Nor do I,' Conrad answered, 'and Spider tells me that the Don's servants came on board and literally ordered our men off the ship. Apparently, before we had come ashore, they had instructed him that everything we owned was to be packed. Maybe it is Spanish hospitality, but even so, it seems a little high-handed.'

'What does Señor Quintero think?' Kamala asked.

'He is as puzzled as I am,' Conrad replied, 'and he has also suggested, Kamala, that we must be very careful what we say to each other in the Sitting-room. He tells me it is quite usual in grand houses for the Spaniards, who love intrigue, to listen to whatever their guests may say.'

'How do you know someone is not listening now?' Kamala asked.

'They may be for all I know,' Conrad answered. 'But the Señor thought that your bedroom was the most likely room to be safe. The Spaniards have a low opinion of women, as they themselves would be unlikely to discuss anything of importance with their wives or sweethearts.'

'I am so glad you do not think like that,' Kamala remarked.

'I want to discuss everything with you always,' Conrad said. 'I want you to be with me, a part of me, I cannot bear you to be out of my sight!'

She heard the rising note of passion in his voice, and because she loved him so desperately she sat up on the bed so that her face was close to his.

'I love you because you feel like that,' she said. 'All I want is that we should be together.'

Her nearness broke Conrad's control.

He took her in his arms and his lips found hers.

He crushed her close to him so that she could hardly breathe. Then as she throbbed and quivered beneath the hungry desire of his lips, he suddenly set her free. He pushed her back against the pillows and pulled the fine lawn sheet up to her chin.

'The woman tempted me!' he said softly with laughter in his eyes.

Before Kamala could say any more, he pulled the curtains back across the bed and she could only see him silhouetted against the sunset as he went out onto the balcony.

She waited for a moment still throbbing from the ardour of his kiss. Then she rose and followed him to see with horror the danger he had risked to reach her.

Each balcony on the seaward side of the house was divided from the one next door by a huge screen of wrought-iron, fashioned exquisitely in the manner the Spaniards guarded the windows of their women.

To come to her Conrad must have climbed round the screen where it jutted out over the balustrade. Had he fallen he would have crashed down onto the terrace below which was flagged with stone.

'How could he be so foolhardy?' Kamala wondered.

She stood on the edge of the balcony looking out to sea. She could see the *Aphrodite* with its broken top-mast at anchor, and noted how many other small ships there were on the Lagoon.

Then as she stood there, she saw coming through the entrance from the sea the sails of another Clipper.

It came in swiftly, looking like a great bird, its slim lines reflected in the clear blue water of the Lagoon.

'Perhaps other guests are arriving,' Kamala thought, and watched the Clipper with fascinated eyes as it came nearer and still nearer the house.

She could hear the anchor splash into the water as finally it heaved to. And she saw the sailors clambering up the masts like small monkeys to furl the sails and fasten them to the yard-arms.

The new Clipper was larger than their own.

She had thought that the *Aphrodite* was the most beautiful ship she had ever seen, but now she knew that the new-comer, whoever owned it, was smarter and perhaps a good deal faster.

'I must ask Conrad about it,' she thought excitedly and turned back into the bedroom.

She was wondering how she should summon the maids when they came into the room and told her it was time to dress for dinner.

They opened a door which she had not previously noticed, and she found it led to a sunken bath made of silver edged with gold in which she could bathe.

The water was cool and scented, and after she had washed the Indian maids enveloped Kamala in huge towels dyed a soft shade of blue and rubbed her dry.

One of the maids arranged her hair, another brought her a chemise and her silk petticoats. Then when she looked towards the wardrobe expecting the maids to fetch her evening gown, there came a knock on the door.

One of the maids opened it and an elderly woman, also an Indian, came in carrying in her hands the most elaborately beautiful dress Kamala had ever seen.

It was of white draped and frilled over white satin, and dazzling on the low décolletage and on the small sleeves were stones which seemed at first sight to Kamala to be diamonds.

She looked closer and saw they were in fact diamonds, dozens of them encircled with pearls.

'For you, Señorita, a gift from His Supreme Excellency,' the elderly maid said dropping a curtsey.

'For me!' Kamala exclaimed, 'but I could not take anything . . .'

Her voice died away. She wondered suddenly if to refuse such a present would be an insult?

She had the feeling that it would not be wise to insult their host, and he was certainly not the type of man who would expect anything but humble and grateful subservience from those he honoured with a gift.

'It is very . . . kind,' Kamala said hesitatingly, 'but it may not fit me.'

'It will be a little big in the waist, Señorita,' the elderly Indian replied, 'but I have here my needle and thread and if the Señorita would be gracious enough to stand still, I will make any alterations that are necessary.'

It seemed to Kamala there was nothing she could do but acquiesce. She allowed the maids to dress her in the gown and she had to admit as she looked at herself in the mirror that it was very beautiful.

'The dress came from Spain, Señorita,' the elderly maid said as she stitched away at the waist which, as she had anticipated, was too big for Kamala.

'And the diamonds?' Kamala asked.

'I sewed them on,' the maid replied with a touch of pride in her voice.

'You have done it very beautifully,' Kamala remarked.

'I was taught, Señorita, by my Mother,' the woman answered.

When Kamala was ready, she wondered what Conrad would say at her appearance.

In some ways she was thrilled at the thought that he would admire her, that he would think her perhaps even more lovely, wearing a gown which was grander than anything she had ever imagined.

At the same time she felt a little apprehensive that he might think that she should not have accepted so expensive a gift.

'When we leave I will not take it with me,' she told herself. 'The diamonds could easily be used again.'

At the same time she could not help thinking that the gems must be very valuable and if indeed His Supreme Excellency meant her to keep them, already she was the possessor of a small fortune.

She put the thought from her. She was certain Conrad would not wish her to accept jewels from a man. Anyway she thought it was up to him to decide what she should do.

It gave her a warm feeling inside to realise that she could in fact rely on him.

He would protect and look after her because he loved her. She felt herself thrill and knew a sudden urgency to be with him, to be beside him.

She thanked the maids prettily and went from the bedroom into the Sitting-room next door. The Señor was there, but not Conrad.

'Where is my brother?' she asked.

She realised, as she spoke, it was an indiscreet question and the Señor did not wish to answer it. She remembered that Conrad had warned her that in the Sitting-room they might be overheard.

'He must not be late for dinner,' she said, 'I am sure that would be extremely impolite.'

'I shall be surprised if we get our dinner as soon as 9 o'clock,' the Señor replied. 'Spaniards eat late and what is more they are naturally unpunctual.'

'Then we must wait and see,' Kamala said seating herself on the sofa.

It made her feel a little frightened to think that every word she said might be overheard, that perhaps through the carved panelling someone could not only hear her, but see her and anything she did.

'It is very hot,' she said after a little while and walked across the room and out onto the balcony.

The Lagoon was certainly lovely, in the crimson, saffron and amethyst of the sky. Overhead the first star was twinkling like one of the diamonds on Kamala's gown.

The Señor came to her side.

'Where did you get that gown?'

'His Supreme Excellency sent it to me.'

'It is certainly magnificent, and the diamonds must be worth thousands of pounds.'

'That is what I thought,' she said a little nervously. 'Was I wrong to accept it?'

The Señor shrugged his shoulders.

'The sunsets are always beautiful,' he said aloud.

At that moment they heard Conrad come onto the balcony behind them. Kamala glanced round at him and knew at once something was amiss. There was a frown between his eyes and his mouth was set in a hard line.

'What has hap . . . ?' she began.

But before she could finish the sentence she saw that the Spanish Aide-de-camp had followed Conrad. He kissed her hand, bowed to the Señor and said:

'His Supreme Excellency will receive you in the Saloon.'

Feeling as if they were school children being shepherded along by a teacher, Kamala preceded the men to the Sitting-room where the Don entertained them on their arrival.

He was not in the room when they entered it, but appeared five minutes later, again dressed in black but with a white frilled shirt and high cravat with diamond studs, each one the size of a shilling.

It seemed to Kamala as she curtsied to him that he looked her over as if appraising the gown he had given her in a manner which made her feel insignificant and unsure of herself.

Then he talked smoothly and conventionally to Conrad, ignoring Señor Quintero as if he was beneath his condescension.

Finally after an exchange of commonplace conversation they went in to dinner.

The Banqueting Hall was almost as impressive as the Throne Room. Again the walls were of gold, magnificent pictures were set in carved frames several feet wide.

The table at which they were to eat was covered with a lace cloth and seemed to be groaning beneath the weight of gold ornaments set with diamonds.

They were so fine that Kamala could not resist a little exclamation of astonishment.

The Don sat in a high-backed chair of Spanish leather at the top of the table; Kamala was on his right and Conrad on his left.

'You are admiring my ornaments?' he asked.

'Yes, indeed, Your Supreme Excellencey,' Kamala answered, 'they are fabulous! I cannot believe we could see finer ones anywhere in the world.'

'I like to hear you say that,' the Don remarked. 'Perhaps it will surprise you to know that they have been made here to my own design by my own craftsmen.'

'It is incredible,' Conrad interposed. 'I imagined they were of great antiquity and came from Spain.'

'The originals did come from there,' the Don told him, 'but I have taught the Indians to copy almost exactly what is set before them. Of course, the metal and the jewels were my choice.'

'Señor Quintero was telling us on our voyage here of the

beautiful diamonds you have in Mexico,' Kamala said.

As she spoke she put her fingers up to those that ornamented her dress.

'And I must thank Your Supreme Excellency for lending me this magnificent gown to wear tonight.'

'Lend you?' the Don said sharply. 'It is a gift!'

'I do not think ...' Kamala began then saw Conrad frown at her and added quickly '... I can find words in which to thank you for such a generous present.'

'I do not wish to be thanked,' the Don said loftily.

He changed the subject.

'Tomorrow,' he said to Conrad, 'you will see the *Santa Maria*, my new Clipper which I have recently had built in America.'

'I saw it arrive tonight,' Kamala interposed. 'It is superb, like everything else here!'

'I am glad you should think so,' the Don replied. 'Only the best is good enough for me. I will not accept anything that is not superior in every way to that owned by other men.'

His eyes rested on Kamala for a moment and then he said:

'Many of the Indians are clairvoyant and have the power of prophecy. It was foretold at my birth that I should reign over this land. Recently I was told something else.'

'And what was that?' Kamala asked with interest.

'That I should find a Queen,' he answered.

'Do such prophecies ever come true?' Kamala asked.

'This Seer has never been wrong,' the Don replied. 'She said my Queen would be white-skinned and would come to me from over the sea.'

He was speaking again in the strange tone he had used when they first arrived.

'Your Clipper is certainly Queen of the Sea,' Conrad said.

He had understood only a little of what the Don was saying.

176

'I saw her come into the harbour this evening and realised how manœuvrable she is—apart from the fact that I expect she could easily show a clean pair of heels to any other ship afloat.'

'In a few days I intend to visit Spain,' the Don said. 'After that voyage I shall be able to tell you if your judgment is correct, and I am sure it is!'

'I will not offer to race you back to Europe,' Conrad said lightly.

'No indeed, that would be useless,' the Don answered.

Conrad hesitated a moment and then he said:

'What I am hoping to find while I am in Mexico is a cargo. As you well know, Your Supreme Excellency, our Clippers have excellent cargo space.'

The Don looked at Conrad as if he had been impertinent.

'A cargo?' he questioned.

'Yes, Your Supreme Excellency.'

There was silence. It appeared the Don had no intention of suggesting a cargo for Conrad.

Kamala wondered if the Aide-de-camp who was sitting at her side would be more helpful. She felt however it was not the moment to speak of it and started to talk of other things.

The dinner was long and drawn out but the dishes were delicious, many of them quite different from anything Kamala had tasted before.

There was quail and red partridge, cooked with herbs and strange mushrooms. There were alligator pears, medlars, apricots and pomegranates to decorate the dishes and a number of other tropical fruits for them to sample at the end of the meal.

Everything was served on gold and silver plate except the dessert, which was presented on Sèvres porcelain.

Kamala hoped that the seamen were also being well fed.

Everyone on board had all been feeling hungry when they finally reached the Gulf and although Conrad had improved the food in the galley, it was still monotonous and unappetising after so many weeks at sea.

When dinner was over they walked for a few minutes in the courtyard admiring the flowers of many colours which were clustered round the fountain and feeling the cool of the evening delightful after the heavy tropical heat of the day.

Finally they repaired once again to the Saloon which Kamala gathered the Don liked the best of the many different rooms.

He asked them to seat themselves then spoke to his Aide-de-camp.

The young man went from the room and returned a few minutes later with a black leather box. The Don took it from him and opened it.

Resting on black velvet was the most amazing diamond necklace Kamala had ever seen. The diamonds were enormous—clustered together they shone brilliantly.

'How fabulous!' she exclaimed.

The Don rose and holding the necklace in both his hands, he walked up to Kamala and put it round her neck.

She was too surprised to prevent him. In fact the Don had fastened the clasp before she realised what he was doing.

Then, as she told herself he was only showing it off to her and giving her the fleeting pleasure of wearing it, the Don said:

'I told you at dinner that it had been prophesied that I should find a Queen, who the Seer said would come to me from the sea and be very beautiful. I knew as soon as I saw you enter my house this afternoon, that the prophecy had come true!'

Kamala stared at him feeling that she could not have heard him right. And yet the Don was looking straight at her, his dark eyes appraising her.

Conrad had not quite understood what was said, but he

had watched the Don give Kamala the necklace with a frown on his face. Now he stared at the Spaniard suspiciously.

'I do not ... think I ... understand Your Supreme Excellency,' Kamala said nervously, feeling as if her voice was very small and lost in the great room.

'Then let me make it very clear,' the Don replied, 'and if you wish I will say it in English: You are—to be my—wife and my Queen.'

Conrad turned angrily to Señor Quintero.

'What the devil is he talking about?' he asked.

The Señor looked perturbed.

'He is asking your sister to marry him.'

'That is ridiculous and an insult!' Conrad exclaimed getting to his feet.

'An insult!'

The words seemed to echo across the room and the note in the Don's voice was one of hardly suppressed fury.

'No! no!' Kamala cried quickly, 'do not be incensed, Conrad!'

She rose and went to his side putting her hand on his as if to calm him. Then looking at the Don she spoke slowly but in English so that Conrad could understand.

'I am deeply honoured, Your Supreme Excellency, by your most flattering and gracious proposal of marriage. I thank you for it, but I am unable to accept such an important position as that of your wife.'

'You refuse me?'

The question expressed incredulity, but it seemed to Kamala that there was also a menace behind the words.

'Your Supreme Excellency must realise we are barely acquainted.'

'Here in Mexico, and in my domain, marriages are arranged without the woman presuming to have a say in the matter.'

The Don again spoke in Spanish. Kamala had a strong sense of unease, that they were all in danger.

She could feel that Conrad was barely able to restrain himself, and she knew instinctively that somehow she must keep the peace. They must not insult the Don, which was something he would never forgive.

'I think, Your Supreme Excellency,' she said, 'we are all over-tired tonight. Can we not talk of this tomorrow? My brother is of course my Guardian, and as I am under age in my country it would be impossible for me to marry without his permission.'

'I understand that,' the Don conceded.

'Then with Your Supreme Excellency's permission, we will now withdraw to our own bedrooms', Kamala said. 'Tomorrow there will be time to discuss such matters. Nothing so important can be decided so quickly.'

'When I have made up my mind I act,' the Don said.

Again there was a menace behind his tone, but fortunately the words spoken in Spanish were too complicated for Conrad to understand.

'Please be patient,' Kamala said with a smile, 'we are grateful for Your Supreme Excellency's hospitality and it has been a privilege to meet you, to see your wonderful house. I am also overwhelmed by your generosity but we have had a long and difficult journey, we are in fact exhausted.'

Just for a moment it seemed as though the Don was about to say more.

Then he walked towards Kamala, lifted her hand to his lips and, ignoring Conrad and Señor Quintero, went from the room.

'What the hell does this mean?' Conrad demanded of the Aide-de-camp.

'When the Supreme Excellency makes up his mind, he expects obedience,' the Spaniard answered.

'Does he really believe that my sister . . .' Conrad began.

'Please do not let us discuss it tonight,' Kamala pleaded. 'As I have already said, we are all tired and we will say things we do not mean. Tomorrow we can consider the matter without losing our tempers or saying anything we might later regret.'

She put her hand on Conrad's arm as she spoke and he felt the pressure of her fingers.

'You are right,' he said, 'of course you are right.'

But she saw the expression in his eyes and knew that he would be hard to hold.

'Good-night, Señor,' she said and curtsied to the Aide-de-camp.

He opened the door for her and she stepped out into the passage where there were a number of servants in attendance. Her maids took her to her room. She allowed them to undress her and got into bed.

She was hoping and praying as she did so that Conrad would come to her as he had come before, but although she lay awake for a long time there was no sign of him.

Finally, miserable and apprehensive, she fell asleep.

Kamala awoke to find the sun pouring in over the balcony, and rising she walked across the room to look out onto the Lagoon.

Had it been true what happened last night or had she dreamt it all? It seemed as though it must be only a dream. It was too fantastic, too absurd!

Things like that did not happen in real life.

She was quite convinced that the Don was mad, but that did not help their present predicament. The mast of the Clipper was broken, they could not put to sea without provisions.

Kamala felt anxious and afraid, then she told herself she was being faint-hearted.

Conrad would find a solution, she was sure of it, and whatever else happened she must prevent him arguing with the Don. That might have far-reaching and dangerous results.

She heard a sudden movement on the balcony next to hers and saw Conrad come out onto it fully dressed.

She snatched up a large embroidered shawl which ornamented a sofa in her room and wrapped it round her. Then she stepped out into the sunshine so that he could see her.

He went to the edge of the balcony and stood looking at the Lagoon.

'Come as close as you can,' he said in a low voice.

Kamala obeyed him leaning over her own balustrade as near to the iron partition as she could get.

'Why did you not come to me last night?' she asked.

'I intended to do so,' he answered, 'but I found there were sentries at each end of the balconies.'

'Sentries!' Kamala exclaimed.

'Fully armed too,' Conrad said. 'I had no desire to be taken for a robber and shot accidentally. There would be every reason for their doing so, if I were seen clambering round this damned iron-work.'

'Why should there be sentries?' Kamala asked in a frightened voice.

'It may be quite usual. After all, he gives himself tremendous airs. He might have quite a number of enemies. But I dared not give him an excuse for being rid of me.'

'No, of course not,' Kamala said, 'that would be very stupid. But what are we to do?'

'That is what I have to decide,' Conrad answered. 'Spider is trying to discover what has happened to the crew. I cannot help feeling that it was an intentional action on the part of the Don, that they should all be taken off the ship and brought ashore. It is impossible for us to leave without them.'

'Are you inferring that in truth we are prisoners?' Kamala asked.

'We may be—I do not know,' Conrad replied, 'The man is a lunatic, crazy as a coot!'

There was a contempt in his voice which Kamala could not help thinking owed something to jealousy.

'He cannot really mean he wishes to marry me,' she faltered.

'Quintero tells me that Spaniards are extremely superstitious. The Mexicans, having always believed in their own clairvoyant powers, convinced their conquerors they could see the future. It has often been used to their advantage.'

'The Don cannot be ... serious,' Kamala murmured in a frightened voice.

'Why did I ever bring you on this blasted voyage?' Conrad asked angrily. 'I might have known that everything would go wrong if there was a woman on board!'

His words hurt Kamala and she did not answer. And after a little silence he said:

'My darling, I did not mean to be unkind, it is just that I am so desperately worried and so afraid. We thought that Van Wyck was dangerous, but this lunatic is infinitely more so. If he wishes to be rid of me there is nothing and no-one to stop him, and then you will be in his power.'

'He cannot want me ... he cannot!' Kamala said.

'Do not deceive yourself,' Conrad said harshly. 'If he has been told that a fair-haired woman will come from across the water to reign beside him he believes it. We know it is a lot of damn nonsense, but not to him. He will do everything in his power to make the prophecy come true.'

Kamala shivered.

'I would rather ... die than marry ... him.'

'Then somehow we have to escape,' Conrad declared. He was silent for a moment then he went on:

'We will have to be clever, very clever, to outwit him.

But it could be impossible—I will start by discussing the terms of your marriage and play for time.'

'I will not have to ... marry him?' Kamala faltered.

'Only over my dead body,' Conrad said fiercely and she knew that he meant it.

'Go now and dress,' he said harshly. 'We must not arouse suspicion.'

As he spoke he turned and went into his own room and Kamala withdrew into hers.

She was nearly dressed and one of the maids was just putting some finishing touches to her hair when there was a knock on the door.

The other Indian opened it and there came into the bedroom a woman at whom Kamala stared almost open-mouthed. She was in fact the most beautiful person she had ever seen.

She had dark hair elaborately dressed, perfect features, huge eyes, dark-fringed eyelashes, an exquisite mouth, and a figure which was almost Grecian in its perfection.

She stared at Kamala for a moment. Then she snapped her fingers and the two maids hurried from the room shutting the door behind them.

'Good morning,' Kamala said because she felt that the silence was uncomfortable, 'my name is Kamala Veryan.'

'I know that,' the woman replied in Spanish, 'I am Josefa.'

Her dress was very elaborate and must have been extremely expensive. She wore a necklace of huge diamonds rather coarsely set, but the stones were magnificent, and long diamond ear-rings dangled from her ears.

Her bracelets set with precious stones were so wide and obviously so heavy, they seemed to weight down her wrists.

'You will not have heard of me,' Josefa said after a moment's silence, and in a voice which Kamala felt was harsh with dislike. 'I was not allowed to dine with you last night.'

'Why not?' Kamala asked in surprise. 'My brother and I would have been delighted to make your acquaintance.'

She realised as she spoke that Josefa's skin was coffee coloured and guessed that she was a Mestizo which the Señor had told her was a mixture of Indian and European. She remembered that he had added, 'The women are often very lovely.'

Josefa was breath-takingly beautiful and Kamala said with a smile:

'I am so glad you have come to visit me. I am sure you can tell me so many things that I wish to know.'

'Why have you come here?' Josefa asked angrily.

'We had no choice,' Kamala answered. 'There was a terrible storm at sea and we were blown ahead of it. Even if we had wished to stop at Havana it would have been impossible. When we reached the coast of Mexico two ships belonging to His Supreme Excellency guided us into the Lagoon.'

'You did not come here purposely?'

'No, indeed,' Kamala answered. 'This place is not even charted on our maps.'

She felt that some of the aggression and hatred faded from Josefa's face. Then Josefa said:

'Is it true that His Supreme Excellency asked you last night to marry him?'

There was almost a note of pain in her voice as she spoke, and Kamala guessed that the Don meant something special to this beautiful woman.

'I think His Supreme Excellency must have been joking,' she answered hesitantly. 'I cannot take him seriously.'

'If you marry him I will kill you!'

Kamala stared at Josefa in astonishment. Then she said quickly:

'I have no wish to marry him, I assure you. I am in love with someone else, someone to whom I am already promised.'

It seemed to her that Josefa's eyes cleared a little before she said:

'You will have no choice in the matter. Women have to do as they are told.'

'Not English women,' Kamala rejoined, putting up her chin.

As she did so, she remembered Uncle Marcus and how little choice he had allowed her. But she knew that she had to convince this beautiful jealous woman that she had no interest in the Don.

'You will do what he wishes,' Josefa said in a dull voice. 'Then he will send me away.'

'No, no,' Kamala said quickly, 'he will not do that. I will not marry him, I promise you!'

Then as she spoke, Conrad's last words came to her mind:

'Help me,' she said, 'help us all to escape and then there will be no chance of his trying to marry me.'

'Help you—escape?'

It was obvious that the words came as a surprise to Josefa.

'Please understand,' Kamala said, 'that we had no wish to come here. It happened quite by chance and now we want to go away. But our ship is damaged, our seamen have been brought ashore, and as far as I can see we are prisoners.'

Josefa came nearer to her. Kamala could smell a strange exotic perfume she used.

'Do you mean that?' she asked. 'Swear to me on the Cross of Jesus that you tell me the truth.'

'I swear to you that my brother and Señor Quintero who is with us wish to go away, to escape from here.'

Josefa looked into Kamala's face for what seemed a long time and then she said:

'I believe you.'

'Then you will help us?' Kamala asked.

'It will not be easy,' Josefa said. 'If he wants you he will take you. He will make you his.'

'There must be some way,' Kamala said desperately.

'I will think of one,' Josefa said. 'Swear to me you will not mention to him that you have seen me. Swear!'

She put out her hand as she spoke and grabbed Kamala's arm. Her fingers dug into the soft skin and were painful.

'I swear,' Kamala said, 'and I beg you, to give us every assistance so that we can go away from here and never return.'

'Then I will help you,' Josefa promised.

She released Kamala as she spoke and walked across the room. She opened the door and went out without looking back. Kamala stood staring after her.

Then she felt a sudden hope rise within her heart. Josefa wished to be rid of her, that might be the key to freedom.

9

Kamala went in to breakfast thinking that Conrad would wonder what had happened to her. Josefa had delayed her so long that she imagined he might be worried.

To her surprise when she entered the Sitting-room, where she had been told breakfast would be served, she found only Señor Quintero holding a book in his hands.

He had obviously finished his breakfast which was set out on the balcony and protected from the sun with a deep blue awning.

'Good morning, Señor,' Kamala said in Spanish.

'*Buenos dias, Señorita.* I have here a book which I am sure will interest you enormously.'

'What is it?' Kamala asked indifferently.

She felt surprised at his interest in any book when there was so much else to concern their thoughts.

He held the book out to her and she took it, looking out on the balcony as she did so to make quite sure that Conrad was not somewhere just out of sight.

'This is the passage,' the Señor said insistently. 'I would particularly like you to read it. It was what we were discussing last night.'

She looked to where he was pointing and saw with a sudden start that there was a piece of paper inserted in the book, on which was written in English:

'*Danger. We are overheard. Agree to everything that is suggested.*'

It was the first word which made Kamala feel as though

her lips had suddenly gone dry, and she could not think how to answer the Señor.

Then with an effort she managed to remark as casually as she could:

'Perhaps I could read it later. Just now I am longing for some coffee.'

'My apologies, Señorita,' the Señor said, 'I am always so thrilled to find something new in literature, that I forget the ordinary needs of the human body.'

'Has Conrad had his breakfast?' Kamala asked, walking towards the balcony.

'I think not. I am the only one who is punctual,' the Señor replied.

The door opened, but it was the servants bringing fresh food for Kamala. A large meal had been arranged for them. There were at least a dozen dishes of fish, fowl and meat and all with French sauces.

There was coffee and also Bordeaux wine and sherry for the men, while what most interested Kamala were the many strange and delicious fruits.

It was difficult for her to eat much when she was worrying as to what had kept Conrad, and when finally he appeared she knew from the look of his face that he was extremely perturbed.

His mouth was set in a hard line, his chin was square and there was a darkness about his expression which told her he was angry, but keeping himself firmly under control.

'Good morning, Kamala,' he said, and to the Spaniard: 'Good morning, Quintero.'

The eyes of the two men met for a moment, and Kamala knew instinctively that this was not the first time they had seen each other that morning.

It must have been Conrad, she thought, who had told the Señor to tell her that they were being overheard and also to agree to everything that was suggested.

Could he have already seen the Don, she wondered, but

then thought it was unlikely. What then could have occurred since she last spoke to him?

She and Conrad ate in silence while the Señor, still holding his book, sat near them on the balcony making commonplace observations about the weather and the heat.

Kamala began to feel that the tension was almost unbearable. She was wondering how she could tell Conrad about Josefa, when the Aide-de-camp came from the Sitting-room onto the balcony.

'I am at your disposal, Señorita,' he said to Kamala in Spanish, bowing elegantly and kissing the hand she extended to him. 'His Supreme Excellency sends you his greetings. He hopes most fervently you have spent a quiet night and hopes you will honour him by visiting the Estate which he has the greatest desire to show you.'

'I would like that very much,' Kamala answered.

'We must accommodate you on horseback,' the Aide-de-camp said. 'There are only a few carriage-paths but His Excellency has a spirited horse which he feels will meet with your approval.'

'It will, I am sure,' Kamala smiled, 'but unfortunately I have no habit with me.'

'That is being arranged,' the Aide-de-camp said.

'I hope I may accompany my sister,' Conrad interposed.

'But of course,' the Aide-de-camp replied after only an infinitesimal pause, 'I am sure His Supreme Excellency will be delighted. And you, Señor Quintero, do you wish to ride?'

'If you will excuse me,' the Señor replied, 'I have a headache and I would rather walk in the garden and sit in the shade, if His Supreme Excellency will permit me to do so.'

'It is of course as you desire,' the Spaniard said courteously.

'At what time will His Supreme Excellency be expecting us?' Conrad enquired.

'In an hour's time,' the Aide-de-camp replied. 'It is wise to set off before the sun becomes too hot.'

'That is of course very sensible,' Conrad agreed.

The Aide-de-camp left the room and Kamala rose to her feet.

'How clear the Lagoon looks!' she exclaimed. 'The water is so transparent that I am sure one could see anything that was lying on the bottom.'

'Such as a pearl,' the Señor remarked with a smile.

'As we have time why do we not walk down to the edge of the Lagoon?' Conrad suggested. 'I am sure it would amuse you, Kamala, to see if there are any fish that are identifiable.'

'I am convinced the Señor will be able to tell us their names,' Kamala smiled.

'You two go ahead,' the Señor said. 'As I have a head-ache I will go first to my bedroom to find a hat, I am always afraid of getting sun-stroke.'

Kamala guessed he was making an excuse so that she and Conrad could be alone. They all three went from the Sitting-room, and now Kamala noticed that at the bottom of the silver staircase leading down to the courtyard there was a sentry on duty.

He was wearing a red uniform, but not so flamboyant as that of the Major-domo who had greeted them on their arrival the day before. Kamala wondered how many sol-diers the Don employed in what was apparently his private Army.

She and Conrad passed from the courtyard out onto the terrace and started to descend the steps to the Lagoon. He did not speak and only when they reached the water's edge did he say in a very low voice:

'Quintero warned you?'

'Yes, indeed,' Kamala answered, stooping down to feel the temperature of the water with her fingers.

She was wearing the white and pink gown that Spider

had made her and she looked very lovely, very fragile and at the same time very English.

It was hard, Conrad thought as he watched her, to believe that the menace which overshadowed them was real.

He drew in his breath and then he said:

'The seamen have all been taken to the mines. Be careful, do not appear distressed.'

With an almost superhuman effort, Kamala did not look up at him, but held up her hand wet from the sea and let drips of water fall iridescent in the sunshine back into the Lagoon.

'What mines?' she asked.

'His gold mines,' Conrad replied. 'Spider tells me that the Don is always in search of new workers and that the crew of every ship you see here on the Lagoon has been taken away to work there.'

'How terrible! What can we do about it?'

'Nothing,' Conrad answered staring out over the water as if he was looking at the ships. 'The only chance for the men to escape is that I paid them before we left the Clipper and gave each man treble his expected wages.'

'How will that help?' Kamala asked.

'The reason so many workers are lost from the mines,' Conrad replied, 'is that as soon as the Mexicans accumulate a little money, they bribe the guards who allow them to escape.'

'I can hardly credit that our seamen have been sent there,' Kamala said.

'It is incredible,' Conrad answered, 'but it means that it is impossible for us to escape by sea. And there is something else I must tell you.'

There was a note in his voice which frightened her. She rose to move a little way along the Lagoon.

There was a marble seat set almost at the water's edge and she settled herself upon it, deliberately arranging her full skirts as if she was more interested in her appearance than anything else.

'Tell me,' she said wanting to share with Conrad the feeling of apprehension and fear that she could sense emanating from him.

'After I had spoken to you on the balcony this morning,' he said in a low voice, 'I started to dress and sent for Spider. Before he arrived a servant came into the room carrying a silver dish.

' "What is that?" I asked as he set it down beside me.

' "Some fruit, Señor."

' "Thank you," I said, "show me what fruit you have brought."

'He took the lid off the dish, and when he did so a small black snake, which I later learnt is one of the most deadly reptiles in all Mexico, struck at his hand.

'He gave a scream of terror and ran from the room. I managed to kill the snake, but I know quite well it was not by accident that it was there, and for whom it had been intended.'

Kamala clasped her fingers together in an effort to prevent herself from crying out.

She wanted to turn to Conrad, to hold on to him, but fearing that they were being watched, she forced herself through stiff lips to say:

'You are alive! Thank God you are alive! Why should he want to kill you?'

'What I said last night about his proposal of marriage being an insult, is, I suppose, something he will never forgive,' Conrad replied. 'I have not told you this story to frighten you, my darling, but merely to make you realise what we are up against and how careful we have to be.'

'And the man who was bitten by the snake?' Kamala asked. 'What . . . happened to him?'

'Spider informed me that he died within ten minutes,' Conrad replied.

'It is monstrous, evil, unbelievably primitive!' Kamala stormed.

But she was careful to keep her voice low.

'I know! I know!' Conrad replied. 'Somehow we have to get away. And now I imagine our only chance is to go overland.'

'In a country of which we know nothing?' Kamala queried. 'He would quickly catch up with us. I cannot believe we should get far.'

'At least when we are out riding this morning,' Conrad said, 'we can look to see if it is in any way possible.'

But she knew by the tone of his voice he was not very optimistic.

'There is something I have to tell you,' Kamala said.

Then she related what had happened when Josefa had come to her room, and how she had promised to help them to escape.

'She must be the Don's mistress,' Conrad remarked. 'The Aide-de-camp made some reference to her last night. I cannot quite remember what he said, because I was not listening very carefully. But it is of course obvious that a man like the Don would not live here without a woman.'

'She is very beautiful.'

'When are you seeing her again?'

'I have no idea,' Kamala answered, 'I hope that she will come to my room when we rest.'

'Impress upon her that we must get away as quickly as possible,' Conrad said. 'It is not that I am afraid for my life, Kamala—God knows that is of no particular consequence—but I cannot bear to think of you at the mercy of a madman.'

'If you die, I shall kill myself also,' Kamala said. 'But if only one of us can be saved, it must be you!'

'My love, do you think I could wish to live without you? I adore you! But, my darling, I am afraid, as I have

194

never been afraid in my life before, that we shall lose each other.'

'I shall pray,' Kamala said very quietly, 'I shall pray that Josefa will help us and somehow we shall get away.'

She gave a little sigh.

'I had thought this was to be Paradise.'

'To me it is the darkest hell I have ever encountered,' Conrad said bitterly.

'We must go back,' Kamala said, 'we must not be late for the Don.'

'Blast and damn his black heart! It would give me the greatest pleasure to throttle him to death.'

Conrad spoke so bitterly that his voice automatically grew a little louder. Kamala rose to her feet. She looked anxiously up towards the house.

'Be careful,' she pleaded. 'I am so afraid ... so desperately and terribly afraid.'

Conrad put out his hand to take hers.

It was a gesture which might have been interpreted merely as one of politeness to help her from the seat back onto the steps leading up to the house.

But at his touch Kamala felt herself quiver, and there was a warm sweet tingling in her veins because he loved her.

Very slowly they walked up the steps. When they reached the top the Aide-de-camp was waiting for them.

'We have been looking for fish in the Lagoon,' Kamala said with a smile.

'I am sure that you, Sir Conrad, have been admiring the *Santa Maria*,' the Spaniard said. 'You must admit she is the most elegant ship you have ever seen.'

'Yes, indeed,' Conrad replied. 'I was just remarking to my sister that I am sure she is without exception the finest Clipper in the world.'

'And certainly the fastest,' the Spaniard smiled. 'After this you will be dissatisfied, Sir Conrad, with your own ship.'

It was almost as if he wished to goad Conrad into being jealous.

'I am worried about the broken mast on the *Aphrodite*,' Conrad said. 'I hope His Supreme Excellency will be gracious enough to allow my men facilities for repairing it and for mending the sails.'

'Yes, yes of course,' the Spaniard said lightly.

But he turned away as he spoke and Conrad's eyes were hard as he thought of his seamen in the darkness of the mines.

Kamala found a riding-habit of thin green silk ready for her in her bedroom.

The maids assisted her into it and fixed on her head a wide-brimmed hat trimmed with a pretty gauze veil which would protect her from the sun.

When she was ready, she was escorted to the other side of the house by one of the flunkeys to find, as she had been promised, a spirited horse carrying a leather saddle beautifully ornamented with silver.

The bridle was of silver as was the handle of the whip with which she was provided. But this paled into insignificance beside the accoutrements of the horse which the Don was to ride.

His was a magnificent beast and the saddle with a high front was highly ornamented in gold. The stirrups were gold and so was the bridle.

When the Don himself appeared, Kamala had to admit that, although she hated him, he looked extremely smart. As usual he was all in black with his clothes so well cut it seemed as if he was poured into them.

His boots shone so that they reflected like mirrors the shining gold of his stirrups, and when they set off he showed himself immediately an extremely experienced horseman.

Conrad had also been provided with an exceptionally fine horse and the Aide-de-camp accompanied them. The Don had greeted Kamala with courtesy but not with any special demonstration of regard.

He gave Conrad a curt good morning and ignoring the low bows of his servants, they set off through an elaborately designed flower-garden with fountains towards the woods.

If Kamala had not been so frightened, she would have enjoyed her ride tremendously. Just as the Señor had promised her, the birds were incredibly beautiful.

The brilliant colours of the parrots and parakeets kept her continually exclaiming with delight. She recognised toucans and spoonbills and even had a glimpse of the gorgeous quetzal, which the Aide-de-camp assured her it was unusual for anyone to be lucky enough to see on their first visit.

After they had passed through the garden they entered a narrow ride which the Don had had cut with great skill through the semi-tropical forest.

Here on either side of them Kamala could see half buried amongst palms and ferns trees of ebony, mahogany, rosewood and Spanish cedar.

The trees and the palms were all enveloped in a curtain of epiphytes and creepers which clung, curled and entwined themselves over the trunks, creating a mystic and enchanted scene.

The trees and the creepers were abloom with brilliant flowers to paint the deep grey foliage with vivid patches of colour.

When they emerged from the forest, they came to the slopes of a hill covered with cacti and Kamala found herself gasping at the glorious kaleidoscope of colour.

'I thought this would please you,' the Don said with a faint smile on his thin lips.

'Indeed, Your Supreme Excellency, I have no words in which to express my admiration.'

'You agree that my land is beautiful,' the Don said as if he compelled her approval.

'I had never dreamt anything could be so lovely,' Kamala replied.

She felt that he was pleased at her enthusiasm and they rode on further.

For the first time she saw Indian women working in the fields with small children slung on their backs. They wore wide straw hats and had short petticoats of two colours.

Everywhere Kamala looked there was beauty. They saw crystal-clear fresh rivulets falling from rock to rock and little Indian huts perched among the cliffs.

On the rough road they passed men with swarthy wild-looking features driving droves of loaded mules. They all greeted the Don with the utmost respect. But he ignored their salutations passing them with his aristocratic nose held high.

Finally, as if he felt he had shown her enough, the Don pulled his horse to a standstill on the top of a hill looking down over the forest to where his white house could be seen, framed like a jewel in a green velvet setting.

The Lagoon below them was vividly blue, enclosing the ships at anchor as if with protecting arms, and beyond, stretching towards the horizon, was the sea.

It seemed unbelievable that they were captives, prisoners in this land of flowers of such incredible beauty.

Yet when Kamala looked at the Don's face and the sharp lines of his mouth, it was easy to credit that he would unhesitatingly send free men to slave in his mines and that he believed himself omnipotent.

There was something cruel, almost primitive, about him. Something which told her that he was completely and utterly ruthless and that he would stop at nothing to get his own way.

Because she was frightened and she wished to placate him Kamala said:

'The *Santa Maria* looks very fine from here. My brother and I were saying only this morning what a marvellous ship she is.'

'You will be sailing on her in three days' time,' the Don answered casually.

His reply took Kamala by surprise. Then as she stared at him searching for words he went on:

'We are going to Spain. I have had her built specially for that purpose. It is ten years since I appeared at Court in Madrid. Her Majesty Queen Isabella is my relative. She will greet us as is befitting to my rank and power.'

'You must speak of ... this to my brother,' Kamala said in a voice which sounded braver than she felt.

He did not reply, and she went on quickly:

'My brother is very important to me and to my happiness. I am sure Your Supreme Excellency would not wish me to be miserable and distraught, and that is what I should be without him.'

The Don turned his face to look at her and she saw he was apprising her as he had done before. Courageously she managed to keep her eyes on his.

She felt she must force him to understand that he must not harm Conrad, that he was essential to her.

The Don looked at her for what seemed to be a long time, and then he said, his voice completely unemotional:

'It is time we returned.'

They started to descend the hill and Kamala wondered frantically if she had made things worse or better. Had she managed to convey the message that if the Don disposed of Conrad, he could not expect her to acquiesce in any way in his plans?

All the way back she talked of the birds.

They saw an armadillo and a raccoon scuttling through the forest, but she was almost distraught with worry lest the Don should have already made up his mind to kill Conrad by one method or another.

Then as they reached the garden and they could see just ahead of them the grooms waiting to take their horses, the Don said:

'We will be married the day after tomorrow. I will discuss the arrangements with your brother.'

There was nothing Kamala could say. She longed to protest, longed to tell him that she would not marry him if he were the last man on earth. But she forced herself to remain silent.

She even bit back the questions which hovered on her lips.

She wondered if Conrad had overheard what had been said. She stole a quick glance at him and thought by his expression that he must have done so and understood even though the Don had spoken in Spanish.

They drew their horses to a standstill. The grooms ran to their heads and then before one could assist her to alight, Conrad was at her side.

He put up his arms and lifted her down. Just for a moment he held her close against him and she knew that he was trying to comfort her and to give her some reassurance.

She wanted to hold on to him, wanted to cry out it would have been better for them to die together than be separated.

Not for one moment must the Don suspect they had any desire to escape.

'Our only hope,' Kamala thought to herself as she went to her bedroom, 'lies with Josefa.'

The Don had disappeared to his own apartments and the Aide-de-camp officiously, it seemed to Kamala, had escorted her to her room so there was no chance of her having a word with Conrad.

Her maids were waiting for her. She pulled off her habit and they showed her that a scented bath was ready for her. She washed almost impatiently.

It seemed ridiculous to spend so much time on ornamentation when her thoughts were all concerned with the danger in which they found themselves and the terror of what lay ahead.

'Supposing,' a voice seemed to say inside her, 'that Conrad is killed and the Don is waiting to marry you? Would you have the strength of mind, would you have the will power to kill yourself? Would you not have to submit to his domination and become his wife?'

She wanted to scream because she was so afraid, but instead she had to allow the Indians to dress her, had to sit still while they arranged her hair.

She noticed in an almost detached manner that the huge diamond necklace that the Don had given her last night had been placed in its black velvet box and was lying on the dressing-table.

She had no desire to look at it or to touch it. She felt as if it was a chain as ominous as those which the convicts wore.

At last she was ready and because she was so anxious she asked one of the maids in a low voice:

'Where is Josefa?'

The maid instinctively looked over her shoulder as if afraid that they were overheard.

'Josefa will see the Señorita during the siesta.'

'Thank you.'

It was an expression of gratitude from the heart. Josefa had not forgotten. Josefa must by now have some plan by which they could escape. But how? How? Kamala asked herself.

She had seen this morning the wildness of the country, the impassibility of the forest. Unless they had a guide, it would be completely impossible for them to find the way.

Outside in the Lagoon there were many ships, but no crews with which to man them!

It was luncheon-time and she dared not linger any longer

in her room. She went to the Sitting-room and almost immediately the Aide-de-camp appeared.

Kamala thought they would be lunching in the great Banqueting Hall where they had dined the night before, but instead he led them to another room, also magnificent, with large windows looking out on the north side of the house where it was cool.

It was a view of the forests which Kamala had not seen before and in the far distance she saw a huge pointed hill.

'What is that?' she asked.

'It is a pyramid built by the Aztecs,' the Aide-de-camp replied.

'How interesting!' Kamala exclaimed. 'I would love to see it.'

'There is nothing there of interest,' the Aide-de-camp replied casually. 'All the treasures have been dug up and removed long ago.'

'By His Supreme Excellency?'

'But of course! They were sent to Spain as curiosities,' the Aide-de-camp replied. 'I imagine one day they will be put in a museum.'

Kamala saw that Señor Quintero was listening intently.

'I would like very much to speak with His Supreme Excellency about the Aztec ruins,' he said.

'You will find he is not interested,' the Aide-de-camp replied. 'His Supreme Excellency will leave a far more enduring memorial of his reign.'

He spoke with an unmistakable sincerity and Kamala had a strong desire to laugh.

'If it were not so serious,' she thought, 'one might be living in a childish fairy story with the Don just a preposterous ogre puffed up with his pride and terrorising the countryside!

'How could this modern Spaniard imagine for a moment that he could build anything as fine or as enduring as the remains left by the Aztecs? What madness had infected his head into believing that he was a King?'

It was easy to have these thoughts, but harder to substantiate them when the Don came into the room arriving last, like Royalty. He waited for Kamala's curtsey and the subservient bowed heads of his male guests before seating himself at the table.

'You may sit here, Señorita,' he said to Kamala and obediently she moved as he had indicated to the chair on his right.

The meal was delicious and to Kamala's relief a light one compared with the enormous dinner with which they had been served the night before.

When finally the Don rose to his feet to indicate the meal was at an end, he said to Conrad:

'You will come to my Sitting-room at 4 o'clock, Sir Conrad, and we will discuss the details of your sister's marriage.'

'It will be a pleasure, Your Supreme Excellency,' Conrad said.

Only Kamala noticed a flash of fury in his eyes while his voice was quite steady and respectful.

Again the Aide-de-camp escorted her to her bedroom where the maids undressed her. But the moment they had left the room, Kamala sat up, waiting impatiently for Josefa.

She came gliding in as softly as a snake moving through the grass. As she closed the door behind her, Kamala exclaimed eagerly.

'I have been waiting for you! Have you any news?'

Josefa came to the bed pulled back the mosquito-netting and stood looking at Kamala with her beautiful dark eyes.

'Sit down,' Kamala pleaded patting the edge of the mattress.'

'The Señorita permits?'

'But of course.'

And then because she was so worried Kamala added desperately:

'You must help us, Josefa! There is no-one but you. My brother has learnt that the seamen have been sent to the mines.'

'They are always sent there,' Josefa answered.

'They will not be cruelly treated?' Kamala asked.

Josefa shrugged her shoulders. Then she said:

'But there are two other men who will help you. Englishmen!'

'Englishmen!' Kamala echoed.

Josefa nodded.

'There are two who came here with their ships. They are Captains.'

'Then why have they too not been sent to the mines?' Kamala enquired.

'His Supreme Excellency thought they might be clever enough to find a way to escape and show other Mexicans how to get away.'

'Then where are they?' Kamala enquired.

'They are locked up,' Josefa said. 'But if I had money I could get them released.'

'Two English Captains,' Kamala repeated almost as if she was speaking to herself. 'But that would only make four men with my brother and Spider who is not much good as a sailor . . .'

She paused a moment. Then went on:

'But still if we could take a small ship I am sure they could manage.'

'No! No!' Josefa said quickly. 'You must sail in the *Santa Maria*.'

'The *Santa Maria*!' Kamala exclaimed, 'but that is impossible!'

'No, it is not impossible,' Josefa said. 'There are ten men on board. The ship is so precious to him that always His Supreme Excellency leaves ten men to guard her.'

'They would not work under my brother and the Englishmen!' Kamala expostulated. 'If we tried to board the ship they would fight us.'

'No they will not fight,' Josefa replied. 'They will obey and that is where I will help you.'

'Explain . . . please explain,' Kamala pleaded.

'There is only one person who can help us,' Josefa answered, 'and that is Zomba.'

'Who is Zomba?' Kamala asked.

'She is the Seer, the Magic One, who predicted to His Supreme Excellency that a fair woman would come from over the sea, whom he would wish to make his Queen.'

'But if that is what she said and we know that he believed her, how can she help us?' Kamala asked in bewilderment. 'I swear I will never be his wife or his Queen.'

'Zomba is my cousin,' Josefa answered, 'but at the moment she is angry with me because I would not give her one of my diamonds. She says it is powerful magic and she needs it for her work. But really she craves it because she is greedy.'

Josefa, who was glittering with the diamonds that she was wearing the night before, drew from her breast another stone. It seemed to shine like a light as she held it out towards Kamala.

Attached to a thin gold chain was the largest and strangest diamond Kamala had ever seen. It was round and it was yellow.

'This is mine,' Josefa said defiantly, 'but Zomba wants it! She has wanted it ever since His Supreme Excellency gave it to me. So she makes predictions which will make him supplant me.'

'You mean she lies?' Kamala questioned.

'No, she does not lie. She said a fair woman would come from the sea whom His Supreme Excellency would want to marry and to make his Queen.'

Josefa paused to let her words sink in.

'I was there when she made the prediction,' she continued. 'She did not say they would be married. She said that it is what he would want! And it has come true! He does want you.'

'I see,' Kamala said slowly.

At the same time she could not help feeling glad that even if she did not believe in Zomba's magic powers, the Seer had not actually predicted she would marry the Don.

'So you think that Zomba will help us.'

'She will help you if I give her my diamond,' Josefa replied.

'Then give it her . . . please give it her!' Kamala begged. 'If it is the one thing that will save us, if we can disappear and you will have His Supreme Excellency to yourself again, surely that is more important to you than all the jewels in the world!'

Josefa looked at the yellow diamond reflectively.

'I suppose you are right,' she said, 'but I do not wish to go to Spain with His Supreme Excellency, and that is why you must take the *Santa Maria* away. It will take a year, perhaps two, for him to have another ship built and by that time he may have changed his mind.'

Kamala sat looking at her wide-eyed.

'In Spain I should be no-one,' Josefa explained. 'I realise that. He will not take me to the Court, no-one will wish to meet me because I am only his mistress—a woman of no importance.'

Her eyes flashed angrily.

'But here it is different. When there are no guests I eat with him and I ride with him. The servants are frightened of me because I have the ear of His Supreme Excellency and also because I am the cousin of Zomba.'

'I can understand what you feel,' Kamala said. 'But how can we ever sail away in the *Santa Maria* without being stopped? Would the patrol vessels let us go? They have guns on board, I have seen them.'

'That is quite easy,' Josefa replied, 'the only difficulty is how to get you aboard. If the sentries see you trying to escape from this house they will shoot you. They already have orders to shoot if they see anyone strange moving around the house at night.'

Kamala thought of how Conrad might have been shot climbing from his balcony to hers and gave a little shiver of fear.

'But I feel something can be contrived,' Josefa went on speaking slowly. 'There are some pretty girls in the house, and after all the sentries are men. If a man is busy making love to a woman he would not notice a soft movement in the water!'

'Oh, Josefa, how can I ever thank you?' Kamala cried.

'You can thank me best by going away,' Josefa answered. 'I am jealous of you! You are so pretty with your fair hair and white skin!'

'But you are beautiful!' Kamala exclaimed, 'the most beautiful woman I have ever seen! I thought that as soon as I first saw you.'

Josefa smiled.

'You are kind!' she said. 'You are different from the stuck-up Spanish ladies who would look down their long noses at me.'

She spat.

'They would kick me out of the way with their pointed toes because though I sleep in the Supreme Excellency's bed, I do not wear his ring on my finger!'

'Perhaps one day he will marry you,' Kamala suggested.

Her soft heart was moved to compassion at the thought that Josefa must suffer so many slights.

Josefa shook her head.

'No, he will not marry me, I am not grand enough. But when he sends me away I shall be rich. There will be many men who will desire me! However I do not yet have enough. That is why I do not wish to part with my diamond.'

'But you will do so! Please say you will do so!' Kamala pleaded.

'Yes, I will do so,' Josefa agreed. 'It is best for me that you should go away and of course it is best for you.'

She gave Kamala a little smile and then she said:

'I must go now. The servants will not tell His Supreme Excellency I have been talking to you, but I do not trust his Aide-de-camp. He is sneaky and he wants to curry favour. I would not wish him to see me.'

'No, indeed,' Kamala agreed, 'and somehow I must tell my brother what you have told me. When will you be able to release the Englishmen and when will Zomba help us?'

'You must go tonight,' Josefa said. 'But first you must obtain some money for me. His Supreme Excellency never gives me money. Diamonds, fine gowns from Spain, many things that I desire, but never money.'

'My brother is next door,' Kamala said, 'he has money with him but we are afraid to speak in that room in case someone is listening!'

'It is likely,' Josefa agreed. 'This room I think is safe, but always someone listens in the Sitting-room.'

Kamala did not tell her that was what they knew already because she thought that even to Josefa it was a mistake to say too much.

Josefa appeared to be thinking for a moment and then she said:

'I am almost certain it is safe. Come, I will show you how to speak to your brother!'

Immediately Kamala rose from the bed and taking up the embroidered shawl she had worn before she put it round her.

She followed Josefa across the room wondering what she was about to do. The room was panelled with wood, elaborately carved and painted white. There were flowers and birds on every panel.

In the far corner Josefa felt with her small fingers in the folds of the panelling. She appeared to be trying to find something, moving from one carving to the other.

Suddenly, unexpectedly, three whole panels swung forward leaving an aperture just wide enough for someone to squeeze inside.

Kamala looked and saw that the wall was hollow.

'So that,' she thought, 'is how they listen to what the occupant of a room is saying!'

'There is nobody here,' Josefa said in a tone of satisfaction.

She stepped through the open panel and again felt with her fingers on the other side of the narrow passage. A second later the panel opened, this time into Conrad's room.

He had not undressed and was not lying on the bed as was usual in the siesta. He was reclining with his feet up on a chaise longue in the window, having removed his coat and his cravat.

He looked across the room in surprise, and when Josefa beckoned him he rose to his feet without speaking, and came to the open panel.

Josefa put out her hand and taking him by the arm drew him into Kamala's room. She pushed the narrow doors closed behind her and said:

'Someone may be listening in the passage on the other side of your room, I am not sure.'

'This is Josefa, whom I told you about,' Kamala explained.

Conrad took the Mestizo's hand in his and raised it to his lips.

'You have given my sister hope, Señorita,' he said, 'I am very grateful.'

Kamala knew by the expression of Josefa's face she was pleased at his courtesy.

'Josefa has told me how we can escape,' Kamala cried.

'Can we talk here?' Conrad asked quickly.

'This room is safe,' Josefa replied, 'but I am not sure about yours.'

'Then if we are not overheard,' Conrad said, 'tell me what you suggest.'

Josefa walked across the room until she was near the window.

'We must speak very quietly,' she admonished. 'The servants know I am visiting your sister, but they will not expect you to be here. If they hear a man's voice, they would think it strange.'

'You talk and I will listen,' Conrad replied in a whisper.

Josefa told him of all that she had told Kamala, about the two English Captains who were imprisoned and guarded; of her insistence that Conrad should take the *Santa Maria*, and that through Zomba she would arrange that the men would obey him once he was aboard.

'And the sentries?' Conrad asked.

'I have already told your sister that I will contrive that the sentries will not be watching the Lagoon. But swim very quietly and do not wear anything white. If they see you they will shoot.'

Conrad looked at Kamala.

'Can you swim?' he asked curiously.

She nodded her head.

'There is no end to your accomplishments,' he said with a little smile.

'What I must have,' Josefa said finally, 'is money. The sentries who guard the English Captains must be bribed. The girls who will keep the sentries on the balcony and on the terrace amused will also require to be paid!'

She paused, then explained.

'It is not jewels the people here need, but money, so

they can get away to the towns or villages where they will be free.'

Conrad rose to his feet. He crossed the room, pulled open the panel which Josefa had not closed completely and went back into his own room.

When he returned he carried the leather case which Kamala had noticed he carried when he left the Clipper.

'This is all the money we have,' he said. 'Take what you need.'

He opened the case and Kamala saw there were a great number of notes besides some gold and silver coins.

Josefa, slowly as if she was calculating, took out a number of notes one by one. When she had a thick handful, she looked up at Conrad with a smile.

'And for yourself?' he asked quietly.

She stared at him for a moment. Then she said:

'You will need money for the voyage, but what I would best like you to give to me, would be some English gold coins. I will have them linked together to make a bracelet, different from those any other woman possessed.'

'Then help yourself,' he said.

She took nine sovereigns and laid them against her wrist.

'I think they will look very smart,' she smiled.

'There is nothing we can give you,' Conrad said in his deep voice, 'to thank you adequately for what you are doing for us. My sister and I will always remember you as a very kind and gracious lady.'

He spoke slowly because the Spanish was difficult for him, but Josefa understood. Kamala saw her flush with pleasure because he had spoken to her as to an equal.

'It is an honour to help you, Señor,' she said.

Conrad rose to his feet.

'I should go back,' he said, 'in case the Aide visits my room and finds I am not there. What time shall we be ready for you?'

'Be in this room,' Josefa said, 'at 1 o'clock in the morning. The tide will be right and there should be the dawn breeze to take you out of the Lagoon and out to sea.'

'You are really sure that the men who have been left on board will work for us?' Conrad asked with a note of anxiety in his voice.

'Zomba will see to that,' Josefa assured him.

'Then I can only thank you from the bottom of my heart,' Conrad replied.

Once again he lifted Josefa's hand and pressed it against his lips. She looked so beautiful that Kamala felt a little pang of jealousy.

'How could he ever admire me again?' she asked herself. 'Josefa must be the most beautiful woman in the world.'

But as Conrad walked towards the panelling she looked into his eyes and knew that she need never be afraid of any other woman. He loved her. There was no mistaking the expression in his eyes, the sudden softening of his whole face.

'I love you!' she wanted to cry aloud.

But already he had slipped through the panelling and Josefa closed it behind him with a little click.

'And now, little Señorita,' she said to Kamala, 'there is no reason to look so frightened. We need only the help of the gods to be sure that you leave in safety.'

'I will pray to my God,' Kamala answered, 'and please will you pray to yours?'

Josefa gave a little smile.

'I put my trust in Zomba,' she replied, 'and my diamond.'

10

Kamala dressed carefully for dinner wearing the white dress covered with diamonds and the necklace the Don had given her.

She kept thinking how careful she must be so as not to raise his suspicions by appearing excited or even unusually alert. The smallest difference in her behaviour might be noticeable.

She would not allow herself to think of what would happen if they failed to escape.

Instead she forced herself to pay attention to the small details of her toilette. Being meticulous about the back of her head, making the maids arrange and rearrange the full skirts of her gown.

Finally, feeling like an actress stepping onto the stage to commence a difficult and complicated part, she walked down the passage to the Salon.

Conrad was already there and so was Señor Quintero and the Aide-de-camp. As soon as she appeared the latter said as he kissed her hand:

'His Supreme Excellency craves a word with you, Señorita, in his private room.'

Kamala looked quickly at Conrad and saw to her consternation that the request was as much of a surprise to him as it was to her.

There was however nothing she could do but acquiesce, and the Aide-de-camp led her to the far end of the passage where two flunkeys gorgeously arrayed in gold-braided livery opened a high mahogany door.

The Don's Sitting-room was very ornate like the rest of the rooms in the house.

As Kamala entered he was seated at an enormous desk inlaid with silver and, as he rose to his feet, she could not help noticing how smart he looked and how his black suit accentuated his well-proportioned figure.

Again there were fabulous diamonds glittering in his shirt front and he wore the huge diamond on his finger.

Kamala advanced towards him slowly, conscious that the door had been shut behind her and that they were alone. When she reached him she sank down in a low curtsey and he kissed her hand.

'You are very beautiful, Señorita.'

'I thank Your Supreme Excellency for the compliment.'

'I am not flattering you but expressing the truth. I have seen many fair women in my life, but none to compare with you.'

His eyes flickered over her, and Kamala felt as if he were enumerating her good points to himself, pleased that the woman he intended to make his wife was in his judgment exceptional.

There was something almost impersonal about his scrutiny, something which Kamala felt was actually an insult.

However she dropped her eyes and hoped that she was projecting the appearance of someone humble and grateful for his approval.

'I have a present for you,' the Don said, 'something which I believe will make you the envy of all the other ladies at the Palace in Madrid.'

As he spoke, he took a small box from his desk and opened it. Kamala saw that it contained the largest and the most brilliant diamond she had ever seen.

If Josefa's yellow diamond had been spectacular, this was even more so. Blue-white, pointed at both ends, it glittered blindingly in the light from the window.

The Don drew the jewel from its box and taking Kamala's hand slipped it onto her third finger.

'I thank Your Supreme Excellency,' she said a little breathlessly, 'it is very . . . kind of you.'

'There are many more jewels that are being prepared for you and which will be ready before we sail.'

'This is the largest diamond I have ever seen!' Kamala exclaimed, feeling he would expect her to be enthusiastic.

'It came from my mines five years ago,' the Don answered, 'and I have been keeping it until I found a woman worthy of its brilliance.'

'Thank you,' Kamala said again.

She would have curtsied, but the Don put out his long thin fingers and lifted up her chin.

She realised what he was about to do and with an almost superhuman effort, prevented herself from turning away and running from the room.

Instead, clenching her fingers until her nails cut into the palms of her hands, she forced herself to stand still.

Slowly and deliberately the Don bent his head and she felt his lips on hers.

She knew then how different a kiss could be when one was not in love. When Conrad's mouth possessed hers she felt herself thrill and a flash of ecstasy run through her so that almost instinctively her lips responded to his.

Now all she felt as the Don kissed her was a feeling of revulsion and a longing to escape.

His hard and possessive mouth held her captive and his arms went round her. She knew then that beneath the iron control forced on him by his breeding and his pride, there was a fiery smouldering desire from which every nerve in her body shrank in fear.

His lips became more insistent, and now he was kissing her brutally with a passion which even in her innocence she knew was lewd and lustful.

Finally when she could no longer breathe and she felt she must faint in his arms, he set her free.

'You are very desirable,' he said in a hoarse voice, 'and tomorrow you will be mine!'

She put the tips of her fingers to her bruised mouth.

'To . . . morrow,' she stammered.

Then because she could bear no more, she turned and ran from the room frightened as she had never been afraid in her life before.

She wanted only to find Conrad and throw herself into his arms. She wanted his protection, the sense of security he always gave her and a feeling that she was safe as long as he was there.

Then as she sped down the passage she remembered. Everything depended on their chance of escape. If Conrad saw her upset and frightened, he might insult the Don or even challenge him to a fight.

She stopped running and made herself stand still in the middle of the passage. She was aware that the servants were staring at her but it did not matter.

All that was important was that Conrad should not be incensed, and that meant he must not know that the Don had kissed her.

Walking slowly, Kamala stopped in front of a large gilt-framed mirror. Her hair was a little untidy at the speed at which she had run. Automatically she smoothed it into place and as she did so the huge pointed ring on her left hand was reflected in the glass.

She felt it was another chain to imprison her.

Then afraid the Don might be coming from his private room, she walked down the passage with some semblance of composure to join Conrad and the other two men in the Salon.

Dinner appeared to take a century of time.

Every minute that passed made it seem more of an effort to talk conventionally, to discuss the countryside, to listen to the Don boasting of his possessions, his achievements and his plans for the future.

Finally when Kamala felt like screaming, they were at last able to retire to their bedrooms.

It was not yet midnight and Kamala realised that over an hour must pass before Josefa came for them.

She allowed the maids to undress her, and then when they had gone from the room she rose, wrapped herself in the embroidered shawl and walked to the window to look out onto the Lagoon.

Mercifully it was a dark night. There was no moon and although the stars were bright, the Lagoon itself circled by the forests seemed to be overshadowed.

She stood staring out, striving to pray and finding somehow that even the familiar words of the prayers she had said since a child would not come to her lips.

She heard a sound and turning saw Conrad come into the room through the panel in the wall. With a little cry she turned and ran towards him. He put his arms round her and held her very close.

He could feel that she was trembling and after a moment he said with his lips against her hair:

'What has upset you, my darling?'

'Nothing ... nothing,' Kamala said quickly, 'it is just that I am afraid for ... you and of course for ... myself.'

He took his arms from her and said quietly:

'That is what I have come to speak to you about.'

'Is it safe for you to be here so early?' Kamala asked.

'Spider is in my room,' Conrad answered, 'he will let me know if by any chance anyone wished to speak to me. But I do not think anyone will disturb us now.'

As he spoke he drew Kamala across the room to a small sofa near the window.

She sat down as he obviously expected her to do and he seated himself beside her. He did not take her in his arms and she waited apprehensively for what he might say.

217

'I talked to the Don about your marriage,' he began. 'He has fantastic plans for the ceremony and the feast that will follow it, but that is of no importance.'

'Then what is?' Kamala asked alarmed by the seriousness of his voice.

Conrad did not look at her and after a moment he went on:

'I thought it only right that I should tell you how rich the Spaniard is. He has in fact unlimited sources of wealth not only from his mines of gold, silver and diamonds, but the fact that he owns great tracts of land which he assures me are capable of development. He has as well vast properties in Spain and is already investigating the possibility of investing money in America.'

'What has this to do with us?' Kamala asked.

'Not us—but you,' Conrad answered. 'I want you to realise the position you would hold as his wife.'

'His wife!' Kamala ejaculated. 'But you know I could never marry him!'

'Are you sure of that?'

He turned for the first time to look into her face, at her eyed wide and frightened, at her lips trembling a little, at her hands linked together as if she was already pleading with him.

'What have I to offer you?' Conrad asked harshly. 'I love you and I think you love me, but would that love survive, the miseries of deprivation, of not knowing where our next meal will come from? And do you think it would be easy for me to watch you suffer?'

'Are you saying,' Kamala asked in a whisper, 'that you no longer . . . want me?'

'God no! How could you think such a thing?' Conrad asked sharply. 'I am only trying to think what is best for you, my precious one. I love you so desperately! You mean my whole life to me! But I must make you understand what you are relinquishing if you choose to come with me rather than remain here with the Don.'

With a little cry Kamala put out her hands to hold onto the lapels of Conrad's coat.

'You cannot leave me ... behind,' she said desperately, 'I love you. How can you imagine for one moment that I could stay with the Don or let him ... touch me?'

Her voice broke on the words and now she hid her face against Conrad's shoulder.

As she did so the shawl dropped from her shoulders and his arms went round her to clasp her close to him, wearing only the soft chiffon night-gown he had seen her in before.

'If you leave me behind I will ... kill myself, I swear it,' she murmured passionately, and tears were now running down her cheeks.

'My darling, my sweet, my little love,' Conrad cried. 'Of course I will take you! Do you not imagine it would crucify me to lose you? It is just that I had to be fair to you.'

'You are not being ... fair,' Kamala murmured through her tears, 'you do not ... understand how much I ... love you.'

Conrad held her so close that for a moment she could not breathe. Then he said:

'Very well. If we die we die together. If we escape, then we will face the future as bravely as we are facing the present.'

She looked up at him, the tears still wet on her cheeks, but her eyes shining ecstatically.

'You will take me,' she pleaded.

'Tonight and forever,' Conrad answered. 'You are mine and I will never let you go.'

He kissed her and she felt again a rapture that was indescribable. It was like quicksilver running through her veins, and now she knew that nothing and no-one would ever part them again.

Finally after a long time he set her free and bending down to pick up the embroidered shawl from the floor, he wrapped it round her.

She blushed that he should have seen her without it. Then he said softly:

'Time is getting on, Josefa should be here soon.'

'Is Señor Quintero ready?'

'He is not coming with us,' Conrad answered. 'For one thing he cannot swim, and for another, while we were out riding today, he managed to persuade one of the grooms in the stables to procure him a horse and to accompany him as a guide.'

'He is escaping by land!' Kamala exclaimed.

'They will have a long ride,' Conrad said, 'because after looking at the maps, the Señor has discovered that his nearest friends are about a hundred miles away. The country is rough, snake infested, and we can only pray that he will get through safely.'

'The Señor told me he has many important friends in Mexico,' Kamala said. 'Will he be able to help the seamen in the mines?'

'That is what he is determined to do,' Conrad replied. 'He does not think the Government, which is weak and undoubtedly on the verge of a revolution, can have much authority over the Don, except to compel him to release any foreigners he is employing.'

'That at least would be something,' Kamala said.

'The Señor can be very determined if he wishes to be,' Conrad answered. 'I am sure he will do everything possible.'

'I am sure he will,' Kamala agreed.

'I will see if Spider has everything we require,' Conrad said.

He moved across the room to the open panel. He stepped through it and Kamala could hear him talking in a low voice to Spider.

A few minutes later her bedroom door opened and Josefa came in with the strangest and most extraordinary-looking woman Kamala had ever seen.

By the darkness of her skin Kamala guessed that she was a mixture of Negro and Mexican. She had large fine dark eyes and rather coarse features. But there was no doubt as to her personality.

She wore Mexican dress with several coloured petticoats, a red fringed shawl over a cambric blouse, and round her head a turban made of crimson and gold lamé which gave her a very bizarre appearance.

What was extraordinary was that from her neck hung dozens and dozens of necklaces of every sort and description which Kamala realised were all connected with magic.

There was a necklace of sharks' teeth, there were others made of shells, coral, gold, silver and bones and long chains in which glittered pearls of peculiar shapes and small strangely coloured diamonds.

On her wrists there was also a multitude which jangled as she walked, and every finger of her hand was ornamented with rings of every shape and size.

'Greetings, Señorita,' Josefa said in a low voice. 'As I promised I have brought you Zomba.'

Kamala curtsied.

'I am very grateful,' she said.

Holding out her hand to the Seer she added:

'May I tell you, Señora, how much I welcome you and how deeply grateful I am that you should come to our rescue.'

'My cousin Josefa tells me you are in danger,' Zomba said.

Her voice was very deep and hoarse, and sounded almost like a man's. Then as she spoke, Conrad came back into the room through the panel in the wall.

He walked up to the women and lifted Josefa's hand to his lips.

'You are our—good angel,' he said in his halting Spanish.

Josefa smiled at him flirtatiously and looked so beautiful as she did so that once again Kamala felt a little pang of jealousy. Then Conrad held out both his hands to Zomba.

'You are our hope and our salvation,' he said.

It was clever of him, Kamala thought, to speak in the extravagant language that the Mexicans and Spaniards understood. She saw Zomba's dark eyes flash approvingly before she replied:

'It will not be easy! You know that?'

'We are aware of the difficulties,' Conrad replied, 'but we hope that with your help we can achieve the impossible.'

'The Englishmen are waiting below,' Josefa said. 'Zomba will take you to them and no-one will prevent you. But once you are in the water you realise there is nothing more we can do.'

'I realise that,' Conrad said, 'and we are both, the Señorita and I, prepared to take the risk.'

'The girls are already busy with the sentries,' Josefa went on. 'They have wine and they are pleased with the money you sent them.'

'You have added what I gave you to the wine?' Zomba asked in her masculine voice.

Josefa nodded and explained to Conrad.

'There are some herbs in the wine which will make the soldiers a little sleepy. Not enough for them to be reprimanded, but enough to prevent them being too alert, too suspicious.'

'Once again I can only say "thank you",' Conrad told her.

'When you reach the ship, Señorita,' Zomba said speaking to Kamala, 'you must first speak to the men alone.'

'Will that be safe?' Conrad asked quickly.

'It will be safe because of what she carries,' Zomba replied.

222

As she spoke she took from round her neck a charm on a thin necklace made of leather.

It was a large round stone painted red and decorated with strange signs. At the top and bottom of it was an enormous baroque pearl and above each pearl there were tiny pieces of coral sticking out like little pink teeth.

'All the men aboard the *Santa Maria*,' Zomba said, 'know this is my sign—the magic sign of Zomba. Show it them, say it comes from me, and then put it round the neck of your man. They will obey his commands and follow wherever he may lead them.'

She put the charm into Kamala's hands. As she took it Kamala felt, although she told herself it was only her imagination, that some strange power exuded from it.

'It is nearly time to go,' Zomba said.

'One thing more,' Josefa interrupted. 'The patrol ships are unlikely to interfere with the *Santa Maria*, but when His Supreme Excellency is aboard, the ship in which he travels always carries a blue light on the mast. You will find one aboard. Tell the men to fix it as soon as you reach the entrance of the Lagoon.'

'I will do that,' Conrad said.

'And I have brought something for you, Señorita,' Josefa said to Kamala.

She held a bundle out to Kamala as she spoke. She unfolded it and saw a habit made of the thinnest black silk not unlike those worn by a monk.

'I had it copied today,' Josefa explained, 'from what the penitents wear on Good Friday. The only difference is that it is split up the sides so it will be easy for you to swim. You must pull the hood over your hair, which otherwise might show in the water.'

'How clever of you to think of it,' Kamala said.

'You had best put it on now,' Josefa suggested. 'You will not wish to change below when the men are divesting themselves of their garments.'

'No, indeed,' Kamala said.

She glanced at Conrad.

'I will not look,' he said with a little smile.

He turned his back to her as he spoke.

Then as Josefa started to help Kamala divest herself of her shawl and night-gown, Zomba went to Conrad's side and far away in a singsong tone, Kamala heard her say:

'You are a fine man, I see that you will do great things in the future. Many people will depend on you, many people will bless your name. There is a crown over your head, it is a sign of importance.'

'I hope what you say comes true,' Conrad replied.

'Zomba's predictions always true,' the Seer answered proudly.

She glanced over her shoulder as she spoke and saw that Kamala was already dressed in the black silk robe.

It clung to her skin and she looked so strangely pathetic with her pale face and fair hair that Conrad wanted more than anything else to take her her in his arms and tell her not to be afraid. But Zomba was still speaking:

'I can also see your future, Señorita,' she said. 'It is quite simple: you will obtain your heart's desire.'

Kamala looked at Conrad and her eyes as they met his were very eloquent. Zomba looked from one to the other.

'You told me, Josefa, that these two were brother and sister. It is not true!'

'You are not brother and sister!' Josefa exclaimed in surprise.

'We too have our secrets,' Conrad answered. 'All I ask of the future is that the Señorita should be my wife.'

'Do not be afraid,' Zomba smiled. 'But come, we must go.'

'If the Señorita walks down the passage wearing only that black garment she will look strange,' Josefa remarked.

'I have a cloak in the wardrobe,' Kamala said hastily.

Conrad fetched the black velvet cloak trimmed with swansdown they had bought in Southampton. He put it round her shoulders before he went to the open panel in the wall and beckoned to Spider.

The small bald-headed man came quickly into the room. He looked surprised at the sight of Zomba, but he bowed to her politely and to Josefa.

'Come!' Zomba exclaimed imperiously, and opening the door they went down the passage.

She moved like a ship in full sail and they followed closely behind her.

This Kamala knew was the moment of danger, but the servants on duty bowed to the floor at the sight of the Seer. It was obvious they were far too frightened to notice anything but the woman they believed had very powerful magic.

They walked for some way and then descended a small staircase, passing an entrance which led to the Courtyard, and going down apparently into the bowels of the earth.

Conrad took a lantern from the walls to guide them because the steps were very small and twisting.

They went lower and lower until they found themselves in a huge cellar. There were barrels and bottles of wine stacked on shelves each arranged neatly and labelled with the year that they had been grown.

There was no-one in the cellar and they passed through it and down some steps which Kamala guessed brought them on a level with the Lagoon.

At the bottom of the steps in the darkness of a domed cave stood two men. With fair hair and blue eyes there was no mistaking their nationality. Here were the English Captains!

'I have not told them who you are,' Josefa said to Conrad. 'Speak very softly.'

Conrad walked forward and held out his hand.

'I am Conrad Veryan,' he said quietly. 'You have been

brought here because it is our one chance of escape. We may be shot as we swim towards the *Santa Maria*, but if we can board her in safety, I believe we can take her out to sea. Are you agreeable to accompany me?'

The eldest of the men replied.

'I am Neil Macdonald, Captain of the *Heron* and this is Roger Turner who commanded the schooner *Thanet*.'

Conrad shook hands with the second man.

'You are a seafaring man, Sir?' he asked.

'I was Captain of the *Hercules* and the *Norma*,' Conrad replied.

Watching them Kamala realised that both the men had heard of Conrad's ships and there was no mistaking the eagerness in which Captain Macdonald said quickly:

'We shall be very honoured to serve under you, Sir.'

'Then there is no time to be lost,' Conrad replied.

He looked at Spider.

'You have brought what I asked you to?'

'I have, Sir.'

As he spoke Spider held out to each of the men a piece of black material and wrapped in it Kamala saw three sharp knives.

'These were the only weapons we could get,' Conrad said. 'And now, gentlemen, I suggest we repair to the cellar out of sight of these ladies and take off our clothes. We have to swim as quietly as possible. If we are heard or seen we will be shot.'

The men followed him up the steps. Kamala turned to Josefa.

'I can only add my thanks to everything Sir Conrad has already said to you,' she said, 'but I would wish you to have this.'

As she spoke she drew from her third finger the huge diamond that the Don had put there earlier in the evening.

Josefa gave a little cry of delight.

'You cannot mean you are giving this to me?' she asked.

'I know no-one who deserves it more,' Kamala said, 'and if we get away the Don will think I have taken it with me, so he need never know you have it.'

'Thank you! Thank you!'

Josefa looked down at Kamala and hesitated. As if Kamala knew what had crossed her mind she bent forward and kissed the Mestizo on the cheek.

'You are very gracious,' Josefa said in a low voice.

Kamala turned to Zomba.

'I should be very pleased, Señora, if you would accept this,' she said.

As she had left her bedroom she had picked up from the dressing-table the black leather box containing the diamond necklace.

Now she pulled back the lid and even in the shadows where they were standing the necklace picked up the light from the candle-lantern which Conrad had carried with him up to the cellar.

It sparkled and glittered and Kamala knew that Zomba's eyes too were glittering as she drew the necklace from its resting place.

'You have repaid your debt to me, Señorita,' she said. 'It will not follow you into other lives as do all the debts we owe to others.'

'I am glad about that,' Kamala said with a little smile.

There was no time to say more. Conrad came down the steps followed by the two Captains and Spider. They wore only black loin-cloths, with the knives stuck in them.

Conrad kissed Josefa's hand and then Zomba's.

'No more talking,' he said quietly. 'I will go first, my sister will follow me and the rest of you behind. Try to keep in a straight line. It will be less discernible from the shore. When we reach the ship I will take my sister up the side.'

He looked at Kamala.

'You have the special charm?'

'It is round my neck.'

She tucked it into the black robe, then Josefa pulled the hood over her head.

'You will be invisible,' she said. '*Buena suerte.*'

Conrad had gone to the edge of the Lagoon and now without another word let himself very carefully into the water. Kamala stepping out of her slippers followed him.

She had a strange sensation as she did so that she was leaving one world behind and setting forth into another.

The water was not cold, in fact after the first slight shock as it touched her body, it was almost like swimming in milk. There was no ripple on the Lagoon and there appeared to be no wind.

As Kamala swam behind Conrad, she wondered if indeed they would be able to sail away. Suppose tomorrow morning found them in the Lagoon helpless and at the mercy of the Don.

Then she told herself encouragingly that Zomba had seen that she would gain her heart's desire, and what was that but that she should marry Conrad?

He was swimming slowly and steadily ahead, his arms hardly seemed to break the water and although the other three men were close behind, Kamala could hardly hear them.

It was a longer way than it had appeared to the side of the *Santa Maria*. Every second Kamala was afraid that they would hear a shout from the shore followed by the explosion of a gun.

But there was only silence, until looming up above them she saw the side of the *Santa Maria*.

There was a rope-ladder hanging over the side of the stern. Conrad grabbed it with one hand and held out his other towards Kamala. She swam to his side and for a moment he held her close against him.

'Do not be afraid, my darling,' he whispered, 'and you know that everything depends on you.'

She did not answer him. She felt as if her voice had died in her throat. Now the moment had come it was terrifying to think that unless she did her part well, they would all be captured again and perhaps killed.

Conrad helped her onto the rope-ladder. She climbed up it, the hard rope hurting the soles of her feet and the softness of her hands.

She reached the deck and saw as she stood there, feeling a little unsteady, that the seamen guarding the ship were rolled up in their blankets asleep.

Slowly, feeling her hands were numb from the water, Kamala pushed back her hood and drew the strange charm that Zomba had given her, from her neck. Then holding it in her hands she stepped forward.

As she did so a man she had not noticed but who was on guard in the stern gave a shout, which woke the others. They stirred in their blankets, sat up and seeing Kamala jumped to their feet.

Instinctively they reached for the knives that they all wore in a belt round their waist.

This was a moment of danger and for a moment Kamala thought she could not speak. Then in a voice which was quite clear and seemed to ring out almost louder than he intended, she said in Spanish:

'I come to you with a message from Zomba, the Magic One, the Seer, and she sends you this so you will know I speak the truth.'

She held up the charm as she spoke.

In the light from the stars, it was easy to see it quite clearly, the white pearls against the red painted stone, the pink coral jutting out at the top and bottom of it.

'Zomba! Zomba!'

She could hear the men murmuring the name beneath their breath, and now they came nearer to her approaching with curiosity, but they were no longer feeling for their knives.

They were nearly all Negroes Kamala noticed and she knew that they would be even more superstitious than Mexicans.

'Zomba sent you?' one man asked.

'Zomba sent me,' Kamala replied, 'and she sent too someone you will obey because he wears her sign.'

She had known without turning round that Conrad was just behind her. Now she put the leather neck-piece over his head so that the charm lay against his naked chest for them all to see.

'I am now your—Captain,' Conrad said in his slow Spanish. 'We go to sea—raise the anchor.'

It seemed to Kamala as if the whole ship was galvanised into action by Conrad's words. The two Captains and Conrad himself started to set the sails and the sailors followed their lead, manning the yardarms, hauling in the ropes, getting up the anchor.

Kamala stood watching them until she heard Conrad's voice say sharply:

'Go below and take off that wet garment. If there is any shooting you are to stay out of sight.'

Kamala obeyed him.

She found the companionway and climbed down it. She stood for a moment in the darkness, then Spider was beside her and in a few seconds he had lit a lantern.

'We've done it, Miss!' he said excitedly.

'We have still got to get out of the Lagoon,' Kamala answered apprehensively, 'and there are the patrol ships.'

'Don't worry, Miss,' Spider admonished her. 'The Master'll see to everything, you mark my words.'

Worried though she was, Kamala could not help being amused that Conrad had now become 'the Master'.

'Now let's see if I can find you anything to wear, Miss,' Spider said.

Going ahead carrying the lantern high in his hands, he opened the door of the first cabin in the stern.

Kamala looked round and gave an exclamation. There was no doubt who was meant to use this cabin because it was extremely magnificent.

There was a bed of gold draped with velvet and embroidered with the Don's very elaborate Coat-of-Arms. The walls were panelled with ebony and the furniture inlaid with different woods all with gold handles.

'His Nibs certainly intended to impress 'em when he reached Spain!' Spider said dryly. 'Now the Master will sleep here.'

He was about to leave through the door by which they had entered, when Kamala saw there was another door in the centre of the wall.

She opened it and realised that in this Clipper the cabins communicated and there would be no need to slip through a hole in the back of a cupboard.

Spider had followed her and by the light in his hand Kamala saw that this was obviously the cabin which had been intended for Josefa or for her.

The bed was of silver and the drapings were of white satin with flounces and bows of pink and blue. The carpet was the beautiful blue that the Mexicans dyed so skilfully, and so were the curtains which veiled the portholes.

'This will be my cabin,' Kamala said with a smile.

'I can see there is plenty of things on this ship, Miss, from which I can make you a gown,' Spider said with satisfaction.

As he spoke he opened the door of a cupboard which extended the whole of one side of the cabin. Then both he and Kamala stared in astonishment.

The cupboard was filled with gowns of every sort and description fashioned in lovely colours and expensive silks, they were as colourful as the parrots and macaws flitting from tree to tree in the forests.

231

'They must have been put there for Josefa,' Kamala said speaking to herself.

'In which case I can easily alter them for you, Miss,' Spider said. 'The Lady in question is larger in the waist, but she was about your height and from what I've heard, most of her gowns came from Spain or France. A very lucky lady!'

Kamala was sure that she would have been expected to wear them once she had been married to the Don, but what was important now was that she would be clothed.

Spider put down the lantern.

'If you're going up on deck again later, Miss, when we are out at sea, you'll want something warm,' he said in a tone of a nurse fussing over a delicate child, 'and I see that there's a cloak here which'll suit you admirably. Very pretty it is too.'

He took a gown and a cloak from the cupboard and put them on the bed. Then with a little exclamation of delight he found a pair of slippers. He laid these out for Kamala and said:

'On this voyage you'll be the easy one to dress, Miss, if you'll pardon the expression. If I am not mistaken, the Master's going to find that the Spaniard's coats a very tight fit across the shoulders.'

He lit the oil lamps which were fixed to the cabin walls and left Kamala alone. She slipped off the black robe, dried herself with a towel that she found beside the washing-stand and started to dress.

It was however difficult to think of what she wore when all the time she was listening to the sounds overhead of bare feet and of voices deliberately kept low.

Supposing, she worried, there was no wind, supposing after all this they were unable to get the ship under weigh?

She had heard the anchor come up, but it seemed as if the ship was still stationary.

Suddenly Kamala could bear the suspense no longer.

She hurried into the gown with its numerous petticoats, pulled the cloak Spider had chosen for her over her shoulders, and ran up the companionway onto the deck.

Then as she stood there looking around her, she made a sound that was neither a cry nor a sigh of relief, but a mixture of both. They were moving!

Not very quickly, but nevertheless they were further down the Lagoon and ahead lay the sea.

Conrad was at the wheel and she knew by the expression on his face he was concentrating fiercely on getting the great Clipper safely past the schooners and the fishing-boats which were lying at anchor.

She went to his side. For a moment he did not speak and she thought he did not realise that she was there. Then he asked:

'You are all right?'

'We are moving!'

'Yes, thank God, and there will be more wind out at sea.'

'You remembered the light on the mast?'

'You can see it if you look,' he replied.

Kamala stepped to one side to be quite sure it was there and had not by any unfortunate chance gone out. It seemed to glow bright as a star of hope and once again she gave a little sigh.

'You realise this is not going to be an easy voyage,' Conrad said. 'It will take us four or five days to Havana even with a following wind. There are only fourteen of us on board, and a ship this size needs forty or fifty hands.'

'Nevertheless, Sir,' a voice said with a Scottish accent, 'I think that your figure of fourteen of us is an under-statement.'

Kamala looked round to see that Captain Macdonald had approached without their realising it.

'An under-statement?' Conrad asked.

'Yes indeed, Sir!' the Scotsman replied. 'I reckon that three English Captains are each equal to three native seamen. That with Spider gives us a complement of twenty. Only half your requirements, it is true, but you should, Sir, be grateful for small mercies.'

Conrad laughed.

'I am indeed grateful, Macdonald, though you may not think so! Have you got the topsails set?'

'We've set every sail the ship owns,' the Scotsman answered.

'It should be dawn at any moment and we must whistle for a wind,' Conrad remarked.

Even as he spoke Kamala felt a faint movement in her hair and now they were nearing the open sea.

As she looked towards the horizon there was a lightening of the darkness and she knew that soon the dawn would bring them a message of hope.

Afterwards Kamala could never remember the details of what happened the next four days. The patrol vessels, seeing the blue light on the mast, allowed them to pass, and then they were in the open sea and heading for Havana.

The wind increased and soon they were sailing at quite a considerable speed. But despite Macdonald's optimistic words it made almost intolerable demands on fourteen men to manage a ship the size of the *Santa Maria*.

Kamala and Spider spent every moment of the day and night either cooking meals which the crew snatched whenever they could leave the deck, or brewing coffee which, hour after hour, they took to the men to keep them awake.

There was no question of regular watches.

Men slept when they could no longer carry on. Kamala grew used to seeing a man slump down on the deck for perhaps quarter of an hour then get to his feet and continue what he was doing before.

It was Conrad who inspired them.

It was not only that he wore round his neck Zomba's magic charm, it was his own force of character, his personal leadership which made them wish not only to serve him, but to please him.

There was never any hesitation when he asked the men to alter the sails. They would swarm up the ropes looking, Kamala thought, like monkeys as they clung to the yard-arms high above the deck, swinging in the movement of the waves.

Then they would slither down again cheerful and ready to go on until the human frame could stand no more and they slept where they lay.

On Conrad's instructions the best provisions, which had been salted away for the use of the Don himself, were distributed equally to all hands, Captain and crew.

There was rum every evening when the sun went down, but the one thing they were short of were the fruit, vege-tables and fresh provisions which would have been brought aboard just before they sailed.

Fortunately there was plenty of water in the butts, and as Conrad said over and over again—'It might have been much worse!'

Spider had found him a shirt and trousers to wear and was busy altering one of the Don's elegant black coats for when they reached Havana.

Going to stand beside Conrad on the deck one afternoon, Kamala found him giving instructions to the younger Cap-tain, Roger Turner, as to what he was to buy when they reached port.

'Lemons,' Conrad was saying, 'we never have enough and I do not want any man who serves under me down with scurvy.'

'I have already made a note of that, Sir,' Captain Turner said, who was making up a long list of requirements.

When he had moved away Kamala said to Conrad in a low voice:

'Have you enough money to pay for all these things?'

'Thanks to Van Wyck, I have enough for when we reach

Havana,' he said, 'but after that we shall have to think of what we can sell when we reach the Azores.'

'You realise your bed is made of gold?' Kamala remarked.

He laughed.

'I have not seen it yet.'

'I know,' she said, 'you must be exhausted! I will go and fetch you some more coffee.'

'Make it strong!'

'I will.'

Then as she was about to leave she said a little apprehensively because it had been worrying her for some time:

'Can the Don accuse you of stealing the ship?'

'No, it is impossible for him to do so,' Conrad answered. 'Which Court of Law would listen to a man who has imprisoned seamen and taken their ships captive?'

Conrad's voice was grim and then he finished:

'No, Kamala! What I have I hold!'

'You are a pirate, that is what you are!' Kamala teased.

'Why not?' he enquired. 'The English have always been particularly good at the game, especially in this part of the world. What about Drake, Hawkins and Cavendish?'

'I think you look like one too,' Kamala said. 'There is a buccaneering dash about you!'

'Do you find it attractive?' Conrad asked.

Kamala gave a little laugh.

'You are too conceited already,' she answered. 'I will give you my answer to that another time.'

'I shall not forget,' he replied.

During the next twenty-four hours it was hard to be light-hearted or even to laugh.

Conrad was driving himself and the men under him to the utmost limits of their endurance. They had been three days at sea and none of them had been able to rest.

The two Captains performed miracles, but Kamala knew

it was Conrad who seemed almost to sail the ship himself.

Kamala was still afraid that they might be pursued, that the Don would catch up with them, although how, she could not think. But he was cunning, he was clever and it was impossible, however much she told herself she was being over-imaginative, not to be afraid.

'It won't be long now, Miss,' Spider said as she passed him going up the companionway with another huge pot of coffee and a tray of cleanly washed mugs.

Kamala often wondered what they would have done without Spider.

He was an excellent cook and however much he had to do, he was never disagreeable, on edge or anything but unfailingly cheerful and polite.

'We shall have to find some way,' Kamala thought to herself, 'of rewarding him.'

It was worrying to think they would soon run out of money. Still there was always the golden bed, and of course hers was made of silver.

It was 1 o'clock in the morning when Conrad said in a voice hoarse with tiredness:

'There is Castle Morro!'

Kamala looked ahead and by the pale light of a new moon she saw the tower of a Castle silhouetted against the star-lit sky and knew it was the entrance to the Bay of Havana.

'So we have done it,' she said softly.

'Go to bed,' Conrad ordered. 'We will talk about it to-morrow.'

She obeyed because she was too tired to argue. She went downstairs, undressed and got into bed.

When she had searched her cabin she had found a certain amount of underclothes in one of the chests. There had been night-gowns beautifully embroidered, petticoats and lace-trimmed chemises, but at the time she had been too busy to be interested.

Now she slipped into a night-gown trimmed with hand-made lace as fine as a spider's cobweb, and put her aching head down on the pillow. She expected to sleep but instead found herself lying tense listening to the sounds above.

She heard them let down the anchor, heard the shouted instructions of the men who were up aloft, the flap of sails being taken in. Then the noise grew less and less until suddenly coming down the companionway she heard Conrad's heavy footsteps.

He went into the cabin next to hers and closed the door.

She heard one bump then there was silence, and she knew as clearly as if she had been there that he flung himself down on the bed just as he was and fallen asleep.

She smiled. They were in harbour, they were safe and they were together!

II

Kamala awoke to find Spider coming into the cabin carrying a tray in his hands. She looked at him sleepily for a moment before she asked:

'Is it breakfast time?'

'It is after noon, Miss.'

Kamala sat up with a jerk.

'Noon!' she exclaimed.

'And here's your luncheon, Miss,' Spider answered, putting the tray down beside the bed.

'But how could I have slept so late ... ?' Kamala began.

'We have all slept late, Miss,' Spider said, 'and the Master asked me to tell you not to hurry, but he would like to take you ashore about half after four. He has a lot to do until then.'

'I am sure he has,' Kamala said with a little sigh of relief, leaning back against the pillows. 'And, Spider, did Sir Conrad sleep well?'

'Like the dead, Miss,' Spider said with a grin. 'I had a rare job of waking him. But I didn't do that until it was absolutely necessary.'

'He must be very tired,' Kamala said.

'Not the Master, Miss,' Spider replied. 'He's so happy to be here that he looks and sounds like a schoolboy.'

Kamala laughed. She knew what it must mean to Conrad, and to all of them, to have brought this enormous ship safely from Mexico to the haven of Havana.

As Conrad had commanded, she did not make any effort

to rise until long after the time of siesta which she knew people would be taking in Havana.

It was very hot and rather airless, but the sunshine coming through the portholes was golden and glorious.

When finally Kamala rose and dressed herself, she put on what she thought was the prettiest gown in the wardrobe full of lovely dresses.

She had never in her life expected to own anything so fine or so magnificent as any one of them.

The gown she chose, and in which she hoped Conrad would admire her, was of white muslin ornamented with many lace frills and slotted with blue ribbons of a quality that could only have come from France.

There was a blue sash of the same silk, and to go with it there was a ridiculous little hat of muslin, lace and ribbon, and a tiny long-handled sun-shade.

Kamala went up on deck where she knew Conrad would be waiting for her and the look on his face told her without words how alluring she looked in his eyes.

It was hard not to run towards him, throw herself into his arms, and tell him how glad she was that they were safe. Instead of which she curtseyed demurely, her wide skirts sweeping the newly scrubbed boards of the deck.

As she rose she thought how handsome and distinguished he appeared.

He was wearing a black suit which had belonged to the Don and which Spider had altered for him with some difficulty. It accentuated his slim athletic figure while the white crisp frills of his shirt and high cravat were very elegant.

A boat was waiting for them, and now as they were rowed towards the wharf Kamala could take in for the first time the beauty of the bay.

Nothing, she thought, could have been more striking than Morro Castle with its towers and battlements of dark grey stone. By its side was a fortress called Cabana, painted rose colour with the angles of its bastions white.

There was colour everywhere, from the feathery cocoas growing amongst the thick herbage which covered the bank by the Castle, to the irregular houses with their fronts painted red or pale blue, which had a cool and almost empty look owing to the absence of glass windows.

But what was so breathtaking was the enormous number of ships in the Bay. There were large men o' war, vessels from every part of the commercial world, merchant ships, trawlers, schooners, while gliding amongst them with snow-white sails were innumerable little boats.

'How pretty it all is!' Kamala exclaimed.

'Lovely,' Conrad answered.

His eyes were on her face and she knew that he was not speaking of the Bay.

A volante, an amusing-looking vehicle but quite the ugliest sort of carriage Kamala had ever seen, was waiting for them at the wharf.

It was controlled by a Negro who rode astride the horse. He wore a dirty fanciful uniform and an enormous pair of jack boots.

As soon as they were in the carriage, Conrad reached out and took Kamala's hand in his.

'I love you,' he said. 'This has been my first opportunity to say so since we reached Havana.'

'Havana and . . . safety!' Kamala said with a little sigh of relief.

'Yes, we are safe,' Conrad replied. 'It was a mad gamble, my darling, but it came off.'

'Thanks entirely to . . . you.'

There was a little throb in Kamala's voice and he looked down into her eyes, a sudden fire flaring in his.

'If we had failed,' he said quietly, 'we would have failed together, that was all that mattered.'

'I do not believe you could ever fail at anything you undertook,' she said softly.

He would have replied but at that moment the volante

drew up outside a shop. Kamala saw it was a jeweller's and looked enquiringly at Conrad.

'Give me your glove,' he smiled, 'and I will spare your blushes.'

For a moment she did not understand what he meant. Then she drew her white glove from her left hand, and taking it from her he went into the shop.

She guessed what he was buying and felt her heart begin to beat a little quicker. This was what she had prayed for, what she had longed for, what Zomba had called 'her heart's desire'.

In a few moments Conrad came out from the shop carrying her glove in his hand and a small leather box. He put them both down in her lap.

'You had better try it on and see if the size is right,' he suggested.

Kamala opened the box and saw, as she expected, a narrow gold wedding-ring.

She would have taken it from its velvet setting, but Conrad lifted it first and then taking her left hand in his he put the ring on her third finger. It fitted perfectly.

Just for a moment his hand tightened on hers. Then he drew the ring from her fingers and slipped it into the pocket of his waistcoat.

'To the English Church,' he said to the postilion in Spanish.

Kamala looked at him in surprise.

'An English Church?' she questioned.

'Yes, indeed,' Conrad answered. 'Havana belonged to England for many years. The Church was built then and the parson who officiates is an old friend of mine.'

Kamala was silent. Then she asked, her voice very low:

'Are we . . . to be married . . . now?'

'Now, at this very moment,' Conrad replied. 'I will take no more risks, my darling, of losing you.'

She looked up at him, her eyes shining beneath the muslin hat.

'That is ... all I ever ... wanted,' she whispered.

He looked down at her radiant face and lifted her hand to his lips. She felt his mouth against her skin and a thrill ran through her.

What was it, she asked herself, that made his touch a rapture, an ecstasy inexpressible in words?

They drove without speaking through the busy streets until a little way outside the town they came upon a low grey Church with stained-glass windows. Beside it was a white house which fronting onto the Bay had a magnificent view.

As Kamala expected, the house was built in a square and a servant led them up an inside staircase into a large cool apartment with a marble floor. There were marble tables and a number of cane-bottomed armchairs.

The servant left the room.

'This is surely a very grand house for a Vicar?' Kamala remarked.

'My friend is rather more important than that,' Conrad replied. 'He is treated as the father of the English Colony and is greatly respected.'

As he spoke, a large man wearing a mauve cassock came into the room and at the sight of Conrad held out both hands.

'Conrad! My Boy! This is an unexpected pleasure!' he exclaimed. 'I had no idea you were visiting Havana.'

'Nor had I until the last day or so,' Conrad replied, 'but I am here now with a very special request.'

'Indeed!' the English cleric exclaimed, looking at Kamala.

'I want you to meet Miss Kamala Lindsay,' Conrad explained, 'who has promised to be my wife. We are asking you to marry us immediately.'

Everything which happened afterwards seemed to Kamala to be part of a wonderful dream.

The English parson, whose name Kamala learnt was Canon Lovell, toasted their health in wine while the necesary documents were prepared for their marriage.

Then they repaired to the grey stone Church where the altar was decorated with flowers and there was a feeling of cool serenity and peace under its ancient roof.

The service was simple and Kamala thought she would never forget the sound of Conrad's deep voice as he repeated his vows and her own rather tremulous responses.

Driving back to the ship in the volante, Kamala knew there were no words in which she could express her joy. She was Conrad's wife, she was his, they belonged to each other for all time and nothing could separate them!

With her hand in his she felt as if she dedicated herself to him for eternity.

'To love and to cherish,' she whispered beneath her breath.

As they reached the wharf in the volante and the postilion drew his horse to a standstill, Conrad asked very softly:

'Are you happy, my darling?'

She turned her face towards his and he saw the wonder in her eyes and it seemed for a moment as if neither of them could move. They could only sit spellbound, held by a love which seemed to pulsate magnetically between them.

Then still as if she were in a dream, Kamala realised that the boat was waiting to carry them back to the Clipper and she allowed Conrad to assist her onto the wharf.

The deck of the ship seemed surprisingly crowded, until Kamala heard Captain Macdonald say:

'I have taken on thirty men, Sir, as you instructed me. They are good seamen and their papers are in order.'

'Have they all been vaccinated?' Conrad asked.

'Every one of them,' Captain Macdonald replied.

Behind him Captain Turner was waiting to tell Conrad

that the last of the stores were aboard, and Kamala realised she was not wanted. She walked down the companionway to find Spider waiting for her in the Saloon.

'You look lovely, Miss!' he exclaimed almost involuntarily.

'I am happy, Spider,' Kamala replied, 'happier than I have ever been in my whole life. Sir Conrad and I have been married.'

'That's what I hoped you'd say, M'Lady!'

Kamala looked at him in surprise.

'Then you knew that the Master and I were not ... brother and sister?'

'I guessed it when we stopped at the Azores coming out, M'Lady,' Spider said. 'You came back to the ship looking as if you'd both been in Paradise!'

Kamala smiled.

'I think that was exactly where we had been,' she said softly.

She went to her cabin to take off her hat and sat at the dressing-table staring at the plain gold ring on her left hand.

'How much more valuable it is,' she thought, 'than the great diamond the Don gave me or any other jewel the world may contain.'

Nothing could be so important in the mind of a woman than a wedding-ring given her by the man she loved and who loved her.

Kamala must have sat thinking for a long time before she realised that the ship was moving. The sails were being set, they were leaving Havana harbour.

For a moment she thought of going on deck. Then somehow she felt shy of being with Conrad when there were so many people around.

There was so much they still had to say to each other. She would wait until they could be alone, until he could come to her as she knew he would do sooner or later.

In fact she dined alone in the Saloon.

'The Master's at the helm,' Spider told her. 'Doesn't trust anyone except himself.'

'He must be very hungry!' Kamala exclaimed.

'Oh no, M'Lady, I've seen to that. Captain Macdonald has engaged a new cook—a Chinaman. Says he's the best cook this side of the Cape. I'll believe that when I sees it!'

Kamala laughed, there was almost a touch of jealousy in Spider's voice.

'Well at least you and I will not have to work so hard,' she said, 'and there are a lot more clothes to be altered.'

'You're right, M'Lady. I must get back to my proper duties,' Spider said, 'and if you'll take my advice, not meaning any impertinence, you'll go to bed. I have a feeling the Master'll not come down below until he is past the Pan de Matanzas.'

Kamala could not be bothered to ask where that was, but she knew Spider's suggestion was sensible. There was no point in sitting about in the Saloon alone, impressive and comfortable though it might be.

She went to her cabin and took off her white dress. As she got into the big silver bed she thought that it, with the gold one next door, must be the strangest beds any ship had ever carried.

The sheets trimmed with lace and the embroidered pillow cases were luxurious and very soft. The breeze out at sea had swept away the heavy heat of the day, and now the cabin seemed fresh although the portholes had to be kept closed.

Night came with its usual swiftness, so that one moment the sky outside was golden and crimson and the next it was dark as velvet, the stars glittering like diamonds.

Then at last when it seemed to Kamala she had waited nearly a century, she heard Conrad come down the companionway and enter the cabin next door.

She lay waiting, her heart beating quickly in her breast,

her lips a little dry with anticipation, until at length the communicating door opened and he came in.

He was wearing a long, very gorgeous robe of gold-threaded brocade with a high collar and cuffs of black velvet. The frill of his nightshirt was white against his brown throat. He looked so handsome that instinctively Kamala held out her hands towards him.

He shut the door behind him and sat down on the side of the bed. He took her hands and kissed them one by one.

'I love you, my beautiful darling, I love you!' he said, and she felt herself quiver at the deep note of desire in his voice.

She waited expecting him to kiss her lips. Then he said:

'I have something to tell you.'

She looked up at him a little apprehensively. It seemed to her there was something strange in the manner in which he spoke.

'To tell me?' she questioned.

'I suppose really I should have told you before,' he answered, 'but I have been too much of a coward.'

'What is it? What is wrong?' Kamala asked quickly.

'It is not exactly wrong,' Conrad replied, 'although you may think it so.'

'What is it?' Kamala asked again and now she was frightened.

Conrad's fingers tightened on hers.

'I know,' he began slowly, 'that you were surprised when I told Van Wyck that I was Sir Conrad Veryan. You thought it was part of our pretence. In fact I am a baronet. However I have another title we will both use in future.'

'Another ... title?' Kamala asked trying to understand what he was telling her.

'I am the Marquis of Truro.'

For a moment Kamala stared at him trying to remember where she had heard the name before. Then with a little cry she took her fingers from his.

'The Marquis of Truro!' she repeated. 'You mean the Marquis who was to marry Sophie?'

There was a moment's silence before Conrad said:

'It is difficult to make you understand now how at the time that seemed the only way out of the problems by which I was beset.'

He rose as he spoke to walk across the cabin to the porthole. He pulled aside the satin curtains and stood staring out into the darkness.

'I have already described to you,' he went on, 'the situation as I found it at home. My Mother dying, debts piled up, people who were my responsibility starving. And there was a letter from my Trustee.'

He paused. Kamala could remember Uncle Marcus saying that it was the Marquis' Trustee who had arranged everything.

'He happens also to be the solicitor to Marcus Pleyton,' Conrad continued. 'He found that his client wanted a title for his daughter and he knew that the fifty thousand pounds that Marcus Pleyton offered to a bridegroom would be a godsend where I was concerned.'

'Fifty thousand pounds!' Kamala ejaculated.

'That was what he was prepared to pay for a title,' Conrad said, 'and the dowry for his daughter was to exceed one hundred thousand.'

'So much ... money!' Kamala exclaimed almost beneath her breath. 'How could you ... refuse it?'

'I did not intend to,' Conrad replied, 'until unexpectedly and inexplicably I fell in love for the first time in my life.'

He turned from the window to look at Kamala, She appeared very small and fragile in the draped bed, her eyes unnaturally large in her pale face.

'Yes I fell in love,' he repeated, 'and I knew then that however much Marcus Pleyton was prepared to pay for my title, I could not sell myself.'

'So you were not ... going to ... Southampton in search of a ... ship,' Kamala said.

'I had just arrived at Southampton from Falmouth,' Conrad answered, 'when we met. I was on my way to Castle Bray.'

There was silence in the cabin, Kamala was no longer looking at Conrad, but staring ahead of her.

'Kamala ...!' he cried and moved towards her.

As he did so the cabin door was burst open. Spider stood there.

'Sir! Sir! Come quickly! You must see for yourself! You must look! I can hardly believe it's true!'

'What has happened? What has gone wrong?' Conrad exclaimed.

'There's nothing wrong, Sir! It's wonderful! Marvellous! But you must see. Come with me, I beg you, Sir, come with me!'

The little man turned as he spoke and started back up the companionway. Conrad looked after him in astonishment, then followed, closing the cabin door behind him.

Kamala put her hands up to her face and even as she did so asked herself why she should mind?

It was because of her that Conrad had not sold himself to Marcus Pleyton and had not married Sophie. No man in his position could pay her a greater compliment.

It is just the shock, she thought, the shock of realising somehow she could not escape her past, and even Conrad was in some way concerned with her uncle. Then she told herself that Uncle Marcus should not spoil her wedding-day.

He had ruined three years of her life and caused her so much suffering and unhappiness that even now it was a nightmare from which she could not entirely escape.

It would, she thought, be giving him an undue importance to let him come, even in the smallest way, between her and her husband.

Conrad was hers! He had taken her with him on the most foolhardy, wild, crazy adventure which no sane man would have undertaken, and he had done it because he loved her.

'I love him! I love him!' Kamala told herself. 'How can it matter for one moment who he is ... if he has one name or twenty? He is mine ... my husband!'

She was smiling when Conrad came back into the cabin, but to her surprise he did not look at her, only closed the door behind him.

Then he blew out the two oil lamps leaving a light only from the candle-lantern which Kamala had placed beside her bed. It stood behind the pink and blue silk curtains and the room was in shadows.

Conrad turned towards the bed and as the ship lurched, he flung himself down upon it, lying on the outside of the satin cover. Then placing his hands behind his head he stared up at the ceiling.

Kamala waited, then as he did not speak, she said in a frightened voice:

'What has happened? What is the ... matter?'

'Spider had been looking at the cargo.'

'The ... cargo?'

'He is insatiably curious,' Conrad answered, 'and actually I had forgotten about it. In fact I had not expected there would be any cargo on board, seeing that the Don was going to Spain on what he considered was a State Visit.'

'But ... there is a ... cargo?' Kamala said.

'Yes indeed.'

She knew this was the key to Conrad's strange behaviour.

'What is it?' she questioned.

Just for a moment Conrad did not answer. Then he said, his voice entirely expressionless:

'Spider opened one crate and it contained diamonds. There are five others. The rest of the hold is filled with gold.'

250

Kamala gave a little gasp.

'Diamonds . . . crates of them?'

'The Don must have been collecting diamonds for years. He intended to make a splash in Spain and he would certainly have done so.'

'And now,' Kamala said almost in a whisper, 'they belong to . . . you.'

'As I have already told you,' Conrad replied, 'what I have I hold.'

'But why are you not . . . pleased and happy about . . . it?' Kamala asked. 'You have money for everything you wanted, you will be able to reward Spider and the Sea Captains who have lost their ships. There will be enough for everything you have ever desired and more.'

'All those things will be done and done generously,' Conrad said.

There was a pause before he continued slowly:

'I think for the moment I am just knocked out at the thought of so much money. So much that I cannot even begin to count the value of what I carry. I was expecting to have to sell pieces of the bed or furniture when we reached the Azores.'

'And does it . . . not make you . . . happy?' Kamala asked hesitatingly.

In reply he turned on his side and raising himself on his elbow, looked down at her as he had done that afternoon in the Azores when she had lain among the flowers in the shadow of the rock.

'What I am realising,' he said slowly, 'is that it is not of the least importance. I wanted money so desperately, I wondered frantically all the way across the Atlantic how I could find it, how I could take enough back to England to do all the things that had to be done.'

He sighed.

'Now that I know how rich I am,' he explained, 'I find

it is not of any consequence, I have already the only thing I want in the whole world.'

'What is . . . that?' Kamala asked.

'You know the answer. It is you who have altered my life and changed my whole outlook,' Conrad replied. 'You who have made me realise that money is not the only essential thing in the world. That there is something infinitely greater, infinitely more necessary to a man if he is ever to know happiness.'

'What is . . . that?' Kamala asked again.

'It is love, my sweet darling, the love you have given me and which has been there in my heart for you ever since I first saw you.'

Kamala felt herself throb with a new wonder and a little quiver of excitement went through her because of the passion in Conrad's voice.

'You are . . . sure . . . quite sure,' she asked, 'that now you are a very . . . very rich . . . man, that you still . . . want me? You are not . . . sorry that you . . . married me?'

'Are you really asking me such a nonsensical question?' Conrad asked with a hint of laughter in his voice.

Very slowly he bent his head and found Kamala's lips. For a moment his mouth was gentle against the softness of hers almost as if he was afraid to frighten her. But as her arms went round his neck, his kiss became more passionate, more insistent, more demanding.

It seemed to Kamala as if he swept her into the golden world where he had taken her once before. They were together and everything else was forgotten, everything else had vanished except themselves.

Then as she felt her whole body respond to him as she quivered because his hand was touching her breast, Conrad lifted his head.

'I love you—I love you!' he said. 'How can anything else be of consequence except that you are mine and I will never let you go?'

252

'That is ... all I have ever ... wanted,' Kamala mur-mured.

She looked up into his eyes and saw even in the faint light from the candle a fire burning in them. She sensed his burning desire but was not afraid.

'Nothing matters, nothing except you, my precious one.' Conrad said again and he began kissing her wildly, frantic-ally, like a man who had passed through deep waters and was afraid he might not survive.

'I love ... you.'

There were no other words in which Kamala could ex-press the ecstasy and the joy that made her whole body tremble with the intensity of her feelings.

'I love ... you,' she whispered again.

'You are mine! Mine!' Conrad said hoarsely.

Then his mouth, masterful, passionate, demanding, hold-ing hers completely captive, lifted her into a paradise where there was only the glory of their love.

If you would like a complete list of Arrow books please send a postcard to P.O. Box 29, Douglas, Isle of Man, Great Britain.

THE COMPLACENT WIFE

BARBARA CARTLAND

When the Earl of Droxford hears that only a married man
may be appointed Lord Lieutenant of his county, he asks
his attractive mistress Lady Sibley to find him a wife – 'a
complacent, comfortable wife'.

All seems to be resolved when the beautiful and unconven-
tional Karina Rendell strikes a bargain with the Earl . . . however, their marriage of convenience is soon threatened by
a series of scandals and misunderstandings, in which lust
and jealousy play a major part, but love is doomed to
suffer. . . .

LESSONS IN LOVE

BARBARA CARTLAND

Miss Mitton found it impossible to look like a governess. She was far too beautiful with glorious red hair and a delicately white, heart-shaped face graced by a pair of long-lashed green eyes.

She was, in fact, Lady Marisa Berrington-Crecy masquerading as a governess in the household of the Duke of Milverly, determined to write the book which would expose the corruption and heartlessness of Edwardian Society.

She found herself responsible for a lonely, loveless child. And also found the arrogant, philandering Duke capable of loving, and of being loved.

Marisa had much to learn – and much to teach.

THE AUDACIOUS ADVENTURESS

BARBARA CARTLAND

The Duke of Windleham was certain that he had seen the Marquis of Lynche coming from his wife's bedchamber. 'I was in fact asking my cousin Druscilla to do me the great honour of becoming my wife,' said the Marquis, desperate for an alibi – one that was to lead him and Druscilla into many exciting adventures.